# "You don't w... do you?"

His eyes glittered with challenge, daring her to answer.

"No." She shook her head. "I don't."

"Why not?"

"Because you never seem satisfied with what I say."

It was enough of the truth for now. She just didn't add that a part of her was very busy noticing him as a *man*. She had from the very beginning. And that his physical presence made her suddenly aware of herself as a *woman*.

She swallowed and added, "And because you never take anything at face value. You always seem to suspect a hidden meaning, an ulterior motive—and you make me…uneasy." It was a better word than nervous. Or self conscious.

"Maybe I wouldn't have to look for *hidden meanings* if you would *talk* to me. If I didn't have to pry out every bit of information you held…!"

**Harlequin Historicals is delighted to
introduce new author Wendy Douglas**

**Here is what some of her fellow authors
have to say about her debut novel
SHADES OF GRAY**

"A heartwarming voice
and a story about the power of love."
—*New York Times* bestselling author
and three-time RITA Award winner Jennifer Greene

"An exquisite love story of hope and healing,
and a stunning debut for Ms. Douglas!"
—*Romantic Times* Career Achievement Award winner
Mary Anne Wilson

# SHADES OF GRAY

## WENDY DOUGLAS

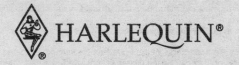

HARLEQUIN®

TORONTO • NEW YORK • LONDON
AMSTERDAM • PARIS • SYDNEY • HAMBURG
STOCKHOLM • ATHENS • TOKYO • MILAN • MADRID
PRAGUE • WARSAW • BUDAPEST • AUCKLAND

ISBN 0-373-29202-3

SHADES OF GRAY

This edition published by arrangement with Harlequin Books S.A.

® and TM are trademarks of the publisher. Trademarks indicated with
® are registered in the United States Patent and Trademark Office, the
Canadian Trade Marks Office and in other countries.

Visit us at www.eHarlequin.com

**Printed in U.S.A.**

*Available from Harlequin Historicals and*
*WENDY DOUGLAS*

*Shades of Gray* #602

For Doug

For giving me the time and freedom to finally
achieve my dream. For teaching me about the miracles
that come from taking chances. And for being
my best friend…my very own hero. *I love you.*

## Acknowledgments

This book was a labor of love, a book of my heart.
Even so, I could not have written it without the help
and support of some amazing people:
Alison Hart, who volunteered
to read the manuscript and offered unlimited time,
advice and understanding. (Thanks, Petunia.)
Tracy Green, Cheryl Johnson, Lynda Mikulski
and Carolyn Rogers, who brainstormed,
listened, read and critiqued my baby
with sincere enthusiasm and encouragement.
Mary Anne Wilson, who taught me that a hard man
is good to find—and knew just the hard men
I would need for this book.
Dana Stabenow, who made exactly the suggestion
I needed, just when I needed it, to find the right ending.
Laurie Miller, who generously shared her
medical knowledge, particularly with home remedies
suitable for the post-Civil War era.
My Texas "expert," Betty Sue Crain,
who offered pictures, maps, stories, an exclusive
Texas tour in seven whirlwind days, and for cooking
dinner—more than once—so I could keep writing.
The "Thursday LaMex girls," Kathy Hafer and
Jean Whitley, for proofreading and years of unflagging
support. (Margaritas are on me next week!)

# *Prologue*

*Texas, April 1868*

He rode damn near to the edge of nowhere before he found it. For days now, the landscape had sauntered by with indifferent sameness, offering little more than mesquite, prickly pear cactus and Indian paintbrush. Finally, a new image appeared in the distance.

The Double F Ranch.

Derek Fontaine reined his horse to a standstill and examined the far-off buildings. At the same time, he grappled with the sound of a hundred noisy voices, all shouting inside his head and demanding his attention. The lies, the accusations…the angry recriminations. He'd been so sure he could hold them under the strictest control—and had done so for years. Suddenly they were back…and for what?

He scowled at the scene before him as the memories forced themselves upon him: the lies from all the years they'd pretended Richard Fontaine was his *uncle;* the unfair accusations he would never forget; the names with which they had branded him. Troublemaker, traitor…bastard.

Betrayals all, and from those he'd trusted most. His own family.

The anger and loneliness of a childhood spent unwanted and unloved festered up inside him like an old wound that had never quite healed. Derek swallowed, forcing back the memories as he had always done before. He couldn't afford to open himself up to it all again, reexamining those tired, ancient emotions when he'd come so close to losing himself to it once. Later, when the pain finally went away, or when he regained his strength, he would think about it.

But not now. *Now* he had all he could manage just trying to figure out what the hell he was doing here.

"That it?"

Derek blinked, turning as he swept a distracted gaze over his companion. Gideon—the only name he'd given, back three hundred miles or so—said nothing more. Willing enough to shoulder his share of the work and more, and evenly divide the few costs they'd incurred along the trail, he had also established himself as a man of few words. He didn't disclose personal confessions and he didn't ask questions. That suited Derek just fine.

He nodded, shifting as imperceptibly as he could. It was sufficient movement to prod a creak from his leather saddle, and he took a moment to appreciate the noise. It sounded familiar, reassuring somehow, and it settled him, reminded him of who he was and where he'd been.

Turning back to study the terrain, he noticed, then dismissed, a patch of bluebonnets waving brightly in the breeze. More interesting was the view of the sprawling frame ranch house and outbuildings that squatted earnestly in the distance.

He answered after another moment. "I expect it is."

"It doesn't exactly look deserted."

Derek aimed a sharp gaze over the details: a lazy plume of smoke wafting from a chimney, while a cloud of dust billowed from what he suspected was the corral. Definite signs of life.

He shrugged. "I didn't know what I'd find."

"You still don't."

"True enough."

"You expect trouble?"

Derek urged his horse forward without answering, and Gideon followed a moment later.

"I always expect trouble," Derek finally replied. "It's just a matter of what kind."

Gideon nodded again, but said nothing more, leaving Derek free to consider the possibilities of what lay ahead. He knew what he wouldn't find: Richard Fontaine alive and well and waiting for his arrival. If he had been, there would be no reason for Derek to be there.

But Richard was dead and Derek wasn't. He was here in south Texas, looking out across the love of the other man's life: the land. More than his ancestry, more than family...perhaps more than life itself, Richard had loved this place.

*That doesn't mean you have to love it the same way,* Derek reminded himself. He doubted that he ever would. He didn't have enough emotion left within him for that. But it was the perfect answer, for now.

He had more than twenty-five years behind him as Jordan Fontaine's *son.* And later, he'd survived four long—agonizingly so at times—years of civil war. In his life, he'd faced enough strife, enough pain...enough *everything.* He just wanted a little peace and quiet.

The Double F would give him that. The space and freedom to be alone, to forget...to heal?

Well, no. He shook his head and urged his horse to move faster. He wouldn't go that far. He knew better. But maybe, if he had any luck left to him at all, he might get the chance to discover if there was anything left of the man named Derek Fontaine.

# Chapter One

"Riders comin'."

Amber Laughton heard the call but held her response, choosing to concentrate on her work for another moment. Separating the troublesome weeds from the healthy plants in her fledgling dill bed didn't take that much thought, but the mindless chore gave her a chance to think.

The Double F Ranch rarely welcomed visitors these days. Invitations were no longer extended or accepted, and she could think of no one interested in seeing that change. No one, perhaps, except Derek Fontaine, arrived at last.

"Amber-girl, you hear me? Riders comin'."

She looked up, shading her eyes with one hand. High, thin clouds gave the day a deceptively overcast appearance, but they didn't entirely stop moments of fierce brightness. Blinking, she picked out Micah standing at the corner of the house.

She smiled softly. The little man, as much grandfather as friend to her after so many years, stood as straight and tall as his size and aging body would allow. Alternately he stared out toward the curved front drive, then sent her sharp, pointed looks, intended no doubt to make her take him seriously.

She did, and he had to know it. "I heard you."

"You expectin' somebody?"

"And who do you think I'd be expecting?"

"Them crazy Andrews brothers ain't been out here in a while. It could be them," Micah suggested, scowling.

"That doesn't mean *I'd* be expecting them. Clem and Twigg come to see Whitley, and you know it." Amber dropped the last few weeds into a dilapidated wooden bucket, already half full of wilting green plants, and stood, wiping her hands on her stained apron. For once she had remembered to put on her gardening apron, and she refused to change it now simply to impress uninvited company. Even if it was Derek Fontaine.

Besides, a dirty apron hardly mattered under the circumstances; she looked every bit the part of the hired housekeeper she was. Her plain brown cotton dress and sturdy work shoes hadn't been new in years. She'd pulled her hair back into a serviceable, tidy bun early that morning, but tendrils had loosened by now and clung with damp persistence to her forehead and neck. Her hands were red and chapped from the scalding hot, then icy-cold water and strong lye soap of yesterday's laundry, while her fingertips seemed permanently tinted to a faded black from the rich dirt in her garden.

"They might *say* they're comin' to see Whitley," said Micah, disapproval wrinkling his already weathered brow, "but they don't care nothin' that he's their nephew. They just wanna stick around till you invite them to supper."

"Well, if it's them, they've run out of luck today." Amber stepped around the bucket and headed in his direction. "Whitley went to town again, and I don't have time to entertain them until he gets back."

"Nah, I don't think it's them, anyway." Micah narrowed his eyes. "That don't look like their horses."

She rounded the corner of the house and stopped next to him, shading her eyes with one hand as she looked out across the prairie.

*There were two of them.*

Amber swallowed the words, along with a clipped gasp for air—or thought she did, until Micah demanded, "What's wrong with you, girl? Course there's two of them. I said *riders* comin'. We was talkin' about the Andrews brothers, fer cryin' out loud. Addin' them esses at the end of a word usually means more'n one."

"I'm sorry. I...don't know what I was thinking. I assumed it would be Derek Fontaine, but I thought he'd be alone."

"Fontaine!" She might have said Jesus Christ for all the stunned amazement that crackled in Micah's voice. "Why d'you think it's him *now?* We been wonderin' fer durn near a year iffen he'd come."

She shot a weary glance at the old man. His wide, rheumy eyes and gaping mouth matched his astonished tone. "I got a note from Frank Edwards a few days ago," she admitted.

"You shoulda told me! We coulda got things ready fer him."

"What difference does it make? It's his, no matter what condition it's in."

Micah's gaze raked her with uncomfortable deliberation. "What's wrong, Amber-girl? This is Richard's nephew. You loved Richard an' he was good to both of us. How come you don't want Derek here? You don't even know him."

Amber sighed. It might shock him to realize it, but Micah didn't know everything about her. He thought he understood her, and she would never tell him any differently—for both their sakes. She couldn't face him if he knew all her secrets.

She shook her head. "I'm sorry. I'm just tired. I haven't slept well the past couple of nights."

He nodded. "It's the change in season. Spring ain't your fondest season anymore."

Turning, she watched the newcomers approach ever nearer. As a child, spring had always been her favorite time of year, and part of her still marveled to see the earth renew itself. But spring had also seen an end to much that she held dear, and she could no longer take the same joy in it.

''No.'' Her answer, finally, was clean and simple, allowing her to concentrate on the new arrivals. ''I don't suppose it is.''

The riders reached the edge of the crushed rock-and-shell driveway, close enough that she could make out the first details. The men both appeared to be thirty or thereabouts, lean and fit. Their features remained indistinct, but they rode well, straight and easy, one on a gleaming red sorrel and the other on a powerful black stallion. The horses looked healthy and lively, even from a distance.

Pausing at the front of the house, they shared a brief exchange that didn't carry before Micah caught their attention with an abbreviated wave and a sharp ''Halloo.''

The man on the sorrel led the way around back. ''Is this the Double F Ranch?''

Amber lost, in that moment, any doubts that may have lingered about the man's identity. It was Richard's voice asking the question, Richard's face looking down at her. His eyes remained shadowed under the brim of his dusty brown hat, but that changed nothing. Derek Fontaine was clearly his uncle's double, though separated by a span of thirty years.

She had never given much thought to Richard's looks; he had simply been her father's friend. Suddenly, though, looking at Derek and his younger version of Richard's face, she discovered with some surprise that he was quite possibly the most handsome man she'd ever seen. The high curve of his cheekbones gave his face an elegance that was apparent even under a reddish-brown beard and mustache. The whiskers provided a subtle accent for his full, finely drawn lips, but at the same time concealed the cut of his jaw. His nose presented the only unremarkable feature on his face.

"Ma'am?"

Amber blinked and swallowed. For pity's sake, what was the matter with her? Standing here, staring at this man—any man—like a smitten schoolgirl.

She frowned and shook her head. "I beg your pardon, sir. We don't often have visitors. This is the Double F Ranch. And you must be Derek Fontaine."

He stiffened, but nodded with a sharp tilt of his head. "I am. You were expecting me?"

"Mr. Edwards—the banker—sent word a few days ago."

"And you are?"

"I'm sorry." She flushed, both embarrassed and irritated by her lapse in manners. "This is Micah Smith, and my name is Amber Laughton. We worked for your uncle."

Derek nodded and removed his hat in a gesture of respect Amber had long ago forgotten to expect. She stared up at him, bewildered, and neglected for a moment to blink.

Blue. His eyes were blue, similar to Richard's, but Derek's were a bright, pure color that looked nothing at all like his uncle's, with lashes so long Amber could see them from where she stood. Derek's hair fell well past his shoulders, longer and lighter than Richard's, a pale brown color the sun had bleached to mostly blond-red. He resembled heaven's own angel, strong and fair, she thought in an odd moment of whimsy—or he would have if the expression in his eyes hadn't looked so...bleak.

"How d'ya do, Mr. Fontaine?" Micah's welcome dissolved the stillness, much to Amber's relief. She blinked and looked away. "I knew yer uncle well. We shared many a fine glass a' whiskey. He was a good friend, and I'm real sorry he ain't here with us now."

"Yes, well, thank you." Derek turned to the other

mounted man before Amber could offer her own condolences. "This is Gideon."

Was the change in subject as deliberate as it appeared? Amber stared at Derek a moment longer, but his stark expression provided no clue. Perhaps he still grieved over the loss of his uncle. With no other choice, she fixed her gaze on the second man.

Nothing about Gideon could be termed light except for his long blond hair. Everything else was dark. Hat, shirt, pants and boots—even the stallion's shimmering coat—shared the same deep ebony color. And the leather patch that covered his left eye was black as well.

"Mister...Gideon." Amber looked directly in his good eye and did her best to ignore both the patch and the mean-looking red scar that snaked out from beneath it. The scar bisected his left cheek into two crooked halves. The right side of his face, however, remained as beautiful and flawless as any angel in heaven above.

Were they suddenly beset by fallen angels?

"Ma'am," Gideon said, his voice as low and polite as his good eye was cold and distant.

"It's miss. I'm not married." Something compelled her to correct the assumption, though she couldn't imagine why it should matter.

Gideon nodded, then introduced himself to Micah.

"We'd like to settle in, if you don't mind," said Derek.

"Of course. Micah, if you'll take Gideon to the bunkhouse and see to Mr. Fontaine's horse, I'll show him the main house."

"I prefer to take care of my own horse, if you don't mind, Miss Laughton."

"I...er, yes, of course." Amber glanced at the sorrel, focusing her attention on the animal rather than its owner. The man seemed to have a talent for making her feel like a blundering fool. "I'll be over there, in the garden—" she turned to point behind her "—whenever you're ready."

"Come along then, boys, an' I'll show ya the way."
Micah headed toward the corral with a wave, and the
younger men followed his lead without comment.

Well, then. So this was it. Amber watched them make
their way across the yard, an anxiety she didn't recognize
putting an awkward brittleness into her shoulders, her
limbs.

*Remain calm,* she told herself. *Don't think, just breathe.*
But a hollow had opened up low in her stomach, and it
transformed even simple breathing into a sketchy, labored
effort.

"This kind of weakness is completely unacceptable,"
she insisted softly, aloud this time, hoping it might give her
strength. Now, of all times, she must keep her wits about
her.

A year of grace. She'd had that long to prepare herself
for this moment. She'd even thought, until now, she'd done
a credible job of it. Why, then, did she feel on the sharp
edge of such panic and...*emptiness?*

*Stop it! Don't waste your time on emotion. It's useless.
Be practical. Look at the facts.*

The facts? Yes, they were simple enough: Derek Fontaine had arrived at last to claim his inheritance. The
Double F Ranch was his, bought and paid for with the life
and death of his uncle Richard. And Richard had been a
friend to Amber—and more—when she had needed him
most.

But none of that would matter to Derek. The bleak look
in his eyes, his stiff back and unyielding shoulders told her
that much. He was the kind of man whose loyalties belonged only to himself, and that could mean anything for
those who remained at the ranch. He was free to do whatever he chose with the Double F and its employees. He
could keep them on or not.

Amber's breathing settled with a soft grunt as the men
disappeared into the barn. Derek, she was coming to real-

ize, had a marked presence that put her on edge. Nothing about him gave the impression that he was simple or easygoing, nor did he seem much like Richard. Rather, he unnerved her with a hardness, a fierceness, that had become all too familiar in the last few years—ever since men had begun returning from that cursed war.

But that didn't matter right now, and she couldn't afford such distractions. Amber brushed the back of one hand over her forehead and turned toward the garden. The past was over and couldn't be changed. All that mattered now was Derek Fontaine's arrival, and his right to be there.

She had prayed this day would never come, but it was here—and with it, the choices she had always known would be hers. Really, there was no choice at all. She had never expected a guarantee once Derek Fontaine arrived.

Now what?

Amber swallowed and knelt among the dill plants to take up where she had left off. If he wouldn't let her stay, where in the world could she go?

*What the hell were you thinking to head south again?*

Derek couldn't stifle the question, any more than he could ignore other, similar sentiments that had occurred to him countless times since he'd left Chicago. And he had no better answers now than when he'd started. In fact, he had nothing but more questions.

He left the barn, his bedroll slung over one shoulder and a knapsack in the opposite hand. Charlie was bedded down safely, leaving Derek with nothing but questions— serious ones—about the ranch and its operations.

He slowed, glancing around, then stopped shy of the drive, flexing his shoulders with an absent frown. Now that he'd arrived and faced the reality of inheriting a cattle ranch, a new and deeper tension settled at the base of his neck.

Shit. The place was a damn mess! The barn door hung

crooked, the corral fence had broken and missing railings, and he'd gotten just close enough to the bunkhouse to recognize the unmistakable stench of rotting food. What would he find when he looked closer?

*Just your luck.* The mocking snicker came from inside his head, a voice that sounded remarkably like his father. No—not his father; the correction came quickly. He'd never heard his *father's* voice. He was thinking of the man who had married his mother.

Precisely. It sounded like Jordan Fontaine at his most sarcastic, and the voice continued. *Your inheritance is falling down around your ears. Just as you deserve.*

"Well, so what if it is?" Derek muttered. The defiance in his tone sounded disagreeably childish, and he sighed. "It doesn't matter." He added that for himself, certain it was true. He'd never expected to like this place to begin with.

But it was his now…and he had nowhere else to go and nothing to do.

He blinked, then cast another look around him. What counted was the ranch—*the land.* In that way, he must be like Richard, for that's what he was after. Land, and nothing more. No emotions and no regrets. Land…with the isolation it offered, the solitude he craved.

In a perverted sort of way, he supposed, he'd earned it. The hard way. Being the bastard son of a man who could walk away without a backward glance—not one in thirty years—should afford Derek some advantage.

He shifted the weight of his bedroll and started for the house again. He found it laughably ironic in a sad, sick sense that Richard had left his ranch to Derek. Richard, the man who had been there for the biological part of fatherhood and nothing more, then had disappeared into the wilds of Texas, seeking adventure and fortune. And Derek, the son nobody wanted.

Oh, yes. He would say he had earned every damned acre

of this place. But if his father—if Richard—had loved the place so much, why had he let it go to hell this way?

Nearing the back of the house, Derek realized that the house proper, the cookhouse and the yard all appeared to be better cared for. He credited Amber with the improvement, since she had taken responsibility for the garden.

And what a garden it was.

The plot was large and thriving, with long, straight rows of young, healthy-looking plants. They stretched to the creek that ran in the near distance, bright yellow puffs of flowers standing as sentries at the end of each row. A large cottonwood and several smaller trees provided ample shade along the creek bank.

Amber had positioned herself in the midst of it all. She crouched in a sea of green, plucking at the plants around her and dropping her harvest into a bucket. And she was humming. Her light soprano voice made the strains of *Dixie* a happy, festive tune, a melody full of joy and life as it had once sounded, before pain and death transformed it into something melancholy and mournful.

She seemed content. Derek slowed, blinking as he considered the possibility of contentment…happiness. Both seemed foreign to him. Had he ever known a life that held any part of such simple emotions?

He dropped his bedroll and knapsack to the ground and moved closer, drawn almost against his will. "I heard Abe Lincoln asked for that song to be played at the White House just after the war and before he was assassinated. Said it had always been a favorite of his."

Amber shrieked, a small yip of surprise, and shot to her feet, trying to spin around at the same time. She scrambled for balance and almost knocked over her bucket in the process.

"You frightened me!"

"Sorry." He frowned, chastising himself. Why had he said something like *that*? Referring to Lincoln—to the war at all—was a foolhardy thing to do for a man in his position, even with old friends. And he didn't know a damned thing about Amber Laughton.

He examined her with a slow, deliberate gaze. He had never seen hair quite the color of hers, a rich reddish-brown that shimmered with burnished bronze highlights. Reckless curls escaped at her forehead, her neck, and tempted him with a hint of wild beauty. Her thin, elegant nose angled above full, raspberry-red lips. Her eyes flashed with a verdant, sparkling green, and seemed to see far more than they revealed.

Her hands appeared nervous as she wiped them on her apron, already stained brown and green, and her voice intrigued him with its anxiousness. "I'm not usually so skittish. I was thinking. About the garden, I mean. The summer squash looks good, and we may have some black-eyed peas ready in a week or so."

Derek flashed a quick, mostly disinterested glance over the greenery behind her. "I'll take your word for it. I don't know anything about gardening."

"Of course."

"Are you responsible for all this?" He motioned in a grand gesture.

"Keeping house for your uncle wasn't difficult." She shrugged, making no attempt to meet his gaze. "He was very tidy in his habits. It made sense that I take over the cooking and the gardening as well. It kept me busy."

Derek nodded slowly, as though he accepted her explanation—and he supposed he did. At least in part. She said all the right things, the things he expected a woman in her position to say, and yet she spoke with singular deliberation, as though she weighed every word with particular care.

Why?

"What about the rest of the place?" He went on the offensive.

"What about it?"

"It's a mess."

"I beg your pardon!" Her eyes popped wide, and her lips tightened with obvious irritation.

"Please, Miss Laughton." He made no effort to disguise his impatience. "It's obvious the place is falling apart. I'd like to know why."

"I don't know what you're talking about."

Derek reached up to the back of his neck, massaging the tense muscles that refused to relax. Maybe this wasn't the best time for this discussion; he'd only just arrived and hadn't yet done a proper reconnaissance.

He opted for courtesy. "How long have you lived here?"

She narrowed her eyes with notable skepticism. "More than two years now. I came as your uncle's housekeeper—and his friend—and stayed after he…" Her voice trailed off, and her eyes darkened with what Derek assumed was remembered pain.

"Died." He supplied the word with a trace of impatience. It may have been a heartless reaction, but it shouldn't have been necessary. Richard's death wasn't recent. And his housekeeper still grieved?

And what about his housekeeper? Derek couldn't ignore his doubts. Why would a beautiful young woman confine herself to keeping house at a remote ranch, and for a man old enough to be her father?

Unless…she had no family or friends to whom she could turn. Or none who would claim her. He blinked, startled by the innuendo. Unless she defined *friend* differently than he did.

"Did you know Richard before that?"

She smiled thinly, as though she recognized his suspicions. "Yes. I knew him for more than ten years."

She didn't give much ground, he noted. "I hope you understand that I'll have many questions about the ranch, and my uncle. We weren't close, and I find myself at a sudden loss here.''

"Richard was a wonderful man." She shot him a spirited glare. Intrigued, he looked closer. "He was a good friend, especially when—others needed him most.''

"If you say so.''

She drew in a sharp breath and stepped back, away from him. Her eyes flared with fiery green sparks, an eloquent conviction that she'd hidden until now. She blinked slowly and then expression and fire disappeared as she fixed her gaze beyond his shoulder.

"I think it's time I showed you the house.''

Guardedly he studied the woman who stood before him, uncompromising and proud. She wasn't nearly as detached as she wanted him to believe. She cared, and passionately, about certain things, certain people. And Richard seemed to be one of them.

Had she been his mistress?

# Chapter Two

Amber arched across the mattress, stretching to tuck in the sheet. After three days of making Derek's bed, she concluded the man was a persistently restless sleeper.

*His sleeping habits are none of your business.* Her cheeks flushed with a dull heat that seemed to haunt her whenever she was in his bedroom. *Proving your worth as his housekeeper is the only thing that should concern you at the moment.*

Surely he would retain a good worker.

The subject hadn't come up yet, but she didn't delude herself. It was only a matter of time.

And then?

Amber ran her hand across the sheet, smoothing out the smallest wrinkle. She continued to hope that she could convince him to keep her on as his housekeeper, but he'd given her little encouragement thus far. Any plans he had for the ranch he was keeping strictly to himself. He *had*, however, begun to ask questions. Questions about ranch operations, about Richard, about everyone and everything. Questions she'd done her best to avoid.

*Tell him too much, too soon, and you won't need to worry about keeping this job.* She'd seen the expressions on other people's faces when they realized who she was, and she knew exactly what she could expect from Derek once he satisfied his curiosity. When he discovered *the truth*—or what so many people thought they knew and were so very eager to tell—she would have one chance to convince him to let her stay.

She didn't doubt what form of persuasion would be expected of her.

An odd sensation, like that of being watched, crawled up her spine, and she shivered. She meant to ignore it, but it persisted until finally she glanced up. Derek stood in the doorway.

"Oh!" She reared back and lost her balance, tumbling awkwardly onto the half-made bed. Cheeks flaming, she scrambled to her feet and gaped at him. He looked back with impressive detachment.

"I'm going into Twigg today. Do you need anything?"

"You startled me!" she snapped. It wasn't the first time it had happened, and she was beginning to feel a little...hunted.

"Sorry," he said instantly, but he didn't look the least bit apologetic. Instead he looked bold, untamed and roguish, leaning against the door frame with lazy grace, his arms crossed over his chest as though he had nothing better to do. He wore dark trousers and a blue cotton shirt that turned his eyes to a dazzling shade of blue.

"I was making up your bed."

He raked her with a sizzling gaze that trapped her words and made them suddenly conspicuous, as if he'd seen her clean unmentionables hanging on the clothesline.

*Making up your bed?* Dear Lord, what did she think she was doing, talking to this man in his bedroom, next to his unmade *bed?* Hadn't she learned how very easily—willfully—a man could misunderstand a woman's intentions? Certainly, if anything could be misinterpreted, it would be a woman floundering wildly on a man's mattress.

Derek remained still, however, simply watching her. He

seemed bigger and taller, his shoulders broad, and a harnessed power filled the room. Amber's cheeks remained flushed, and she clenched her fingers into tight fists. Her breath came out as a sketchy wheeze.

"Making the bed," he murmured softly, breaking the silence. He shook his head and dropped his arms to his sides. "I almost remember when things like that mattered."

Standing across the bed from him, looking into his fallen-angel features and barren eyes, she felt his proximity as keenly as if he touched her. The possibility seemed imminently dangerous.

"I beg your pardon?" She stepped back, some ancient feminine instinct insisting she put more space between them. "Don't you want me to do such chores?"

He shrugged and straightened, his movements a study in carelessness. "Go ahead. I don't care. When you've spent as many nights as I have under the stars with just a blanket, any bed at all seems like a luxury."

Amber swallowed. Was he referring to his trip here? Traveling from South Carolina to Texas on horseback would be a long, arduous journey in these days of reconstruction. Vaguely, she recalled the trip she and her father had made from St. Louis, twelve years ago now. She had been eight years old, and life then had seemed more like high adventure than grueling travel.

Or could Derek mean something else? Something like the war? A deep coldness settled heavily in her chest. To Amber's way of thinking, most able-bodied men in Texas—in all the South—had blindly enlisted to fight for the Confederate cause. They'd rushed off to fight the damn Yankees, intending to teach those sorry boys in blue a lesson they'd never forget, and be home in a month.

Four years later they'd all been dead or whipped, she thought severely, and they'd left the South in a mess from which it would likely not recover in her lifetime. They had paid dearly for their foolish Rebel bravado and forced a heavy price from their mothers and sisters and wives and sweethearts. A price no one ever seemed to consider.

Surely Derek had played his own part in the debacle. She didn't know a man who, at least in some small way, hadn't. And yet how could she blame him, any more than a thousand other men?

"Well, around here I do things like make up the beds," she announced briskly. "Just as I clean and do laundry. And you don't have to eat your meals in the bunkhouse. I cooked for Richard, and I can do the same for you."

Derek stared at her, his eyes narrowing to slivers of blue. "Are you a good cook?"

*What choice do you have?* Amber swallowed the question, reminding herself that sarcasm would do little to improve her chances of retaining her position at the Double F. Instead she shrugged. "I'm better than Six. I've eaten the rocks he calls biscuits and his son of a gun stew. Personally, I think it tastes like paste."

"Son of a...gun stew?"

"Hasn't he fixed it for you yet?"

"Yes."

"Then you know what I mean."

He nodded.

"Oh, don't worry. I know what it's really called. But Micah and Six have gone to such trouble to rename it so I wouldn't hear them say 'son of a bitch,' even about stew, I pretend for their sakes."

Derek angled his head, as though seeing her from a new perspective. "They're protective of you."

Her breathing faltered again. He made her feel as though he could see straight through her, all the way to that secret place where she kept her most treasured memories and dearest hopes. She turned from the intensity of his gaze, moving automatically as she fluffed a pillow into place.

"Yes, I suppose so," she answered finally. "But Micah should know better. My father may not have approved of my saying it, but he never kept me from knowing the truth.''

"Micah must know your father, then. Does he live nearby?''

Derek sounded as though the answer meant little to him, but Amber knew better. It was another of his endless questions and, like the ones she hated most, it was personal.

She looked at him and said flatly, "My father is dead. Did you say you were going to Twigg today?''

He blinked, then slowly nodded, as though telling himself to accept her change of topic. "Gideon will be riding with me. Can we get anything for you?''

"No." Her insides froze at the idea. "There is nothing in Twigg I could possibly want.''

"All right." He hesitated, but finally shrugged and turned toward the door. "I'll see you later.''

Amber stood motionless, waiting long, breathless minutes as his footsteps receded. When she heard the jingle of harness and the crunch of rock and shell under horses' hooves, she hurried to the window, watching as they set out at a brisk pace.

Twigg. She had left the town behind her two years ago, along with everything it represented. Now she shuddered at the mere thought of going back, of seeing the derisive faces and hearing the cruel whispers. She wrapped her arms around her midsection, as though to ward off blows.

What would happen when Derek saw the faces and heard the whispers? When he discovered the stories people told with such gloating? It wouldn't matter how much truth there was to them. He'd meet Frank Edwards, Eliza Bates—and how many others?

Oh, God. She dropped her forehead to the windowpane and gave a soft sigh. She'd hoped for more time. Time enough to prove herself.

*Well, it's too late now, and there's nothing you can do about it.*

She took a deep breath and straightened, mustering every bit of stubborn determination she had. She'd known from the very beginning that Derek would eventually learn it all; she just hadn't determined what she would do when that happened. Now the time was upon her and she could no longer avoid the hard choices.

Amber turned back to the bed and pulled the quilt into place. Truthfully, there was no question of what she would do. As always, she would do whatever she had to.

It was a matter of survival.

Derek approached the outskirts of Twigg with guarded trepidation. He shifted in his seat, at the same time squaring his shoulders in a show of strength that had become automatic to him. It wasn't that he expected anything unusual, but he prepared himself in any case. He hadn't gone out unarmed since the day he'd joined the army, and now was hardly the time to consider a change of habit. Gideon seemed of the same mind.

Alone or not, Derek didn't doubt his ability to defend himself. He had learned his lessons well and quickly, first as Jordan Fontaine's unwanted son and then, from the first day at Shiloh, on dozens of battlefields across the country. Entering Twigg could hardly compare.

His unease, it seemed, could be more directly traced to his lofty ambitions upon arriving at the Double F, and his decided inability to achieve them. He'd been looking for peace and quiet, and instead found himself at the head of a floundering ranch populated by less than a dozen men—a group of individuals more closemouthed than any battle-field spies. Talking to Amber proved little better. He'd learned a bit about her personally, but nothing of particular interest where the ranch was concerned.

Or had he?

Derek thought for a moment. Her father was dead and she hated Twigg. Knowing that, however, only led to more questions. How? And why? And most importantly, could any of it involve Richard?

If it did, then *that* concerned the ranch—and Derek.

He shook his head. It may not have been how he planned it, but if he had anything to spare, it was time. Time to understand whatever secrets lay hidden beneath the surface of life at the ranch, and time enough to resolve them. *Patience,* whispered a sixth sense he'd learned to rely on through all of the war and beyond, *isn't a virtue or a luxury. It's a necessity.*

Reaching the edge of town, Derek cast an indifferent glance at the first house, then, blinking, stared at the tumbled-down old structure. Good God, had he been overly optimistic about everything? The building listed to one side, tattered and disheveled. An overgrown tangle of grass and weeds surrounded the porch and crept up the front steps.

"Looks worse than the ranch."

Derek glanced at Gideon and lifted one eyebrow. "That takes some doing."

Gideon shrugged and a faint sparkle lit his eye—as close to smiling as Derek ever saw him. "You said you didn't know what to expect. I figure that applies here as well as the ranch. Maybe more."

This much of Twigg hardly represented the bustling little township that Frank Edwards's letter had described. "Definitely it applies here," Derek agreed. "Things don't seem quite…right."

Gideon nodded shortly, his gaze tracking left and right with sharp precision. Derek had seen it done too often to mistake the action for anything other than the defensive practice it was. Even with one eye missing, Gideon was more alert and observant than most men—and Derek had known some of the best.

At least at the beginning of the war, he amended regretfully. Many were gone now. Somehow even the best men made mistakes at times, and after four long, bloody years, mistakes began to catch up with a man.

Derek had made his share of mistakes, and most had caught up with him. Even some he'd never considered mistakes. A sour taste tickled the back of his throat, and he swallowed it down.

*Later,* he snapped to himself. *You don't have time for regrets now. You did what you had to do, fought where you had to fight. You don't owe explanations to anyone—especially anyone here.*

"I don't know what it is about this place," Gideon said after a moment, "but I don't like it."

"You're thinking of moving on, then?"

"No, not yet. I want to see just what it is that has my gut twisted like it hasn't been since..."

"Appomattox," Derek finished for him, and neither said anything more. There was nothing left to say. Some things about war didn't change, no matter who a man chose as his enemy. His life and Gideon's might have been far different before the war, but the fighting had changed all that. And later, after General Lee surrendered at Appomattox Courthouse, nothing was the same for anyone. Life before the war seemed all but meaningless now.

Derek's interest sharpened as they neared the center of town, much as Gideon's vigilance seemed to grow keener. He knew well that his uncertainty came from little more than a gut feeling, but he'd learned the hard way that his instincts were right more often than not.

"There's the bank." Derek pointed to his left and reined Charlie to a halt. "You want to look around town while I meet with Edwards?"

Gideon pulled up next to him. "Yeah." He tilted his hat, deepening the shadows that shielded his face, and slanted his good eye toward Derek. "I do."

Derek dismounted and tethered his horse, while Gideon

did the same. "I'll meet you at the mercantile in thirty minutes," said Derek as he headed for the bank.

Arriving, he probed the lobby with a keen gaze. Dark mahogany woodwork dominated the room, polished to a high shine. A marble-topped counter, graced with ornate scrolled bars, divided the room. A sour-faced clerk frowned silently from the safety of the teller cage.

"I'm looking for Frank Edwards."

Wordlessly, the man pointed to a door with Franklin Bacon Edwards, Bank President inscribed on its window glass. Derek knocked once, entered, then closed the door behind him. The man seated at the large, mahogany desk looked up, irritation sketched clearly on his features.

"Edwards."

The man's eyes grew wide, but then a smile lightened his expression and he stood. He was of average height, but his stomach protruded with amazing girth. His large drooping mustache and graying mutton chop whiskers swallowed half his face, except for sharp, rapidly blinking eyes that gave him the look of a large, overfed rodent. His dark, tailored suit enhanced the effect.

"Ah, Mr. Fontaine, I presume?" Edwards said with forced cheer as he offered his hand. "You look remarkably like your uncle."

"So I'm told." Derek accepted the handshake but withheld his smile.

"Your message came from Chicago—quite a distance from Charleston. I tried to reach you there first."

Derek shrugged, not tempted in the least to explain how he had ended up in Chicago after the war. He had no reason to trust this man with his confidences, so he merely said, "There wasn't much left in South Carolina. I decided to move on."

Edwards nodded solemnly. "The war reached us here, as well. The blockade, you know. And south Texas was occupied by Yankee troops for a time."

"So I've heard. Does that explain the condition of the Double F?"

"Down to business, is it?" Edwards's smile seemed to wear a bit thin. Derek studied the man, wondering why he would be reluctant to discuss the ranch. Or was it just Derek himself, imagining things because his own desire for privacy made him impatient with polite chitchat?

Edwards gestured to the chair opposite his desk. "Please sit down, and we'll talk."

Derek sat, resting one ankle on the opposite knee. "All right, Mr. Edwards. What can you tell me about the ranch and its present state of neglect?"

Edwards wrinkled his brow in a frown. "It's never been a matter so much of neglect, Mr. Fontaine. Richard would not have allowed that. He loved that ranch like some folks love a person. He came here just after the Andrews brothers settled this place, and built his ranch up from nothing, just a few wild mustangs and some longhorns he rounded up. He worked and sacrificed—he would have done anything to preserve that place."

Edwards shook his head, as though Richard's devotion quite eluded him, then continued. "When so many men left to join the fighting, there weren't enough left to work the big ranches. The Double F did well during the first years of the war. But being shorthanded for so long took its toll. Supplies and necessities became impossible to get, and what we did have, we shared or donated it to the Cause to keep our boys fighting. Richard did his part—and more. He supported the Confederacy with everything he could spare."

Another staunch Confederate. "I see." Derek blew out a weary breath. "So I've inherited a broken-down ranch years past needing repair, cattle and horses scattered to hell and gone, and nobody left to work it."

"There *are* still hands there, aren't there?" Edwards's cheeks flushed and his eyes widened in alarm.

"Don't you know?" Derek tried to pin the banker with a sharp frown, but the man refused to meet his gaze. "Your letter said you were overseeing the place until I got here."

"I…" Edwards paused as though reconsidering whatever he'd started to say, then merely nodded. "Yes, of course. I haven't been there in a while, though. Busy here, you know." He waved a hand to indicate his desk, which looked remarkably clutter-free.

Derek swallowed a sigh. What the hell was the use? No one seemed inclined to confide in him. "The place isn't quite deserted." He made no effort to keep the displeasure from his voice. "There are two old men, a couple of Mexican families, a boy too young to have seen much of any kind of work and a woman. *Those* are my ranch hands?"

"Six Parker worked for your uncle from the very beginning, and the Mexicans stayed through the whole of the war." Edwards counted off the workers on his pudgy fingers. "Whitley Andrews may be young and inexperienced, but he's willing. As for Micah Smith and Amber Laughton, they came together—a pair, you might say. They moved to the ranch when she was run out of town."

*"Run out of town?"* The incredulous question slipped out before he could think better of it. Derek snapped his mouth shut, effectively cutting off any other indiscreet remark, but his earlier observations taunted him.

Why would a beautiful young woman confine herself to keeping house at a remote ranch, and for a man old enough to be her father?

And his reply to himself: Unless she defined friend differently than he did.

"I am not one to carry tales, mind you," Edwards said in a prim voice that told Derek otherwise. "However, since Amber Laughton is living under your roof, I feel obligated to warn you that she was involved in some trouble with a number of men. She consorted with them after her father died—or so they say. Your uncle—well, I don't know if she bewitched him, or if he thought to do a good deed and take the hussy from our midst. In any case, she moved to the ranch, and she's been there since."

Derek said nothing for the space of a heartbeat. "Amber was Richard's mistress." It was more a statement than a question. Dozens of other questions raced through Derek's mind, but a particular reluctance to ask them of Edwards kept him silent. He'd already said too much. He would get his answers, but he'd get them from Amber.

"Only she can tell you that for sure, now that Richard is dead," said Edwards stiffly, without meeting Derek's gaze. "But I believe so, yes. I, certainly, will have nothing to do with her."

Derek tightened his jaw. He couldn't risk unleashing any emotion over Edwards's announcement. He had certain secrets from his own sordid past that he wished to leave behind him; he couldn't afford to start something he wasn't prepared to finish. He'd already revealed too much in his desire to learn more.

"All right, Mr. Edwards," he said. "And just what is it you suggest that I do as the new owner of the Double F?" He had no real interest in Edwards's opinion, but it seemed an easy diversion for the moment.

He was right. Edwards's mouth flattened in a self-deprecating smile. "It's your ranch now, Mr. Fontaine. Nothing has to remain as it was. You are under no obligation to maintain the same workers your uncle employed. At the very least, I encourage you to disassociate yourself from Amber Laughton once and for all."

"I see."

"Times are changing, people are moving west." Edwards leaned forward as though warming to his topic. "We've had two new families settle in Twigg, a man to take over the newspaper Amber's father once owned, and a man who plans to build a new hotel. More Mexicans are drifting farther north again, without the Yankee army to get in their way.''

He paused expectantly, his features smoothing themselves back into their thin, rodentlike appearance. ''The railroad has come, you know, and here in Twigg, we have plans to be a part of the progress. That can only bode well for you and your ranch. They want cattle up north, and we've got them here. Your uncle had great plans for the Double F.''

''As you said, Mr. Edwards, it's my ranch now.'' Derek offered a sparse, distant smile. ''However, I am not prepared to rush into ill-advised changes at the moment. You will find that I never make rash decisions.

''In the meantime, I have other concerns about the ranch and its financial situation. And I'd like to arrange for a personal account with your bank. If you don't mind...''

Edwards nodded, perhaps a bit eagerly, and Derek felt a coil of apprehension relax inside him. He understood this man and his desires; he was a businessman, and Derek had money. Not a fortune, perhaps—a major's commission hardly made a man rich, but there had been precious little on which to spend it during the war. In these days of reconstruction, it was more than many had. Not that he intended for Edwards to know exactly what he had or how he'd acquired it

No, he would show the overfed rodent just enough to make them friends—*good friends* in Edwards's eyes. And then?

Well, maybe then Derek would have the means to get answers to some of his other questions.

# Chapter Three

Andrews Mercantile looked like a thousand other general stores that had sprung up in the fledgling towns that had begun to dot the West. Derek stopped just inside the doorway and glanced around, inventorying the crowded interior with narrowed eyes. Groceries, dry goods and hardware filled the shelves. Kegs and barrels of sugar, flour and molasses littered the floor, squatting next to half-filled sacks of potatoes, onions and other produce.

Several women stood in a semicircle near the dry goods, murmuring among themselves, while two old men sat crouched on a pair of stubby, three-legged stools next to a cold woodstove. A middle-aged man, the proprietor, no doubt, shifted canned goods on a shelf to make room for more.

"Them wimmen cackle like a bunch a' chickens."

"Flock."

Derek followed the voices and found himself looking at the old men. They stared back. "I beg your pardon?"

The thinner of the two, balding on top and scowling, jerked his head in the direction of his companion. "A flock. A group a' birds is a flock. Clem called them a bunch."

"Dang it, Twigg." The other man, really no heavier, with fewer hairs and an almost identical sour expression, spoke up. "It don't matter about the damn birds. I was talkin' about the wimmen."

The corner of Derek's mouth kicked up in amusement, then faded in bafflement. "Twigg?" He stepped closer. "Like the town?"

"Yep." The old man straightened with peremptory pride. "They named the town after me. We was the first ones here—the founders. Clem wanted to name the place after him, but that ain't no name fer a town. Clem!" He snorted.

"Yer him, ain't you? The new feller at the Double F."

Derek hesitated, then nodded. "I'm Derek Fontaine."

"Ha! I knew it!" Clem slapped his knee with a liver-spotted hand. "Yer Richard Fontaine's nephew, all right. I'd recognize you anywhere. You look just like him. Pay up, Twigg." He held out the same wrinkled hand, palm-up.

"Dang it, Clem, when he come in you said you never seen the man before. Now yer sayin' you knew him all the time. That's cheatin' an' I ain't payin' no cheater."

The old men's quarrel took on a snappish tone, and Derek blocked them out with an ease that surprised him for a moment. But—no. It made perfect sense that the habits of the past remained deeply ingrained within him. Hadn't he spent years listening to Jordan's tirades and lectures, standing at attention before the old man's desk with bright eyes and a thoughtful face, while his mind had darted off to a far different world?

And later, when the noise and stench of thousands of men and animals, all crowded together in the hell that masqueraded as life in the army camps, had become too much, hadn't he stolen away inside himself for his own private solitude? He'd escaped that and more rather than dwell on things far more oppressive. Things like the emotions conjured up by Clem's observation.

When he'd first learned that Richard was his father, Derek had embraced the news with equal parts relief and fury. Relief because it explained so much—and fury for the very same reason. He had never seen a portrait, tintype or photograph of his father, if any had ever existed; even the mention of Richard's name was banned in Jordan's household after the death of Derek's grandmother. As a child Derek had never understood why there were so few opportunities to learn about his "uncle" Richard. Now, none of it seemed to matter.

And how odd to realize that, in order to see his father's face, he'd only needed to look in the mirror. But, damn, he was tired of hearing how he looked just like the man.

"Did they, young Mr. Fontaine?"

The sharp voice recaptured Derek's attention. "Pardon me?"

"You deaf, boy? I asked if the law ever found out who kilt yer uncle."

A thousand denials shrieked in his head, each one fierce with disbelief. Derek blinked, gathering his concentration, before attempting to eye the men with cool calculation. "Killed…as in murder?"

"Yeah, murder. Ain't nobody told you nothin'?" demanded Clem peevishly.

"Apparently not. Or maybe I've been talking to the wrong people."

"You have if you been talkin' to Frank Edwards. He sits over there in that bank, thinkin' he knows so much 'cause he studied that law and he owns the bank. Hell, he's even been pretendin' to run the Double F since Richard died. Well, let me tell you, he ain't done nuthin'—an' he knows even less. He oughta get out here with the rest a' us, and he might figger a few things out."

"What'd he tell you, anyway?" Twigg asked.

Derek hesitated. These men seemed to know more than he did, and his purpose here today was to get answers to his questions. He shrugged. "That Richard was found dead several miles from the ranch. That he'd been out alone and it looked like an accident."

"Accident, my foot!" Clem stamped the floor for emphasis. "He was shot—*murdered*—by rustlers. You mark my words!"

"Rustlers?"

"Rustlers. They been plaguin' us since the end a' the war. An' everybody 'round here knows it. Edwards knows it, too. But maybe he didn't wanna scare you off by tellin' you the truth."

Richard had been murdered, and Derek had had no idea. He hadn't even considered asking for the grisly details; after all the death and mutilation he'd seen during the war, it had seemed enough that dead meant dead.

He should have known better.

He took his time in answering. "Looks like I need to visit the sheriff."

"Bah, don't waste your time on that worthless no-good nincompoop. There's been nothin' but trouble since he took over. First year there was that mess with the Laughton girl an' her daddy, and then last year he let Fontaine git kilt."

"Uncle Clem, Uncle Twigg! Lower your voices, please! There are ladies present!" The middle-aged man strode over, his forehead creased in a harsh frown that looked remarkably identical to those of the men who were apparently his uncles. He turned to Derek, his frown easing until he looked as though he merely suffered from a severe case of dyspepsia. "I'm sorry, sir, if my uncles disturbed you. They can be quite a nuisance, I know. I'm Bill Andrews, and I'm the proprietor of this establishment. May I help you?"

Derek settled his gaze on the man. "I'm Derek Fontaine. Has someone from the Double F been in for supplies today?"

"No, sir, we haven't seen Whitley—"

"Whitley won't be in. I brought another man with me, a new hand named Gideon. Tall, dressed in black?"

Andrews shook his head. "No, sir, I haven't seen him—"

"You lookin' fer help, young Fontaine?" Clem demanded suddenly. "You got enough men to run that place yet?"

"No, Clem, not enough men. But I'm working on it."

"Well, don't you worry. There's a *bunch*—" Clem flashed a triumphant smirk in Twigg's direction "—a' men movin' around the countryside these days. Men who cain't settle down after all the years of soldierin'. You hire you some a' them good Southern boys when they show up at yer door."

"Yes," Derek agreed, though he refrained from acknowledging that he'd hire a good Northern man just as quickly. The war had been over for three years, and it was past time for them to put their lives back together and go on. Now didn't seem the best time to make his point, however. Not if he had any other questions to which he wanted answers.

He blinked, seeking a quick diversion. "Now, about some purchases I'd like to make."

"Yes?" Bill Andrews's response carried a stiff formality as his gaze darted disapprovingly between his uncles and Derek.

"Billy's got some wrinkled potatoes and soft onions he's been tryin' to get rid of," Clem suggested with a sly grin.

"How about them radishes and beets and turnips, Billy?" Twigg asked, his tone far too innocent for Derek to believe. "You ain't managed to find anybody else to take them off yer hands yet, have ya?"

The younger Andrews's eyes bugged out and his face turned a deep, shocking red. Lord, had the old men sent him into a fit of apoplexy? Derek shot a half concerned, half amused glance from one to the other.

The breath rushed out of Bill Andrews in one great whoosh, and he bellowed, "Uncle Clem! Uncle Twigg!"

The old men beamed at Derek and nodded proudly before they turned their attention back to their nephew. Their antics tempted Derek to smile—dammit, to grin—as he hadn't been so persuaded in a very long time.

As a child he'd often wished for a bit of nonsense from the ever-serious Jordan, but jokes and teasing had been beyond the man. Instead, Derek and his older brother—his *half* brother, he knew now—had relied on each other for their all-too-brief bits of fun, and he could almost picture the two of them in thirty or forty years, languishing in Clem's and Twigg's places.

*God, Nathan.* Memories slammed through Derek with all the force of a minié ball. He turned away and closed his eyes. *Where did we go so wrong? I never meant for things to end like they did. I'm sorry…so damn sorry.*

"Mr. Fontaine! Wait a moment…please! My uncles were just making sport, and I—well, I sometimes lose my temper with them. We'll have an excellent variety soon, but at the moment we have only a few early crops and what's left from last year."

Derek swallowed a weary sigh and turned back. "I don't need anything like potatoes or onions, Mr. Andrews. The Double F has a very healthy, producing garden of its own."

"Thanks to that horrid Amber Laughton!" The pronouncement came from the direction of the dry goods, where the ladies present had seemed busy choosing among several bolts of fabric. One of the women, rotund and frowning, separated herself from the group and stalked over to them.

"Now, Eliza, don't get started."

"Bill Andrews, how can you say that? After what she did, why do you men insist on taking up for her? Thank God *some* men, like my dear son-in-law, are smarter than that."

Derek stared at the woman, eyes narrowed to cloak his instant dislike of her and her intrusion. "I'm afraid you have me at a disadvantage, madam."

"Oh, don't listen to these fools, young Fontaine." Clem waved his hand at the store in general. His earlier frown returned, and he stared at the others, blinking rapidly. It put Derek oddly in mind of a demented chicken. "This here's Eliza Bates. Eliza, meet Derek Fontaine, Richard's nephew. If'n he's anything like his uncle, he ain't gonna wanna listen when you bellyache about Amber anymore'n we do. It gets mighty tiresome, let me tell you."

"Clem Andrews!"

Derek ignored the disgruntled cry. "And what is there to bellyache about, Clem?" He rather enjoyed Eliza Bates's sharply indrawn breath.

No one answered for a moment, nor did they meet Derek's gaze as he looked at them, one by one, until Twigg finally said, "There ain't nothin' wrong with Amber. She had her a little trouble a couple a' years back an' some folks cain't fergit it." He shot an angry chicken-blink, identical to Clem's expression, at Eliza. "Some folks just don't want 'er to have a life 'cept'n what *they* decide she kin have." Twigg's eyes sparked with defiance. "Me an' Clem, we feel different."

"Yep," Clem added. "We feel different about a lot a' things from other folks, an'—"

"If you gentlemen—and ladies—will excuse me..." Derek interrupted as smoothly as possible. He sought an even tone, firmly stifling the impatient snap that would have satisfied him far more. He couldn't afford to alienate these people—not yet. Not if there was a chance they could provide answers to other questions he had.

Indeed, they seemed willing enough to talk.

But, Christ! Why hadn't Richard gone insane himself, living with this bunch—Derek fought back an impulsive smile—of lunatics?

"Mr. Fontaine, wait!" Bill Andrews's cry stopped him before he'd taken a step. "You said you had some purchases to make?"

"That can wait, Mr. Andrews. I think I've had enough for one day." He shot a last, amused glance at Clem and Twigg as he turned to leave. Clem winked at him.

"Mr. Fontaine!"

The strident grating of Eliza Bates's voice stopped him just short of the door. He turned, waiting as she bore down on him, but he made no attempt to disguise the impatience in his voice when he said, "Yes?"

"Don't let a pretty face and soft voice fool you, Mr. Fontaine." Her expression offered a peculiar mixture of angry disapproval, authority and earnestness. "Amber Laughton has a history of bewitching men into seeing whatever she wants them to. You listen when I tell you she was responsible for her own downfall and the death of her father."

He stared, withholding any outward reaction. "And why should that concern me, madam?"

She snorted in a startlingly masculine manner. "She is a shameless hussy with no morals or decency! When she couldn't seduce my son-in-law, she became your uncle's mistress, and she's still living at the ranch, from what I hear. *Your* ranch now. If you're looking for a fancy woman of your own—"

"It will be no one's business but my own, Mrs. Bates." The whole ridiculous exchange suddenly irritated the hell out of him. "Good day."

Escaping to the veranda at the front of the house, Amber started the rocking chair in motion with a push of her toes, and settled back for a few moments of relaxation.

It was her first chance of the day to relax. She'd wasted too much time watching Derek ride toward Twigg—too much time thinking—which left her scrambling to catch up on her chores. Even in the garden, where she could usually dawdle for hours, she'd had to rush just to finish the watering. Now, finally, this private time came as a pleasant escape.

Amber closed her eyes and laid her head against the back of the chair, yielding to the enveloping darkness. With unerring precision, she found herself again considering the precariousness of her situation, the uncertainty of life. If she was forced to leave the ranch, where would she go? She had no family save Micah, and they weren't even related. And how could they leave? Micah's rheumatism would never stand the trip, and they hadn't the money to go. Frank Edwards had been stingy with their wages since Richard's death.

Enough of that. The shadows had become oppressive, her perspective distorted, and life seemed only painful—unbearable.

*Stop it.* She jerked forward and opened her eyes, planting her foot flat and bringing the rocker to an abrupt halt. She drew in a ragged breath, blinking against the darkness and smoothing her fingers lightly across her brow. She shoved back an errant curl, and then, as she dropped her hands to her lap, she saw him.

Derek stood at the base of the porch steps, his head back, and he seemed to be staring directly at her. Darkness concealed the fine details, but she didn't doubt for a moment that it was him. His size, his bearing, everything about the man marked his identity.

How long had he been there? And more importantly, how was it that she could recognize him so easily, after no more than a few days' acquaintance?

"It's a lovely evening," she said softly, the first thing that came to mind. The politeness of her voice seemed oddly appropriate, considering her earlier bad temper.

"You seem to be enjoying it."

"I am. We won't be so lucky this summer."

He shrugged. "I've endured worse."

*Worse?* Amber kept the question to herself. Derek seemed to care little for the comforts of civilization, yet Richard had described life for the Fontaines of South Carolina as being one of privilege and luxury. Then again, she remembered Richard sharing other stories of living in the bosom of the family.

"Richard described summers in South Carolina as being…*difficult,* I think was the word he used."

"My—he told you of his life there?"

Amber nodded, then realized that Derek couldn't see her through the darkness. "He talked of Charleston and your family on occasion. He loved it, missed it, I think, but he seemed satisfied with his life." She smiled fondly and settled back in the rocker. "He was an adventurer, he said, better suited to conquering new worlds."

Somehow the evening shadows seemed to ease her discomfort with Derek. Perhaps it gave her the illusion of anonymity? Or perhaps it was because she couldn't see his fallen-angel features and bleak eyes, that face of Richard's that wasn't Richard at all.

"An interesting assessment of my uncle. Not one I would have made." Derek's voice carried an unmistakable edge of disapproval. "Since I hadn't the pleasure of meeting Richard, however, I'm hardly qualified to disagree."

"I think it was his love for your family home that kept him from adopting a more traditional Texas style for the ranch house. Adobe was fine for some of the buildings—" she waved a vague hand toward the assortment of shadowy outbuildings "—but it wasn't right for his *home.* I gather there are similarities between this house and the one at Palmetto?"

"I suppose, from a nostalgic viewpoint." Darkness shifted around Derek as he moved, and his boots thudded against the wood of the steps as he started upward. "I understand that Richard started with very little here. He did well for himself.''

"Yes, he did well, but it was never easy. He worked very hard. He told wonderful stories of how he slept out in the open at first, capturing a few wild mustangs and some longhorn cattle.'' Amber smiled, the reminiscence giving her real pleasure. It came as a distinct relief from sidestepping the ceaseless, difficult questions that had preoccupied Derek until now. "He didn't construct the house until he was able to find the original Spanish land grant so he could purchase the property."

"Sounds like the mark of a good businessman.''

An unusual emphasis on the words alerted Amber to some skepticism. "You disagree with his reasoning?''

A rustle of fabric left her wondering if he shrugged, then she caught the dismissive wave of his hand. "You tell me how effective it was. The place is all but falling down around us.''

"It is not!'' She surged forward, and her goodwill toward him disappeared with the last emphatic word.

"Of course it is. Why are you so defensive? Have you taken a good look around you lately? There's more to fix than there is right.''

Amber found herself on her feet, the rocking chair clattering behind her. "That may be, but it's not because of incompetence or mismanagement on Richard's part. Don't even think such a thing! There may be some problems, yes, but aside from his death, it's because of—''

"The war, I know.'' He cut her off, his voice sharp. "I know all about the war. Frank Edwards gave me the same excuse. I didn't believe it any more coming from him.''

"Of course it was the war,'' she snapped, unable to stop herself. "Everything goes back to *the war* these days. But there's more to it—you must know that. There was the cattle rustling. And Richard's death.'' The words ran out as hastily as they had come, leaving Amber momentarily breathless.

"Ah, now there's another interesting topic." Derek sounded indifferent—disturbingly so. It sent Amber's nerves screaming and did nothing to restore her breathing. "Rustling," he continued. "And murder."

"What do you mean?"

"I get the impression your father didn't exactly die of natural causes." He neared the top step and stopped, but his words continued as her heart began to pound. "Nor did Richard, it seems. Why didn't you tell me he was murdered by rustlers?"

Amber gaped at him, but the darkness revealed nothing. "You didn't know how he died?"

"How did you think I would find out?"

"The same way you found out you'd inherited the Double F. From Frank Edwards, I suppose."

Derek laughed, but it was a sharp, hostile sound. "It seems there was a lot Mr. Edwards neglected to tell me."

Amber nodded in spite of herself. She never would have expected to agree with Derek, but he was right about Frank Edwards. Still, she chose her words carefully, fearful that saying the wrong thing would shift his attention back to probing for details of her father's death. "It has been my experience that Mr. Edwards has a habit of...reordering the truth to suit himself."

"You mean he lies."

"He likes things tidy. Arranged as he wants them."

"Dammit, Amber!" The words erupted from Derek, startling her with their strength and volume—and his use of her given name. Until this moment, he had not referred to her by any name at all.

"Why is everything such a holy secret around here?" he demanded irritably, climbing the final stair. "Why won't anyone *talk* to me?"

"We *are* talking to you," she said softly, firmly, holding

her ground despite the temptation to step back. "You just don't want to hear the answers we have. There's nothing we can do about that."

The night fell quiet for a moment that grew painfully long.

"Perhaps you're right." Derek's voice sounded mild enough, but it carried a razor's edge all the same. "That reminds me, I have a message for you."

"A message?" Her fingers began trembling, and she wove them together tightly.

"Regards. From Clem and Twigg Andrews." Derek stepped forward until he was within arm's length of her.

"You met the Andrews brothers." Ordinarily she would have smiled to think of the eccentric old men, but she couldn't seem to muster one now.

"Among other people. They're an interesting pair. More intelligent than their nephews. Bill or Whitley. Bill's a bit fussy, but he doesn't have Whitley's temper. The old men are more honest than Frank Edwards. And friendlier than Eliza Bates."

Amber blinked and wished the darkness away, feeling an acute need to see Derek's face.

He'd met Eliza Bates.

Dear Lord, why her, of all people? Had she been alone, or had Melinda—or, worse, Jeff—been with her? Amber couldn't ask such questions, but she managed what she could. "You met a number of people."

"I should have stopped in Twigg before I came to the ranch. They're an entertaining, informative bunch."

"Entertaining?" God in Heaven, why couldn't she *think?* She knew very well that Derek was toying with her, but she couldn't seem to do anything about it.

She put one hand to her forehead, as though it might help. It didn't. She could only stand there and stare into the darkness, wishing away the shadows that now offered Derek their protection instead of her.

"The Andrews brothers are quite smitten with you. Some of your other neighbors didn't seem quite so enamored."

*He knew everything.* At least everything the people in Twigg knew—or thought they knew. And that, in all reality, amounted to nothing. Less than nothing. If they thought her responsible for her father's death and her own fall from grace, so be it. Pride—and perhaps a twinge of guilt— would not allow her to dignify such accusations.

She supposed she had anticipated this moment from the day Derek arrived. It should have come as a distinct relief that the wait was over. It didn't, and she could only stand there dumbly.

"Tell me, Amber," he asked in a lazy voice she didn't believe for a minute, "*were* you Richard's mistress?"

# Chapter Four

"So, that's how they remember me in Twigg." Her voice held no discernable emotion.

Derek wished suddenly that he could see her face, her eyes. Dammit, he hadn't meant to broach the subject tonight. He'd planned to wait until tomorrow, when he'd had a chance to think about his questions and how he would phrase them. When his gut had a chance to settle down and not make him all but sick at the thought of Amber with *his father*.

Derek swallowed heavily. If only she hadn't spoken so fervently, her soft, feminine voice defending Richard with such passion. Hearing it, he found his better judgment vanishing like the once-glorious Cause that so many had defended with such ardent belief. And, much as the Confederacy had been left defenseless after Appomattox, Derek's wayward plans had abandoned him to a fierce hunger that all but consumed him.

*Hunger?* He would have liked to laugh at the word, but he couldn't. Not when it so weakly described what he felt: a sudden, thrusting, wholly shocking and entirely unwelcome, red-hot desire. For Amber Laughton, a soiled dove. A seductress. *His father's mistress.*

*Ah, Christ.*

"You expected something different?" he snapped, his voice heavy with equal parts doubt and animosity. Damn his body for betraying him. And damn his mind for reminding him of all the reasons. He shoved a hand under the hair at his nape and rubbed the back of his neck, where the tension of the day always seemed to settle. "I don't imagine they run that many people out of town."

"*Run...out of town?* I—is that what they're saying?"

"It's what Frank Edwards and Eliza Bates said."

"And you believed them," she said softly, shadows shifting as she straightened.

"Why wouldn't I?"

"You're right, of course. Why wouldn't you? I'm sure Frank Edwards has been the epitome of honesty and truth with you. And Eliza Bates is known as the soul of discretion."

Her observation stung; Edwards *had* misled him, and Amber knew it. The man had lied—more than once—and about important things, such as Richard's death and the condition of the ranch. He could have exaggerated the situation with Amber, as well. But why would he?

Then again, why not? Edwards had no reason to do anything that served any purpose but his own, and who knew what the hell that might be? His intentions needn't be any clearer than anyone else's around this godforsaken place.

And what about Eliza Bates? She had made a point of approaching him with her hateful gossip. He couldn't deny that he cared little for her manner or her general outlook. Still, the uncertainties rankled.

"You, on the other hand, have been so very forthcoming in all of our conversations," he pointed out, making no effort to disguise his sarcasm.

A heartbeat of silence passed. "You're right. Again. I keep expecting you to react as Richard would have...and I continue to be disappointed."

"I never pretended to be like my—uncle." He used the

title grudgingly. It galled him to call Richard or Jordan by anything but their names; neither deserved more. ''You and others here insist on a physical resemblance between us, but that doesn't necessarily lead to other similarities.''

''My mistake, I assure you. I apologize if it offends you.''

Derek shrugged. ''*Offense* isn't the word I'd use. I'd have to care to be offended.''

''You don't care? You have no regrets that Richard died a stranger to you?''

''Regrets?'' he asked shortly. She couldn't begin to imagine. There were days when he thought of little besides the many things he had to regret in this life, but Derek wasn't about to explain. Not to her, and not now. ''It's difficult to regret what you never knew.''

''I would think that alone would be reason enough. But then, I don't really know you, do I?''

''No more than I know you,'' he agreed.

''I don't see, then, what else we have to discuss, so I will say good-night.'' She reached the front door before he sensed that she'd even begun to move.

Derek reached out and caught her arm just as she entered the house. The fabric of her sleeve was soft to the touch, from wear and many washings, he'd guess, considering the limited wardrobe he'd seen her wear. She had a brown dress and a gray one, both plain cotton. Which had she worn today?

What did it matter? It didn't, and yet his body felt singularly alive, touching her like this, and he wanted to know. He tightened his fingers around her upper arm, as though the color would imprint itself on his skin, or perhaps to chase away his other, lustful thoughts. It didn't do either.

She went abruptly still, but she stood her ground, silent and stiff. He couldn't even hear the sound of her breathing.

''You never answered my question,'' he said softly. He loosened his grip, enough to save her from bruising. Even so, the muscles in her arm tensed, as if she were preparing for further confrontation.

"No, I didn't. And I don't intend to."

"No?" He lowered his voice to just above a whisper and allowed disbelief to color his tone. "And why not?"

Amber turned, forcing him to step closer or release his grip. He didn't let go. "Would you believe me?"

"I…"

"You see? You can't say for sure, can you? Or if you can, it would be to say no, you wouldn't believe any defense I could give you." She tried to move away. "So why put either of us through that?"

He tightened his hold just enough to keep her still. "You seem awfully sure of yourself."

"Do you really think that?" She gave a delicate snort. "Well, let me tell you what I *am* sure of. I'm sure of all the times I tried to explain myself to people like Frank Edwards and Eliza Bates. If they didn't believe in me, why ever do you think I would expect you to? Did Frank Edwards tell you he propositioned me?"

Derek's stomach churned fretfully, but he swallowed and ignored it. "He didn't mention it."

"No, I don't suppose he would. Well, he asked me to become his mistress both before and after I moved to the ranch. And he's never forgiven me for turning him down."

"I see." Derek drew in a deep breath, and along with it the sweet scent of vanilla. It seemed suddenly familiar, and he realized he had begun to associate it with Amber.

"Do you really? Do you understand, then, why I've stopped answering questions such as yours?"

"Are you saying, in this roundabout way, that you *didn't* try to seduce Eliza Bates's son-in-law? And you *weren't* Richard's mistress?"

He heard a sharp intake of breath, then nothing. "I'm not saying anything," she said eventually. "My answer doesn't matter."

"Doesn't matter? To you or to me?"

"To anyone. Now let me go." She tugged at her arm.

Derek didn't release her, but he didn't tighten his grip, either. "I could argue that I have a right to know."

Complete and utter silence followed his pronouncement, then Amber jerked her arm back with little care, as though she took serious offense at either his touch or his statement. "What gives you any rights where I'm concerned?" she demanded hotly, and darted into the house.

He stepped inside behind her. "I own the Double F. That makes me responsible for everyone here—including you. It gives me the right to know something about you."

A soft yellow light flared suddenly and the smell of sulfur tickled his nose. Amber stood across the hall, next to a small table. She dropped the spent match, its tip blackened and shriveled, into a small pottery bowl, then replaced the glass chimney on the flickering lamp and turned to face him.

"I don't work for you." She spoke evenly but firmly. "I *worked* for your uncle and stayed until Richard's heir arrived. It was part of my obligation to him."

"And that's finished now?" He probed her face, the verdant green eyes that shone like emeralds in the golden lamplight, but her expression revealed nothing.

"Nearly so, it seems. You haven't hired me, and without that, you have no rights where I'm concerned."

"Do you *want* to work for me?" The question came from nowhere.

She watched him for several long, silent moments, then finally blinked. "I don't know." She nestled her hands together and held them in front of her, against her stomach.

It was the faded gray dress that she wore today, with the round white collar and tiny white buttons down the front. Was she trembling? Surely not. She had defended herself and Richard adamantly, fearlessly, at every turn.

Or was it his stare, intense and relentless? But what other

choice did he have? Her crystalline eyes revealed little and saw far too much. And her lips, soft and full, parted just enough to tease him with a hint of white teeth and pink tongue.

"Your position here is secure," he snapped. It had never occurred to him that she would not remain. "I can't afford to fire anyone. There aren't enough of us to work the ranch now. But I expect the same work for the same wages Richard paid. Until we make some improvements and the Double F starts paying for itself, there isn't money for anything more."

He paused, waiting, but she didn't respond. Irritation and relief battled for dominance. Hell, he didn't *need* a housekeeper; why didn't he just fire her?

"Is that what you wanted to hear?" he demanded with some frustration.

"I suppose so, yes. Something like that." Something in her expression flickered, disturbing him. Was that... vulnerability he saw?

"You intend to stay, then?"

She blinked, averting her eyes. "Yes."

"Then you must accept one thing." He meant to regain control of the situation. "There can be no misunderstanding."

"And that is?"

"Honesty. I expect complete honesty from all who work for me. I will not tolerate a lie, under any circumstances. Is that clear?"

Amber drew herself up, tall and proud and sure. "Absolutely. Honesty is a virtue I greatly esteem, myself. I have never lied to you, and you have my word that I will not do so in the future."

She turned toward the back of the house and her bedroom, tucked behind the stairs at the end of the hall, then stopped and glanced back over her shoulder. "I will always be honest with you, Derek. But that doesn't mean I will share my every thought with you. Those are mine, burden or comfort, and I will keep them to myself.''

Amber wielded her broom with swift, sure strokes, cleaning dirt, twigs and leaves from the back stoop. She had long ago accepted the light, gusty breeze as a part of everyday life in south Texas, and the daily routine of sweeping the walkway gave her some comfort now and served as a balm to her fractious nerves and wounded pride.

Derek's questions, followed by his other bold, disdainful remarks, had kept Amber awake through much of the night. The multitude had chased themselves around in her mind like a litter of kittens after their tails. Somewhere in the middle of the night, she had realized the significance of her refusal to answer his direct question. For reasons Amber still didn't understand, he had let her have her way. She had not bested him, and she did not try to delude herself into thinking that she had. It wasn't that he had accepted her answer—or, more accurately, her lack of an answer. Nor had he given up searching for a response that satisfied him. He would ask again—and likely soon.

And then what?

It didn't matter. Nothing mattered as long as she could keep her job.

The words echoed with importance as she reached the cookhouse. Amber swallowed. Derek could fire her as easily as he'd agreed to let her stay. He had given her nothing more than an opportunity to prove herself...a little space in which to breathe. Only a fool would waste it.

She swept the pile of debris into her weeding bucket before she propped the broom against the wall, next to the door. If she hurried, she could start her own recipe for son of a gun stew before Six got to it. She wiped her dusty hands on her apron and stepped inside.

A huge worktable dominated the room, its top nicked and scarred from years of use. Amber used it to assemble the first ingredients for her stew. Banging a large cook pot down on one end, she turned toward the door and spied Derek.

He watched her as he pulled the brown, wide-brimmed hat from his head and tossed it onto the tabletop. He ran his hands through his blond hair, shoving it back from his face.

She swallowed and inhaled a deep breath. He moved with an unhurried, lazy grace she'd never noticed in another man. And his hair—did it feel soft as silk, as it looked? One breath stumbled over another and sent her heart pounding.

*Don't be stupid!* She forbade herself the least physical reaction to Derek. He presented enough complications to her life as it was.

"Were you looking for me?" she snapped. "I was on my way to the smokehouse."

"We need to talk."

*"Talk?"* He wanted to talk? Already?

"Talk. As in engage in a discussion."

"Yes, I know what it means. But…now?" She swept a quick, agitated gaze around the room. "I'm in the middle of son of a gun stew."

He almost smiled. "That's good news. I expected to have to fetch the doctor if Six kept feeding us. Are you sure you can do it?"

"I'm an excellent cook." She drew herself up and threw her shoulders back, emphasizing every capable inch.

"I didn't mean *that.* I meant do you have time?"

Amber nodded. "I can manage. For a while. At least until you hire more men."

"I'll see if I can find us a cook then."

"Well, if that's all you wanted…" Surreptitiously she stepped to the side, hoping he wouldn't notice until she had reached the door. How did he manage to fill a room with little more than his presence, or make her feel as though she needed the open skies and fresh air to breathe?

"Do I make you uncomfortable?"

"What?" She stopped moving and peered at him—and couldn't help noticing differences between them. He stood at least six inches taller and outweighed her by close to eighty pounds. His muscled strength was apparent in his arms and chest, even under the fabric of his brown cotton shirt, and his narrow waist made his thighs look like the trunks of large trees.

She felt like the weakest of saplings next to him.

"You don't want to talk to me, do you?" His eyes glittered with challenge, daring her to answer.

*Will you do it?* they seemed to demand. *Will you tell me the truth, like you promised last night?*

"No." She shook her head. "I don't."

"Why not?"

"Because you never seem satisfied with what I say."

It was enough of the truth for now. She just didn't add that she had trouble concentrating on the things she said because a part of her was too busy noticing him as a *man*. She had from the very beginning. And that his physical presence made her suddenly aware of herself as a woman.

She swallowed and added, "And because you never take anything at face value. You always seem to suspect a hidden meaning, an ulterior motive—and you make me… uneasy." It was a better word than *nervous*. Or *self-conscious*.

"Maybe I wouldn't have to look for *hidden meanings* if someone would *talk* to me. If I didn't have to pry out every bit of information as if you held the secrets to Lincoln's assassination and the rest of us had never heard of John Wilkes Booth."

She glared at him. "Don't be ridiculous. There's nothing to *tell* that you don't already know."

"Just like I knew that Richard was murdered? Like I

know how your father died? Or that you were run out of town?''

''You didn't ask those questions,'' she said tightly as she battled the urge to throttle him. ''It wasn't my place to tell you anything about Richard's death. I thought you knew already. The rest of it was none of your business.''

*''None of my business?''* He shot her a fierce glare. ''I own the Double F. I didn't ask for it, I didn't expect it. This inheritance was thrust upon me with no warning, no explanation, and I'm entitled to some questions.''

''Why accept your inheritance then, if you didn't want it? Why not stay in Charleston with your family and forget about this ranch in godforsaken Texas?''

Derek closed his eyes for a moment, two, then opened them to reveal a very clear, very blue void. He stared at her with blank simplicity and said, ''Will you answer my questions?''

What choice did she have? She recognized his growing frustration in his inability to find satisfactory answers, but she hated remembering the things he was asking about. She knew so little. Only enough to be frightened.

She had already far overstepped her bounds with her impudent questions and brazen observations, however. If she continued with such insolence or refused to answer him, he might reconsider his offer.

She sighed. ''All right.''

''Please sit down.'' He gestured to the nearest chair of four that flanked the table.

She sat, folding her hands together with prim seriousness and resting them on the tabletop. She watched him cautiously, expectantly, but made no attempt to conceal her asperity.

Derek remained silent, studying her with those brilliant blue eyes that shared nothing of the man behind them. Finally he pulled out a chair, and the wooden legs screeched across the plank floor. He sat, never taking his eyes off her.

"Frank Edwards said the Double F was once a successful cattle and horse ranch, that the war caused its present condition. Is that true?"

"For the most part."

His mouth tightened. "What is the rest of it, then?"

She shook her head. "Richard didn't confide in me, and he stopped discussing business in my presence after my father died. I can only tell you what I witnessed or overheard."

"Go on."

She took a deep breath and wet her suddenly dry lips with her tongue. "The Double F did very well for a long time. Once the war started, Richard all but worked himself to death to keep it going. But after a while, around the middle of the war, I suppose, he had to slow down."

She glanced down at her twined fingers and noticed her knuckles had turned white. She tried to relax her grip. "By then, not only weren't there enough men, but the Cause desperately needed money, supplies, whatever anyone could spare." She looked at Derek. "You must know what it was like."

He stared back at her, his gaze distant. Eventually he angled his head in her direction. "Yes."

"Richard gave all that he could. More than he should." She smiled sadly. "He had a little cash besides Confederate scrip, which by then was all but worthless, but he couldn't afford to part with it. He had to start making choices. The cattle and horses came first or there wouldn't be a ranch, he said, so that's what he worked to save. Other things just had to be ignored."

She glanced at Derek, whose eyes were alert with polite interest. "When the fighting was over, things didn't improve. There still wasn't any money, and Richard couldn't afford the wages he'd paid before the war. When men began drifting through...well, too many young, healthy ones didn't come home. Some were unable to do this kind of work, while others couldn't settle down.''

She paused, listening for a moment to the distant sounds of men and horses on a typical ranch workday. Richard had always said they were the sounds of heaven to him. The thought made her smile, and she continued.

''The violence started...oh, more than two years ago. At first it seemed like just something more for Richard to worry about. There wasn't enough law here, with too many strange, angry men moving through the countryside. Sheriff Gardner was new and untrained, and the violence became considerable. Eventually it seemed like rustlers were targeting the Double F.''

''The same rustlers who murdered him?''

Amber closed her eyes, but then immediately reopened them. The question allowed no escape, and the darkness made it all too easy for Richard's image to return in full color and detail. Not the warm, laughing man she had come to love, but as she'd last seen him, cold and still, with a bullet in his chest.

She glanced aside, through the window, and saw Gideon stride purposefully across the yard to the corral. ''I assume so,'' she said in a sketchy voice no more than a whisper. ''No one ever saw them, before or after. I believe Richard had his suspicions before the shooting, but he refused to share them with me. For my own protection, he said. And since he's been gone, the rustling has stopped.''

''Stopped?'' Derek straightened and stared at her, his interest obviously piqued.

''At first I thought it was because Richard was dead. That it may have been a personal grudge, though I can't imagine it. He had no enemies that I knew of.''

She paused, probing Derek's expression. Had something flickered in his gaze? Had his mouth tightened? He stared back, his expression as flat and distant as she had come to expect from him, and she decided she must have been mistaken.

"During the first few months I was here, several others were wounded mysteriously. No culprit was ever found, and they left before Richard died. More left after his murder, until we had only the men who are here now. I've thought about it and decided perhaps the rustlers simply didn't need to continue. Without a leader and enough men to work the ranch—"

"There was no need to steal the cattle. They could just round them up after they wandered off," Derek finished for her.

"Yes. Men on smaller ranches simply turned their cattle loose when they left to fight."

He leaned back, tilting the chair to stand on its rear legs, and nodded thoughtfully. "It's quite ingenious, really. You've heard nothing more since Richard died?"

"No. I don't go into Twigg and only the Andrews brothers visit, so I remain relatively isolated. Men don't often tell women things of that nature, and though my father was an exception, that hasn't been the case here."

Derek leaned forward, resting his powerful forearms on the table. "Who was in charge until I arrived?"

"No one, really." She paused as sudden activity in the yard caught her attention through the window. A man and horse approached, and Gideon strode out to meet them, Whitley close on his heels. Amber smiled to herself, wondering if admiration or jealousy struck Whitley more. Since Gideon's arrival, the young cowboy had rarely let the man out of his sight.

Regretfully, she turned her attention back to Derek. "Six has been here the longest and knows the most about ranching, but he's not a leader and he knows it. Micah does what he can, but he had no one when I left Twigg, so he came with me. He doesn't have the experience and he's not up to the challenge physically. Whitley would like to take control, but he's young and inexperienced, and no one listens to him. Frank Edwards issued instructions from town, but he never came himself. He sent them with Whitley so, again, no one would listen. Juan and Carlos are hard workers and will do what is asked of them, except..."

"Except what?"

"Well, they disapprove of taking orders from a woman."

Derek's eyes narrowed. "You were willing to take on the responsibility if the men had cooperated?"

"Please don't misunderstand." She almost reached for him, intending to make her point with a light touch to his arm as she would have done with Richard, but she stopped herself after merely unclasping her hands. She flexed her fingers, then laid them flat on the tabletop. "I don't want to get anyone into trouble. We all did our best, in our own ways, to keep the Double F going until you arrived. I just thought if the men would have listened—"

"Boss? You in here?" Whitley barreled into the cook-house, scouring the room with wide, sullen eyes. The youngest vaquero at the ranch, he retained the thin wiriness common to boys who had not yet reached their full maturity. Amber had rarely seen him with anything but a brooding expression on his face.

Derek turned, and she heard him sigh. "What?"

"Gideon said to fetch ya." Whitley's voice carried an unmistakable edge, sharp enough to approach the point of disrespect. "There's a man here lookin' fer work."

Derek blinked. "Good." He spoke as though he didn't notice the insolence, but Amber knew better. Derek missed nothing. "I'll be right out."

"I dunno, boss. We need men, but..."

"But what?"

Amber glanced out through the window once more, but she could see only Gideon's back and the well-ridden gelding that stood next to him. Curious, she looked from Derek to Whitley.

"Well, I dunno what he can do. He ain't all there."

*"What?"* Derek stood as he uttered the question, and his chair skittered back behind him. The word came out low and fierce.

"It's his arm." Whitley gave a dismissive wave. "He's only got one."

She looked at Derek, but nothing about him indicated his least emotion as he strode past Whitley. His beard and mustache did a fine job of concealing his expression. She caught a glimpse of things in his eyes now and then—things she never quite understood—but it wasn't enough to reveal anything about the man beneath the fallen-angel features.

# Chapter Five

Derek knew the stranger was another veteran without having to see the man. Doubtless he was, as Clem and Twigg had noted, another man moving across the country because he couldn't settle down after years of fighting.

Or, like Derek himself, because he had no home to return to—until he'd come here, that is. And the case could be made that Derek himself had helped to destroy his own home.

But that was old news. Not entirely true, and it wouldn't matter if it had been. He had the Double F now. It was, at the very least, a place to *be*.

He headed down the brick pathway, passing Amber's tidy herb garden, then cut across the yard. Derek swallowed a sharp grunt of annoyance as Whitley's footsteps scuffled along behind him.

Gideon waited near the barn, standing with the stranger next to a spent, nondescript brown gelding. Derek blinked as he approached, concealing his interest beneath lowered lashes.

The newcomer was tall, perhaps an inch shorter than Derek. His dusty clothes and overlong hair suggested he'd spent some hard days on the trail. And he had both his arms. It was his left hand and forearm, to just below his elbow, that were missing.

Derek tightened his lips. It didn't appear that Whitley cared whether or not he got his facts straight. He formed opinions based on little or no information, and seemed to expect that others would believe even his most outlandish claims if only he repeated them often enough. Worse, he never knew when to keep his mouth shut.

"I'm Derek Fontaine." He held out his hand. "I own the Double F."

The man blinked as though dazed and stared at Derek's outstretched hand. He looked tired, the color washed from his face, and his pale complexion emphasized the dark circles beneath his eyes and the hollows of his cheeks. He raised his gaze slowly to Derek's, revealing eyes unnaturally wide and grave and heavy with something resembling...despair.

"Beauregard Montgomery, Mr. Fontaine." He finally responded with his own introduction and shook Derek's hand.

"What can I do for you, Mr. Montgomery?"

"I…" He looked away, allowing a moment of silence to pass before he glanced back at Derek. Or, more accurately, at a spot somewhere beyond Derek's shoulder. "I wondered if you had any work for a fellow like me."

*A fellow like me.* Derek would go to his grave hearing men—friends, comrades, enemies alike—describe themselves in such terms. They meant a man without an arm, a leg, or perhaps an eye, like Gideon. Men who believed they had lost the best part of themselves—their manhood—as well.

Derek nodded solemnly, betraying nothing of his thoughts. He turned to Whitley. "Whitley, take care of Mr. Montgomery's horse."

"But that ain't my job! I was workin' with Gideon an'—"

"Come on, Whitley." Gideon gathered the gelding's reins and held them out. "You take care of Mr. Montgomery's horse like Derek says."

Whitley glanced from Derek to Gideon, his eyes narrow and angry. Derek stared back in stubborn silence. It took some effort, but he reminded himself of the need to curb his impatience. He had tried to be understanding with the men and Amber. In his experience, many people, Southerners particularly, found change difficult; the War for Southern Independence had displayed that in all its glory— and pain. A South Carolinian, born and bred, Derek didn't need any reminders of Southern eccentricity.

But he'd waited damn near as long as he could afford to for them to accept him. Richard's murder and Derek's unexpected arrival may have made things uncomfortable, even difficult, but the ranch had been limping along without a leader for a year now. He couldn't wait indefinitely for them to adjust to his authority.

"If you say so." Whitley's answer came slowly, petulantly, and only after Gideon cleared his throat with a gruff cough that sounded much like a warning.

"I do."

Whitley shot a last indignant glare in Derek's direction, then snatched up the reins and led the horse away.

"I'll take care of things." Gideon followed after leveling a steady look at Derek.

Trusting Gideon, Derek dismissed the problem for the moment and turned back to his current concern. "Now then, Mr. Montgomery. What kind of work are you looking for?"

Amber draped two colorful rugs, both made of tightly woven rags, over the railing of the long front veranda. She smoothed out the wrinkles in each, one in varying shades of blue and the other in green and yellow, then took up a long wicker club and began whacking it against each in turn. The wide, flat, fanlike end made a dull *whump* when it hit, curling dust up from the fabric until it hovered around her in a cloud. She sneezed and blinked the grit from her eyes.

She'd left the stew simmering, and later she would mix up biscuits—a triple batch, knowing the men's appetites for anything that didn't resemble Six's rocks. If she had the time, a spice cake would make a fine dessert.

In the meantime, she had turned to her housekeeping duties. Her first choice would always be to spend her time in the garden. Sinking her fingers into the cool, rich soil was such a pleasure. With Derek in residence, however, she dare not neglect any of her chores.

Amber took another healthy swing with her mallet, wondering about the stranger who'd arrived. Who was he? Did Derek know him? What was he doing here? She had witnessed their meeting through the cookhouse window, but it had revealed precious little. Eventually Derek had escorted the man to the corral, and she hadn't seen them since.

Flexing her shoulders, she gave the rugs another good smack. Goodness, but it felt good to whack those poor, defenseless rugs, she thought as the action dissipated some pent-up energy. She allowed herself a silly grin and hit them once more, twice, a third time for good measure. Tension she hadn't realized she had began to relax within her, spreading a certain sense of release through her arms and legs.

Drawing back to assail her victims once more, she felt that eerie feeling of being watched begin to creep over her. Instinctively she spun around, every instinct at the ready and the wicker mallet clenched in her hands like a weapon.

Derek raised his arms in mock surrender. "Do you take prisoners?"

She glared at him and lowered the mallet. "Why don't you ever make some noise so a person can hear you coming?"

He shrugged. "Too much time trying to do the opposite, I suppose. I'd like you to meet our new cook."

She blinked, and her irritation evaporated as she regarded the man standing behind Derek. He didn't indicate much interest in her, but the rugs, or perhaps the porch or her roses, seemed to captivate him.

Derek made the introductions, and Beau stepped forward. "Ma'am," he said in a soft drawl.

Georgia? Amber wondered as she tried to place his accent. No, that wasn't right. Virginia, perhaps?

She ignored Derek and candidly eyed Beauregard Montgomery. For pity's sake, he had both his *arms*. Trust Whitley to exaggerate the case. She should have known better; she hadn't trusted the young cowboy since the day she caught him sneaking out of the ranch house study, trying to steal a decanter of Richard's best whiskey. Richard would have fired Whitley if he'd been able to find enough competent workers.

Whitley's shortcomings, however, didn't concern her nearly as much as did Beau. She'd never met a man who seemed so downright skittish, due, she'd wager, to his missing hand. She could well imagine the reality of his situation; her own more limited experience had taught her how cruel and unthinking people could be. She'd stake her reputation—if she had one—that the loss of his hand had caused Beau a host of difficulties that had nothing to do with his physical infirmity.

"How do you do, Mr. Montgomery." She tried to catch his gaze with hers. "Please call me Amber."

He looked at her then, uncertainty etched on his features. "Thank you. And I prefer Beau."

She smiled and stuck out her hand. "Welcome to the Double F."

"Thank you, ma'am." Carefully he accepted her handshake. "Er—Amber." He corrected himself with a crooked smile that, at best, was only half there, but she took it as a start.

"*I* should be thanking you. You're the answer to my prayers. Derek promised he'd find a cook to help me—and here you are."

"You haven't tasted my cooking yet. I'm afraid I learned out of desperation, during the war."

"No matter." Amber smiled in encouragement. "I'll be glad to help at first, if you need. I have a whole book of recipes, and I've learned a few tricks myself."

"I'd appreciate that."

"We're agreed, then," Derek interjected, sounding suddenly impatient. He had remained quiet until now, which had enabled Amber to concentrate on Beau. Even so, she had remained supremely aware of Derek's presence; she heard his every breath, noticed each time he stirred. He seemed to have invaded her very consciousness, and she could never quite dismiss him.

"I'll introduce you to the other hands and show you where to put your gear," Derek said to Beau. "You can meet up with Amber later."

"If I'm not at the house, I'll be in the cookhouse or one of the gardens." She pointed in the proper direction.

Beau nodded.

"I've got stew started already, so tonight's meal should pose no difficulty."

"How's your recipe for biscuits?"

"Light and fluffy."

Beau nodded again and almost smiled again, too. "Then we'll use yours."

"Gideon, Six and I won't be here," Derek announced suddenly.

Amber stared at him. "What? Why?"

He leveled a flat gaze on her. "This is a cattle ranch with a herd that's been neglected for too long. There's work to be done, not enough men to do it, and I can't wait any longer to get started.''

''I see,'' she said slowly. ''How long will you be gone?''

''Overnight.''

Curse him and his stiff, one-word answers. She did her best to settle her features into an even display of indifference. ''Is anything…wrong?''

He raised his brows and angled his head in her direction. ''There's a lot wrong. I told you that. Right now I want to get a better idea of this herd and see how these cowboys work.''

He turned and strode toward the bunkhouse. ''I'll see you sometime tomorrow. This way, Beau.''

Amber couldn't bring herself to look away from the men's departure. Nor could she lie to herself. It was not Beau she watched, but Derek. He carried himself like a warrior, a man she instinctively recognized as someone to be counted on—if he believed in you. He had a presence that threatened her, overwhelmed her, unnerved her… fascinated her.

She whirled around to face the half-beaten rugs. *No*. Fascination suggested something entirely inappropriate, something like—enchanted? Perhaps mesmerized, or even infatuated. And those reactions were completely unacceptable. Utterly ridiculous. She hardly knew Derek. He didn't like her, and she didn't like him. Did she?

*Don't worry. He's leaving, at least for a day.*

Relief spread through her, making her almost light-headed. She wouldn't have to see him, think about him or this sudden awareness that refused to give her any peace. And if he left, even for a day, she could escape his damned questions. A day wasn't much of a reprieve, but it would do for now.

Derek and the others were ready to leave within the hour. Amber packed some food in a canvas bag—smoked meat and bread and cheese—and handed it to him as they prepared to ride out.

"Here. I don't know what provisions might be left in any of the line shacks, or even where you'll be going. This will carry you through, at least until tomorrow."

"Thank you." He took the package, his eyes darkening with what she interpreted as grateful surprise. Didn't he expect his housekeeper to look after his welfare? He gave no indication of his thoughts, however, merely settling his hat on his head. It deepened the shadows over his face and effectively obscured any clues his features might have revealed.

She swallowed a small sigh of frustration and stepped aside as Derek secured the pack to his bedroll. He swung up into the saddle without another word, his movements clean and sparse, and with a style and grace that created a curious little ache in the middle of her chest. For the second time in less than an hour, Amber couldn't make herself look away from him. Merely breathing seemed suddenly difficult.

"You and the new feller gonna be all right cookin'?"

Six claimed her attention as he pulled his horse up next to Derek's. She offered the grizzled old cowboy a grateful smile that eased his frown.

"Rest easy, Six. We'll be fine. We'll miss you, of course. My son of a gun stew and biscuits are nothing like yours, but we'll try to cope without you."

Perhaps she stretched the truth a bit, or meant something different by the words than Six would assume, but that didn't change her sincerity. He was a friend, and she would never deliberately hurt his feelings. She would miss him, as she would miss any member of her family.

"Yeah, well, if I had any recipes I'd leave them here fer ya. But I don't. Just picked up what I know here an' there, and tried to remembered it. Never been much fer readin', ya know."

"I know, Six. And thank you. I understand you're anxious to get out with the herd." He'd spent more years tending cattle and horses than Amber was alive.

"If that ain't the truth." He shot Derek a look of unmistakable impatience. "You ready to go, boss?"

Derek's mouth twitched and he looked at Gideon. "Ready. What about you, Gideon?"

Gideon nodded, pursing his lips as though containing his own amusement. "Ready."

"All right, then, Six. Lead the way."

"Be seein' ya, Amber." The old man flicked his reins and started down the drive. Gideon nodded in her direction and went so far as to tip his hat before following Six's lead. Derek brought up the rear without a word or a glance goodbye.

What a surprise these men could be, thought Amber as she watched their departure. Derek and Gideon seemed almost to joke with each other over Six's anxiousness. Not at the old man's expense, but more with indulgent understanding. They had treated Micah in much the same way, offering an unspoken respect for him. She had noticed it the first day they arrived. And today, by merely hiring Beau, Derek had shown a compassion that had touched her heart.

Despite herself, she smiled. When she thought about it, it astonished her to discover these men had the capacity for sympathy and tolerance; they seemed mostly reserved and serious. But Derek displayed a real affinity for the less fortunate. He treated old, worn cowboys like Six and Micah with tactful deference. He'd hired Gideon, a man with one good eye, and now Beau, with only one hand.

And...her. She had all the proper parts, nothing of that nature missing. Just a scandalous reputation to go with them.

With a soft sigh, Amber turned her back on the disappearing figures, facing the ranch house and the myriad chores that awaited her. *Don't think of that now.* It would do no good. She didn't know Derek well enough to reach any reliable conclusions.

*Instead,* she told herself with firm resolve, *you should be considering your position here.* The house needed a good spring cleaning. She hadn't done anything like it since Richard's murder.

Amber started up the stairs to the front gallery, a new resolve to her step. She had a plan for her days, a purpose in her life. A surge of energy straightened her spine.

The last year had passed in a most aimless way, not only for her but for all of them at the ranch. Derek's arrival changed everything. Not only did he intend to live at the ranch, but he'd been to town and met some of Twigg's citizens. They would be visiting in numbers, and she would give them no reason to question her suitability as housekeeper.

But... She slowed, stopping at the top of the steps as she reconsidered her gratitude. Nothing would please her less than a renewed association with the people of Twigg.

*Run out of town.* Derek's words whispered back to her.

"It doesn't matter what they say about me." She gave the words all the resolve she could muster. *She* knew the truth, and so would the people who had once been her friends and neighbors, if they looked at her with their hearts and not through the hateful eyes of people like Frank Edwards and Eliza Bates.

They'd done their worst, and she'd survived. She even prevailed on occasion, as during her first skirmish with Derek. Yes, his return would mean more questions, and eventually she would have to give him at least some of the answers he so desired. But it wouldn't happen today, and probably not tomorrow. She might even be able to count herself lucky until the arrival of their first visitors from Twigg.

But *they* wouldn't content themselves with gossip and

vague rumors. They would sit with Derek in the parlor or right here, on the veranda. They would drink the coffee or tea she brewed for them and eat the gingersnaps or shortbread cookies she baked. And piece by piece, all the ugliness of the cruel and wicked whispers would settle right here, in the only place she had to call home.

Amber closed her eyes and called upon the courage that had comforted her when she first arrived at the Double F. The welcome, the freedom, the relief. Sanctuary at last.

She had always known that peace was hers on borrowed time. Sanctuary never came free.

The time was coming—and soon—when she would have to pay the price. And, not for the first time, she prayed to God that she could afford it.

# Chapter Six

"Is something wrong?" Beau asked the next evening.

Amber turned from the window, feeling a bit ridiculous. "I don't know." She gave him the best smile she had. "Gideon just rode in, I think, and I wondered why Derek wasn't with him."

Beau lifted his shoulder in a halfhearted shrug. "You don't think there's a reasonable explanation?"

"I don't know."

"Don't worry." He tried on a smile, but he didn't seem very good at it. "I'm sure everything is fine. I'll be back in a minute to keep you company," he added as he headed for the door, then left her staring at an empty doorway. Was he coming back because she had him worried, too?

Amber turned again to the window, but the yard remained empty.

"Where's Derek?"

She whirled to find Gideon standing in the doorway. Her heart pounded as though she'd run all the way from Twigg, and she pressed her hand to her heaving chest. "You frightened me!"

"Sorry." It was a perfunctory apology. "Have you seen Derek?"

"No, I haven't." She recognized the uneasiness in her

voice and swallowed. "Not since yesterday. I thought you two were together."

"We were. He's probably just late." Gideon pivoted and was nearly out the door before she could respond.

"Wait! Where are you going?"

He stopped and glanced back at her. "To the bunkhouse." He shrugged, indicating the bedroll slung over his shoulder.

"You can't!" She planted a hand on each hip and glared at him. "Not until you tell me what's going on. What happened? Why are you alone, and where's Derek?"

He turned slowly to face her full on. She couldn't see his face any clearer, but the keenness of his stare seemed to burn through her. He leaned one shoulder against the door frame. "Fierce tigress, aren't you?"

"What?"

"Nothing."

"Please, Gideon." A hollow had opened up in her chest, an emptiness that seemed achingly familiar. "Just tell me the truth."

"There's nothing to tell."

*"I know better."* The words came out more forcefully than she'd intended, but she let them stand, and straightened, because a man like Gideon would respect nothing but strength. To further the illusion, she grabbed her apron in a wad to keep her fingers from trembling. "There's always a story. No one wanted to tell me the truth when my father died. And I was the last to be told when Richard was killed. Yesterday you and Derek left together. Now you came back and he didn't. I don't want to assume the worst, but you aren't giving me much choice."

Gideon unbent from his casual stance and went so far as to push his hat back on his head. He pinned her with his good eye, his gaze serious and clear. "It's probably nothing," he said evenly. "I expected Derek to get back ahead of me. We left Six at one of the line shacks and split up this afternoon. I followed some tracks we'd seen, and he went to look over a place where Carlos found some dead longhorns.''

"Then surely he must be on his way back here by now." Her gaze darted to the window, but only darkness greeted her. Irritation goaded her into pointing out the obvious. "It's dark out. He can't see anything after dark."

Gideon nodded. "I came back when I ran out of daylight. Maybe he's on his way home, just the same. Or maybe he went farther than he expected to and decided to spend the night."

"Or maybe he found something."

Gideon shrugged. "Derek can take care of himself."

"I'm sure he can, but he's new in these parts. He—"

"We traveled together a ways before we got here," Gideon interrupted, "and he seemed capable enough in strange territory. He made it from Chicago to Texas alone."

"Chicago!" Amber stared at him.

"That's what he said."

"But…the Fontaines are from South Carolina—Charleston. They have been for generations. There's Palmetto and their business there. Richard never said anything about Chicago."

Gideon leveled an impatient gaze in her direction. "And Derek didn't say anything about Charleston or any business. It's none of my business, but after Sherman and his Yankees showed Charleston no mercy, how much do you suppose the Fontaines have left there?"

"I…" Amber fell silent as she realized all she had not considered. Not lately. Often during the long, lean years of war, Richard had shared his questions, concerns and worries about the fate of his family. She had empathized with him, reassured him, and, when his letters went unanswered, she had prayed with him. Since Derek's arrival, she'd had countless opportunities to ask after his family. She never had.

"It's darker than the inside of a goat's stomach out there."

"Beau." Gideon nodded and stepped aside to make room for the other man to enter.

"Hello, Gideon. Amber said you'd ridden in." Beau moved into the room, skirting the table until he reached the cupboard and dry sink. "Have you eaten?"

"No."

Lord, she hadn't thought to ask after Gideon's welfare, either. Amber gave herself a firm mental shake.

"I'll fix you something," Beau offered.

"I'd appreciate it. I'll put my things in the bunkhouse and wash up."

Amber remained still, observing silently as Beau worked at the counter. A man who had witnessed—*experienced*—a hell she couldn't imagine, *he* thought of others' needs. He didn't dwell on his loss; he'd adapted to his handicap with an ingenuity that shamed her at times. Now he anchored a loaf of bread with his stump, then used his good, right hand to cut several generous slices. Appalled by a selfishness she'd never realized, Amber lowered her eyelids in shame.

"Don't worry."

She looked up. Gideon's gaze rested squarely on her. "Derek will be all right. You'll see."

He swiveled around as though the words propelled him, and disappeared into the night. She hoped he was right.

Derek started up the staircase, moving with extreme caution and wishing—not for the first time—that he could risk a light. He couldn't. Not until he reached his bedroom.

He held on firmly to the wooden railing that angled its way up into the darkness, planting his feet carefully with each step, and only then attempting the next. A single misstep could be his undoing, and he dare not chance it. The last thing he wanted was to fall—or wake Amber.

Why the hell did her bedroom have to be next to the stairs?

One, two, three. He stopped for a moment, astonished that the simple acts of walking and breathing at the same time suddenly seemed so difficult. Maybe he could sit down here on the stairs and rest for a minute or two.

*No.* He shook his head and started upward again, before the idea appealed too much. Five, six, seven, eight. If he sat down, he seriously doubted his ability to get back up. But stopping again for a moment, to breathe without the added burden of moving—now *that* was a necessity.

Eleven, twelve, thirteen. Gradually he made it to the top of the stairs, through the darkness that blanketed the second floor, and reached the doorway of his room. He envisioned the layout in his mind's eye. One hurried or wrong move, and he could ruin all his progress.

Concentrating, he remembered the bedside table and lamp that stood off to his left. He let out a heavy breath and headed in that direction, his right hand out, groping as he went. He found both without incident, and even managed to light the lamp with a minimum of fuss, considering how much he favored his left side. Perhaps desperation *did* aid a man when he needed it most.

Derek closed his eyes, breathing through his nose as deeply as he dared. When he looked again, it was with new determination. *You can do this,* he told himself as he carried the lamp across the room to place it on the dresser.

He turned, facing the nearby washstand, when a sudden, horrible thought struck him. He'd told Amber to expect him today—or would that be yesterday by now? She'd probably given up on him. What if she hadn't left any water for him?

*Oh, God.* He grimaced. He'd never make it downstairs to the pump and back.

Gingerly he peered into the white porcelain pitcher. It was full. Relief deflated all other emotions.

Moving with controlled care, he poured as much water

into the bowl as it would hold, then set the pitcher on the dresser next to the lamp. Only then did he allow himself to look at his left arm and shoulder.

Shit. It didn't look good, but he couldn't tell anything for sure until he got his shirt off. It wouldn't be easy, especially working alone, but it had to be done.

Awkwardly, using his right hand with far more dexterity than his left, Derek managed to unbutton his shirt. If he could just move slowly, carefully enough, he could push it off his shoulder and—

*"Son of a bitch!"*

The words escaped him with a fierce grunt, and he fought to stay conscious. He stumbled backward, reeling against the bed hard enough to send it skidding. Vaguely, Derek noticed the sound of wood scraping against wood as the legs of the bedstead skittered over the polished plank floor. He gave it no more attention than he did the groan of the mattress as he collapsed onto it.

Eyes closed, he clutched his left arm tightly against his chest, rocking back and forth. He had no clue how long he sat like that, his breath billowing in and out like a winded horse. Perhaps a minute—or maybe an hour. Time held no meaning as he tried to breathe, in and out, until the ragged edges of pain smoothed out and he could concentrate.

He had moved too far, too fast. *Jesus Christ, that hurt.*

"Derek! Is that you? What happened?"

Amber's voice came from directly behind him. He didn't turn to look at her; he couldn't. The fiery agony had begun to recede, but not to the point where he could face anyone.

"Who else would it be?" he asked through gritted teeth, struggling to sound as normal as possible.

"Are you—you're very late. We expected you hours ago."

"I was delayed."

"Delayed? Are you sure everything is all right?"

"Fine." He shifted, turning to present her with more of

his back. The movement pulled at his aching shoulder, and he sucked in a harsh breath through his teeth.

"No, something's wrong." He could hear her moving behind him. "I can tell. What—"

"Isn't it a little late for an unmarried woman to be in a man's bedroom?" He tilted his head toward his injured shoulder and shot her a hot glare from the corner of his eye. He could only hope she would read it as something illicit. "Or is this the kind of offer you made Richard?"

"Why you—" Derek couldn't see her well enough to gauge her physical reaction, but the fury in her voice was unmistakable. "—you *devil!* I can't think of anything bad enough to call you."

He turned his head away as though dismissing her. "There are words to describe a *lady* like you," he drawled, infusing his voice with all the insolence he could muster. Christ, would she never leave?

Utter silence followed his vulgar question. He waited a heartbeat, then another—as long as he could stand it—and still he heard nothing. *Thank God.* Finally she had left.

He pulled in a slow, deep breath, as slow and deep as he dared, and closed his eyes for a moment. *Get up,* he told himself. *You can't sit here all night. You'll pass out.*

And what a relief that would be. First, though, he had to get the damned shirt off.

He reached up and tried to shove the fabric of his shirt from his shoulder on that same side, doing his best to swallow a deep groan of pain. It slipped past his clenched teeth and came out as every bit an anguished moan.

"I was wrong! I *can* think of something to call you, you son of a—*Derek!*"

He whipped his head around before he remembered what the sharp movement would do to his shoulder. *"Christ!"* The word erupted from him as new torment exploded through his shoulder and plunged down his arm. "Goddammit," he muttered breathlessly.

Amber stood poised in the doorway, and he followed his curse with a savage scowl designed to stop her in her tracks. He'd been so sure that she'd left, dammit!

"Get out of here," he ordered in a ridiculously thin voice.

"I will not. Something's wrong." She moved farther into the room, giving the bed a wide berth until she rounded the end. "I—oh, my God! You've been shot! Derek, how did this happen? Who did this to you?"

He shook his head and looked down at the blood-encrusted shirt. "I didn't stick around long enough to find out."

She'd scooted next to him before he could blink, one knee touching his thigh as she bent low to peer at his wound. "Here, let me help you."

He looked at her, but all he could see was her hair, a burnished bronze color shot with shimmering red highlights in the lamplight. It fanned down her back, over her shoulder, and curtained her face from his gaze.

He couldn't warn her off with a fierce expression if he couldn't see her face. "Amber." He tried to instill the proper authority into his voice.

"What?" She didn't look up.

"This is no place for you. Not now. I'll take care of it."

"The hell you will!" She reared back and glared at him, looking almost as shocked as he did by her use of profanity. "You cannot do this on your own, Derek Fontaine. Maybe you can do most things alone, but this isn't one of them. Now don't be an idiot. Let me help you."

"I—" He started to get up, to show her that he could do anything he damn well pleased, and completely on his own. Another sudden, sharp dagger of pain stabbed his shoulder and he sagged back onto the bed. "Damn."

"You see? I told you." Remarkably, she didn't sound the least bit satisfied. "Now, let me help you get this shirt off."

She pulled the sleeve down his good arm with a care he hadn't known in longer than he could remember, then she moved to the other side and began easing the fabric away from his neck and shoulder blade. "This is going to hurt. I'm sorry. You have dried blood on your shirt, and I think it'll pull."

He nodded and closed his eyes. "I figured as much."

Slowly she worked at separating the material from his skin, and the gentleness of her fingers tantalized him. They felt cool and soothing.

"How long ago did this happen?" she asked.

"I don't know. Hours."

"Here." She brought the bowl of water over and set it on the bed, then moved the washstand closer and placed the lantern on it. "This will help. Let me get some towels."

She hurried to the armoire and was back in a moment, dipping a linen cloth into the washbasin. "It looks like it stopped bleeding, but getting your shirt off is starting it again."

He started to shrug, but reconsidered when the movement tugged sharply at his shoulder. "You got any other solutions?"

She shook her head. "No. I'm sorry. But I'll make it as easy as possible."

Derek watched her actions, but they were beginning to seem as though they happened at a great distance. She wrung out the cloth and held it against his shoulder, soaking the fabric, then dunked it back into the basin. The water turned a sickly pink color as his blood was rinsed from the linen, and looking at it made him feel a little nauseated.

Now that was strange. He'd never had a weak stomach, and he'd seen a lot of things worse than bloody water. One day in the army—the *right* day, a day of battle—could show a man more brutality than he should ever have to face.

"There. That's better," Amber murmured. She used the

damp rag to slowly separate his shirt from his skin. He felt a sharp yank wherever the fabric had secured itself, and yet it didn't hurt so bad anymore.

In fact, now that he had a moment to think, he noticed a certain lethargy beginning to steal over him. It made him feel light-headed, and he frowned as he tried to concentrate.

Gradually the shirt gave way. Amber pulled it from him and tossed it to the floor. "I'm going to clean this wound up a bit and see how bad the damage is. All right?"

"Hmm?" Derek had closed his eyes, and now he re-opened them. He cast a distracted gaze around the room, then slowly looked back at Amber. Lord but he was tired.

"I'm going to clean this up a bit and see how bad the damage is," she repeated. "All right?"

"Fine. Whatever you want." He tried to smile at her, but his lips felt odd, as if they weren't working right. He thought she might have smiled back, but she turned away before he could be sure. He followed the sound of trickling water and discovered she was rinsing the towel again. She wrung out the cloth, then began washing the blood from his shoulder.

"Your hair is down."

"What?" She stopped and looked at him, eyes wide.

"I've never seen you with your hair down before."

"I was in bed when I heard you up here."

He blinked, then dragged a long, lingering gaze over her white, very proper nightgown. With its high neck and long sleeves, it covered everything it was supposed to. "You're wearing a nightgown."

Her gaze seemed to focus on his shoulder. "It's what I usually wear to bed."

"It's beautiful."

"What?" She looked down at herself, then back at him with an odd little frown that made him want to smile. "My nightgown?"

"No. Your hair."

"Oh." She reached up and smoothed some of the loose copper strands back from her face. "Well, uh—thank you."

He nodded and closed his eyes, leaning back just a bit. "You smell good, too. Like vanilla."

"Derek, don't! You're going to fall back on the bed, and I'm not finished."

He opened his eyes long enough to say "Sorry," but then he closed them again. It was suddenly so hard to stay awake.

She touched him once more, and he decided he liked it. Very much, in fact. The way he felt right now, he could sit here all night long and let her touch him. Maybe she'd even want to touch him in other places, places that didn't hurt quite like his shoulder.

"There. That's the best I can do for the moment. I'll heat some water and get my medical supplies, then I can bandage it."

"Mmm-hmm."

"It looks like the bullet went clean through. That's good."

"Mmm-hmm."

"Derek? *Derek?*"

He opened his eyes when her tone became insistent. "What?"

"You need to get undressed and into bed. I can finish bandaging your shoulder after that. I don't think you can stay awake until then."

"I'm tired," he agreed.

"I know. It's from losing so much blood. But can you help me?" He'd never seen her face with an expression of such sweet concern before. "Can you take your pants off and get into bed?"

He winked at her. "Sure, honey, if that's where you want me."

"Stop it."

"I can make you happy, you know. They—women—have told me so."

"Derek, I mean it." Her sweet concern became a severe scowl. "I don't *want* you in bed, not that way. I want you to *get* into bed so you can go to sleep."

"Yeah, I am tired," he repeated.

"I know. Now, please. You've got to get undressed before you can get into bed."

He nodded. *Get undressed.* He looked down at himself, at his bare chest and fabric-clad legs. Undressed meant he had to take his pants off. He could do that. But first he should probably take his boots off, then his belt and gun belt.

The boots didn't cooperate at all. He applied the toe of one foot to the heel of the other, but nothing happened. Maybe he should push. He tried, and his feet slipped apart.

"Here, let me help you." Amber knelt and tugged first one boot, then the other, from his feet.

"How long is your hair?"

She looked up and shook her head. "Why are you preoccupied with my hair? It's long." Was that soft expression a smile? "Almost to my hips… There." She stood. "Now, can you do the rest alone?"

He looked down at his lap. First his gun belt. He fumbled at his waist. The leather didn't want to cooperate, particularly with his awkward, one-handed movements, but finally he worked the buckle free. The belt to his pants required much the same effort, and by the time he'd unfastened it as well, his breath was coming in shallow little gasps.

He tried to take a deeper breath as he hooked his fingers in the waistband of his pants, but he couldn't manage much more than a ragged sigh. Well…damn. The buttons didn't seem any easier.

"Can you do it?"

He looked up to see Amber waiting nearby. She'd put

the room back in order and replaced the lamp on the bedside table.

"It's the damn buttons."

"Do you want me to get Gideon or Micah to help you?"

He looked back at his lap and thought about it. Richard's attraction to her was beginning to make perfect sense. She was a strong, beautiful woman. An experienced woman. Hadn't his father made her his mistress?

Derek raised his eyes and smiled—or at least he thought he did. "No. You could do it. You know how."

"Me?" He couldn't place the tone in her voice.

"You were Richard's mistress."

Her expression presented him with the same confusion. He almost thought he saw pain, outrage…frustration—but that couldn't be right, could it?

Suddenly nothing made sense. Seeing her at all was becoming increasingly difficult. His vision seemed fuzzy around the edges, and the room had begun to grow steadily darker. "Amber?" he managed to croak, just before his last conscious thought: *Is this what it's like to die?*

# Chapter Seven

An unfamiliar anxiousness jerked Amber awake with a start. She shifted, realizing then that she was sitting, and her chair made a wholly uncomfortable bed. She had slept fitfully at best, leaving her body aching, her neck cramped and stiff.

A sudden chill crept upon her, and she shivered, crossing her arms and rubbing her hands up and down. Her thin cotton nightgown provided little protection against the cool morning air.

She glanced out through the window with sleepy interest. White, puffy clouds dotted the sky, while the sun painted the morning with wide, shimmering streaks of blue and yellow. She had overslept, that much was certain, but she couldn't find the energy to be concerned. She'd been up half the night.

Derek!

Full awareness returned in an instant, and Amber shot up straight. She blinked and aimed an anxious look across the room. Derek looked back. His gaze, if not quite clear, was at least steady. It was the first time he'd been awake since he lost consciousness last night. He'd slept through the uproar she'd created rousing the others, Gideon undressing him and Amber cleaning and bandaging his wound.

Dear Lord, he'd been *shot*. She stumbled from the chair and tripped over the quilt, which had slipped to the floor.

"Careful." His voice sounded labored and hoarse.

Amber collapsed on the edge of the bed and stared at him with frantic concern. "Are you all right?" She realized the absurdity of the question the instant she heard the breathless whisper, but she didn't waste time trying to take it back. She offered a sheepish smile instead.

"Fine. Just dandy. Can't you tell?" His scowl matched perfectly his snappish tone of voice.

Amber shook her head and pressed the backs of her fingers to his forehead. It felt warm, but not overly hot. "You're wounded and you have a fever, so I'll forgive your sarcasm."

He grumbled something under his breath, too low for her to hear, and turned his head away. She didn't need to understand the words; she recognized his tone. It was hardly surprising that he was irritable, she consoled herself. Men rarely proved to be model patients. Still, if he showed signs of restlessness already, what would he be like in a day?

"Derek." She reached across him, pressing her fingers against the side of his chin. His beard felt softer than she'd imagined, almost velvety, and tempted her to stroke the line of his jaw. She swallowed and held her hand in place.

He resisted the urging of her touch, but she insisted until he relented and looked at her. "I know you're in pain, and that makes you cross." She withdrew her fingers, curling them up when they would have lingered. "And I know you're angry. But you must put that aside for now. Think about getting better and the rest will come in its own good time."

He shuttered his eyes with lowered lashes and seemed to find the far corner of the room highly interesting. She leaned down, deliberately entering his line of vision, and peered directly into his eyes. Their usually bright, vibrant color was a faded, dull-looking blue, and above his beard, his cheeks were flushed a mottled red.

"Your fever is nothing to worry about," she continued. "I expected it. You put your body through a terrible ordeal before reaching the house. You need time to heal."

"I don't have time." His eyes flashed with sudden life, an intense fierceness she was beginning to recognize. "I have a ranch with some damn serious problems."

"Well, you don't have to concern yourself with that now. The ranch survived for a year without you. A few more days won't matter. It shouldn't be any longer than that before the fever is gone and you regain some of your strength."

"Humph." Though she was no longer touching him, he jerked his head aside with a snort, staring at the door as though planning his escape.

Amber shook her head and sat back. "I have some willow bark to steep for tea. It should help your fever. Now that you're awake, I'll bring you a cup."

"I'm not an invalid." He struggled with his good arm until he managed to push himself into a half-reclining position.

"You're going to hurt yourself worse." She shot him a disapproving frown that he ignored; rather, his mouth curved upward in a tight, satisfied smile. He leaned back to balance himself on his elbows—and then collapsed on the mattress with a tortured groan.

"Derek!" She searched his face and torso for signs of further injury, but otherwise resisted touching him until she was sure of his condition. "You can't put pressure on your shoulder that way. Not with the kind of wound you've suffered."

She reached for a towel left from last night's nursing and pressed it to his forehead, wiping away the sweat that dampened his skin. He ignored her, just laid there and sucked in one deep, heavy breath after another.

"Are you going to be sick?" she asked.

"Leave me alone."

She wiped the towel over his forehead once more before laying it on the bedside table. "Here." She turned back to him. "Let me look at your shoulder."

Carefully she unwrapped the bandage and gauged his injury with a shrewd eye. His restless sleep had caused some seepage, and his stubborn movements had started the bleeding again. Not badly, but he'd lost enough blood that it concerned her to see him lose more. The skin around the bullet hole looked red and angry. She didn't ask him to turn and show her the opening behind his shoulder; she'd seen it last night, and she knew very well how much more damage a bullet did on its way out.

"I'll get a fresh poultice started and then put a clean bandage on for you." She would check the exit wound then. "But first I'll bring you some tea."

"I don't drink tea," he groused in a sulky tone.

She leveled a determined look in his direction and stood. "This kind of tea is good for you. And the bark is precious to come by, so if I make it, you'll drink it."

He grunted but said nothing more. Instead he closed his eyes and breathed deeply.

"Will you be all right alone here for a while? I'm going to dress, and then I'll be back."

He offered no response, prompting Amber to lean forward for a closer look. "Derek? Will you be all right alone?"

He opened his eyes and stared silently at her, then with a blink raked an oddly heated gaze over her. Instinct told her his expression had nothing to do with his fever, and prompted her to cross her arms over her chest or turn her back on him. Stubbornly, she did neither.

"You dress like a virgin," he said without taking his eyes from her.

"What?" She crossed her arms now.

"Your nightgown and your hair down like that. You remind me of a virgin sacrifice in some pagan ritual."

"I…" Her voice tapered off after only a word. Virgins, sacrifices and rituals? A shiver of excitement she recognized as wholly inappropriate raced up her spine, and the scorching look in his eyes fired some previously untested spark in her own blood. Untested, at least, until last night.

His statements and the images they produced were utterly shocking. "You shouldn't say things like that." Her breathless voice made her frown, and she swallowed. "It's not decent."

She paused, thinking of all such a simple word like *decent* entailed. There'd been a time when "decent" men like Frank Edwards greeted her on the street with a polite nod and a smile. Now they approached her with an entirely different attitude. They had the disgusting and misguided hope of gaining sexual favors. When she refused to cooperate, they found ways to make her pay for rejecting them. But still, they remained *decent* men.

Amber had always found strength in her own decency, never responding to their illicit suggestions, never explaining and always maintaining her dignity with haughty pride. Last night seemed to have changed that between Derek and her. The late hour and his injury had overcome her better judgment.

"I should have gotten dressed last night once I realized the seriousness of the situation. It was wrong of me to fall asleep in the chair, as well. I was upset and wasn't thinking clearly. Still, that doesn't make it right, and I apologize." She stepped around the tangled folds of the quilt still puddled on the floor and headed for the door.

"Amber." He said her name just as she reached for the doorknob.

"Yes?" She didn't turn to look at him.

"Thank you."

By the time she had dressed and put up her hair, Amber had regained her composure. She slipped her feet into comfortable work shoes and hurried to the cookhouse. Only Beau was present.

"Good morning," he greeted her. "How's our patient this morning?"

"Irritable," she acknowledged with a sigh. "Already. The next few days aren't going to be pleasant."

"It's not easy being laid up." Rueful compassion darkened his eyes.

She nodded, sharing his understanding. Beau, better than anyone, would appreciate injury and recovery, but for her to make that observation seemed unkind.

"Did Derek say anything more about what happened?" he asked.

She shook her head. "No. He didn't ask any questions, either. He doesn't seem to be thinking clearly yet. He lost a great deal of blood—and he's angry."

"Yes. I know how that feels, too." Beau closed his eyes, for long enough that a certain nervousness began to crawl up her spine. Memories of his own injury no doubt still troubled him, but what could she say to reassure him?

"Beau…" she began, but he shook his head and she fell silent. Perhaps he found it simply too painful to discuss.

Why was it that everyone around her seemed so very wounded, and in so many different ways? And how could she, of all people, help them?

"What can we do for him?" Beau asked after a moment, and Amber welcomed the conversation.

"Whatever we can to make him comfortable. I don't think he's up to eating yet—some broth tonight, perhaps. And I want him to drink willow bark tea laced with honey. It's good for healing. Oh, and I need to replace the poultice

I put on last night.'' She glanced at the worktable, where she'd left the contents of her medical supplies strewn about, grateful that someone had collected them neatly together. "He was determined to move more than he should this morning, and started the bleeding again.''

"Do you think he's all right alone up there?''

She smiled shrewdly. "I'd be more worried if he hadn't tried to get up. It will be awhile before he has the energy for it again.'' She hoped.

Amber set about mixing up her special poultice made of crushed leaves from Richard's prized peach trees, while Beau brewed the willow bark tea. They worked in the companionable silence that had settled between them from the very beginning. With Derek and his fractious mood waiting upstairs, she found Beau's company particularly soothing at the moment.

Whitley came into the cookhouse as they worked, then Micah, and finally Gideon. All asked the same questions that Beau had. When the poultice was ready, she placed it on a wooden tray along with fresh bandages and a few other assorted medical supplies. Beau handed her the tea, and she added it to the tray, as well. "I'll be up later to see if you need anything,'' he called as she left the cookhouse.

Derek was asleep when Amber returned to his room. She moved quietly, depositing the tray on his dresser before tidying the room. She folded the quilt, still crumpled on the floor, and rearranged the sickroom paraphernalia that cluttered the bedside table: a basin, a bowl, several small bottles, a stack of white cloths.

That done, she turned to her patient. He remained asleep, though he shifted restlessly from time to time, displacing the sheet so it covered him from only the waist on down.

She ran a long glance over his body, recalling the ordeal he'd been through. Dull red mottled his skin, while fever dampened his matted hair. Again she leaned down to press her fingers lightly against his forehead. He was still too warm.

Her gaze returned sharply to his face. His lashes fanned across his cheeks, while his lips pressed together in a thin line that belied his pain. Looking at him now, she saw through the caring, compassionate eyes of a nurse a patient in need of care. But awake, with his autocratic demands, he became her employer, the man she must please if she meant to keep this job.

*The man she must please...* As sordid as it sounded, it was also the truth. Not only that, but he *needed* her—as no one else had in a very long time. Things continued to change between them; emotions deep and elemental were beginning to flourish and she didn't like it. One bit.

A cool dampness soothed Derek's brow, and he uttered a soft groan. Mmm, it felt good. He'd been hot—too hot—though what that meant exactly or how to change it eluded him at the moment. But someone had known, some angel of mercy. He smiled, or it seemed like he did.

The moist, cool feeling seeped downward, refreshing his face, his neck, his shoulders. He sighed and leaned into the pleasant touch.

"I'm sorry. I thought I could do this without disturbing you."

He pried open his eyes and looked for his angel of mercy. Amber sat on the bed next to him, holding a crumpled white rag.

Derek blinked, frowning as he tried to make sense of her presence. "Angel..." His eyelids drifted down.

"What?" She leaned forward. "Derek?" Something light, soft, brushed over his forehead. "What did you say?"

He blinked and swallowed. "Hot. Thirsty."

"Here."

He blinked again and gradually focused on her. Slowly she brought a cup to his lips, and he opened his mouth automatically. "It's tea," she said. "The willow bark will help your fever."

Fever. He had a fever. He'd been wounded. Shot. Lucidity came staggering back. He angled a careful look at his shoulder.

"You were shot last night. Do you remember?"

"Yes. I remember." He narrowed his eyes and leveled a disgusted look in her direction. "I was shot, not hit on the head." She didn't have to know it was mostly himself he was disgusted with. He didn't remember everything, at least not at first. Each time he awoke, he had to wade through a mire of hazy, sluggish thoughts before his brain began to function with any clarity.

Thank God he could gather his wits eventually.

He heard the trickle of water and forced himself to concentrate. Amber was rinsing out the cloth, then turned back to him. "Does this feel good?"

"What?"

"The bath." She smiled, but it faltered under his stare, and she looked away, smoothing the rag over his forehead once more. "I don't suppose you can call it a bath, but we need to bring your fever down."

"You said the tea…"

"This will help, too."

Derek lay quietly as she tended to him. He hated feeling weak as a newborn, but he'd already learned the folly of trying to do too much. Why waste his strength on pure stubbornness? Besides, the longer he was awake, the more he understood.

God, it felt so damn good to have her brush that soft, damp rag over his body. He watched every movement as she stroked it over his neck, his shoulders, his chest. The only thing better would have been her hands alone, without the barrier of cotton, touching him that way, skin against skin.

*Don't even think it. Not this woman and not like that.*

They had too many differences between them, not the least of which would be their incompatible—and unsuitable—ties to Richard.

The knowledge made Derek suddenly ill-tempered. "Why are you doing this?" he demanded.

Everything about her stilled before she took a long, deep breath. Her breasts peaked against the brown cotton of her formfitting bodice, and Derek cursed himself for noticing.

"You're injured," she said in a soft voice. "Why wouldn't I help you?"

"You don't like me. You don't want me here."

"I didn't want you injured—and I don't want you dead."

"What do you want?"

"Now isn't the time to talk about it." She slipped the cloth into the basin of water and began shifting the curious arrangement of bottles, jars and bowls on the bedside table. Were her hands trembling?

"Amber—"

"I need to put a clean bandage on your shoulder." She selected a clear glass bottle and plucked a clean rag from the stack next to it, then turned to look at his wound, but not him.

"What is that?"

"It's a tincture, good for healing." She held the bottle up for his inspection. It told him nothing.

"It may sting." Carefully, guarding the edges of the wound with the cloth, she tilted the bottle and poured the tincture all around the bullet hole.

"Son of a bitch!" He all but came up off the bed.

"Derek." She reached across him, holding him down with one arm angled across his chest, though she hardly needed to do a thing. Suddenly weak all over, he lay there panting, his chest heaving and his heart pounding.

"I'm sorry," she said without moving. "I told you it would sting."

*"Sting?"* He had hardly enough breath to say the word. "It hurts like holy hell!"

"I know. But it will help. Truly it will."

Gradually his breathing began to slow, regulating itself as the pain settled to a dull, persistent throbbing. And as the pain faded, he realized how Amber was stretched out across him. Her arm may have been resting on his good shoulder, but even at an angle, the soft cushion of her breasts pressed against his chest. He could raise his arm and—

*Don't even think it.* The reminder came to him again, exactly as it had before. *Not this woman and not like that.*

"If I was in better shape, honey, we might be able to do something about this." It took his best effort to call up the insolence to utter the words.

"What?" She jerked upright and stared at him. Her eyes widened, but where he expected to see the fires of anger, he discovered something else. A glimmer of...pain, perhaps?

She blinked, and whatever it had been disappeared. "How can you say such a thing? I'm trying to help you."

"And I still don't understand why."

She hesitated, her thoughts in turmoil if he could believe the way her eyes darted wildly around the room. Only when he had given up on her answer did she respond. "Because I worked for Richard, and I cared about him. He chose you as his heir, and I agreed to work for you. I don't want you to die. *I don't want anyone else to die.*"

He didn't have a ready response worthy of her impassioned words. She took advantage of the moment, turning back to the table to pick a small bowl from the clutter. She angled it so he could see the moist, pulpy mixture inside. "I'll put this poultice on your shoulder, then bandage it." She spoke with a distant politeness that somehow irritated him, as so much else was doing this morning. "I'd like you to drink the rest of your tea, then I'll leave you alone to rest.''

He'd thought they'd made progress that day in the cookhouse, when she'd finally answered some of his questions. Now he wasn't so sure she would cooperate again. He opened his mouth to ask, but she held up her hand and shook her head. "I know, you don't like tea," she said, ''but it will help you recover. You want to get out of this bed as soon as possible, don't you?''

She had him there—dammit. He scowled and glanced past her, out the window. A host of white, fleecy clouds hastened across the bright morning sky. The sounds of everyday ranch life drifted up from the yard: a distant shout that was quickly answered, the jingle of a harness, a horse's whinny.

Hell, yes, he wanted out of this bed.

Soft fingers brushed lightly over his shoulder, the touch he'd once wished for. He watched Amber smear the cold poultice over his skin. He hated the feel of it, sodden and slimy, but he would endure it if it meant getting back on his feet.

As much as it rankled, he had to admit he couldn't have asked for a finer nurse. No matter what he said or did, Amber's touch remained gentle. She displayed a steady confidence that never wavered. He didn't deserve her kindness, but he wouldn't waste it, either.

Gentle, confident—and beautiful. He'd be a fool to turn away from her.

What was it about *this* woman that seized him, ate at him, made him think of a soft mattress and silken sheets— or the hard ground and her silken thighs? Despite his better judgment or reminders of her reputation, he couldn't escape the need. The where and how of it didn't matter, only that *she* could ease the ache that came upon him whenever he looked at her.

No wonder Richard had made her his mistress.

Her spirited green eyes flashed with life, while her full, pink lips parted as she concentrated on her task, teasing him with a hint of her tongue. The faint scent of vanilla reminded him of last night, when her hair had flowed down all around her and she'd worn the sweet-looking white nightgown, long-sleeved and high-necked, with only her bare toes peeking out.

Most of the time, as now, she disguised her lustrous hair by coiling it up at the back of her head. That at least bared the column of her throat above her modest collar. His fingers twitched as he trifled with the vague idea of reaching for her, of trailing his hands over her skin, from the line of her jaw to where the fabric of her dress would stop him at her throat.

"Can you move so I can see the back of your shoulder?"

Her voice came out soft and quiet and sweet, and for an instant he expected different words, something inviting— even provocative. They weren't.

"I'll help. I need you to roll over so I can see the back of your shoulder," she added.

It was just as well that her words were impersonal. "All right." He held his muscles taut and started to move.

"Not all the way. Just enough so I can see where the bullet went through."

Pain issued from his shoulder immediately, pounding up through his head, throbbing across his chest and shimmering down his arm. He gritted his teeth in an attempt to hold back a groan, but the ragged sound slipped past.

"Here." Amber spoke in a soft, dulcet voice. She pressed one hand against the base of his neck, while the other splayed across his chest. With her direction he moved cautiously, until finally she whispered, "That's enough."

The mattress dipped as she shifted her weight, moving until she slid close enough that something—her hip? her leg?—pushed against his lower back and helped prop him in place.

"I'll try not to hurt you."

She wiped the soft, cool cloth over his ragged skin, touching him with as much gentleness as he could ever remember. Derek identified the sounds of trickling water, then the clink of glass. Recognizing what was happening, he tensed just as the first cold drops of that damned tincture sent the sharp sting of pain coursing through him. He sucked in a sharp, hissing breath.

"I'm sorry. I know it hurts."

By the time he could breathe freely again, she was spreading the soggy poultice over the place where the bullet had exited. Next she applied a pad of light, soft material against the wound, following that with a thicker, larger piece of fabric. "Lie back," she said in a soothing voice he refused to let himself become accustomed to. The prop against his back moved as she scooted away.

He rolled back into place, swallowing a groan as the now-familiar pain passed through him once more. Dammit, this weakness was completely unacceptable. He closed his eyes and breathed heavily through clenched teeth.

"This will make you feel better."

The cool cloth was back, stroking across his brow. Derek opened his eyes to see Amber with the corner of her bottom lip trapped between her teeth, seeming completely engrossed in her task as she tended to him.

Dammit, it *did* feel good. It shouldn't, but it did—and somehow emphasized his infirmity.

"Later, maybe this evening, you can have a real bath," she was saying. "But this will do for now."

She didn't seem to expect a response, nor did she look at him. Rather, she kept stroking the cloth over his arms, his shoulders, his chest, his stomach.

If only she would move her hands a little lower.

Lower? Derek shifted slightly, just enough to recognize the hardness that he felt *lower*. Enough to remember how very naked he was under the bedding. Enough to realize that if she put her hands lower, she'd find his erection, as hot as a fever and hard as stone. And, God help him, he *wanted* her to touch him there.

*Why her?* he demanded of himself. And why now, when he had so much at stake—so much else to consider—and when he was hardly in any shape to do anything about it? He clenched his fingers into tight fists, but groaned and released them when it only aggravated the pain he already felt.

Dammit! He blinked and swallowed, forcing back the ugly urge to blame someone—anyone—for suddenly making life all but intolerable. He would give anything to climb out of this bed and get as far away from the Double F and Amber as he possibly could.

It was all her fault. How could she bandage his shoulder with such calm indifference, yet tease him with her nearness? And worse, refuse to explain herself or answer his questions?

He watched her with an intensity matched only by her own concentration. Her touch whispered over his skin with delicate strokes as she wrapped his wound with long, thin strips of cotton. Her cheeks flushed a warm, healthy pink.

Derek narrowed his eyes and looked closer. If her cheeks were flushed, perhaps she wasn't as detached as she pretended. Could she respond to him, as well?

"You're a fine nurse, Amber." The words came out low, his voice almost husky. And why not? *She* had done that to him, this woman who had been lovers with his father. Had she devoted to Richard the same tender care she now bestowed upon Derek? Or perhaps even more? And did she measure Derek against the memory of his father?

"Thank you." She kept working without looking at him.

"I can see why Richard wanted you in his bed."

# *Chapter Eight*

"How can you *say* such a thing?" He could have said nothing guaranteed to hurt her more.

"What's wrong, angel?" Intelligence sparked in his eyes, contradicting the slow, innocent drawl of his voice. "It's the truth, isn't it?"

Amber scrambled away. "The *truth* is that I am your housekeeper—and at the moment, your nurse. I have ignored your wretched claims, telling myself that you are injured—in pain—and not in your right mind. That your base accusations don't deserve a response." She glared at him, hands on her hips, and huffed in an angry breath. "I have my limits, however."

He narrowed his eyes. "Did I misunderstand something?"

She made no effort to hide the rage or hurt or anger she usually worked so hard to disguise. "You misunderstood everything, just like the rest," she snapped.

"The rest?"

"Men. Like Frank Edwards. Men who look—ogle—but don't see. Not *me*. Amber Laughton doesn't exist anymore. Richard Fontaine's mistress took her place. And you're just like them."

She backed away from the bed until the windowsill

brought her up short. She spun on her heel, presenting Derek with her very stiff back, and stared out at the brilliant blue sky.

How could she allow his words to hurt her so? Her defenses were better than that—or had she only thought so? She had spent two years learning to protect herself; how had Derek managed to reduce her efforts to nothing in less than a week?

"What do you mean I'm just like them?" he demanded from behind her. "What irony! I have no choice. You don't tell me enough to *be* any different."

She turned to stare at him. *"Different?"* She spat the word. "You don't *want* to be different!"

He looked tired—exhausted—but angry, too. "If you don't want to be treated like a whore, then why in hell don't you give me a reason not to?"

*Whore.*

The word loomed between them like a huge, ugly beast, settling wickedly in the middle of the room.

"It seems that we have nothing more to say to one another."

For the first time he looked uncertain. "Amber..."

She walked past his bed to the door. "I will see you are taken care of, but do not expect anything more of me."

"Amber! Dammit!" He shouted her name again as she pulled the door shut behind her.

And, for all the good it did, she remained true to her word. She spent no more time with Derek than her nursing duties required. She changed his bandage twice a day, brewed healing tea and broth, then soup, as often as he would take them. She made no further mention of the "real" bath she had promised, and he didn't ask for it. She spoke to him only when necessary and avoided meeting his eyes at all costs.

If Derek realized the seriousness of her intent, he didn't show it. He didn't, in fact, seem particularly troubled by her distance or coldness. Still, he offered no other disgraceful observations, nor did he express interest in baiting her into any arguments. As the days passed, however, he began to watch her closely, carefully…guardedly, and with eyes increasingly lucid. The growing intensity of his gaze provided her with another reason to avoid him and the sickroom.

She could not, however, dismiss him from her mind so easily. The ranch hands pestered her constantly for news of his recovery. Worse, thoughts of him—memories— haunted her when she was alone.

After two days of increasing tension, Amber sat on the veranda and forced herself to look at the situation with all honesty. The shooting had forever changed things between them—not all for the good or bad. They could not seem to ignore the familiarity that had sprung up between them; she had touched him, soothed him…seen him as she expected few others had. Both had said things they could never take back.

If his comments were cruel and biased, her self-defense was bitter and furious. The more she reflected on it, the more convinced she became that he'd wanted to hurt her, to make her angry, to send her running from the room. She just couldn't figure out why.

Not that it seemed to matter, she reminded herself wearily. With some dismay she had come to realize the memory of Derek's words no longer hurt with the same intensity as when he'd initially said them. He wasn't the first to suggest such things, nor even to say them blatantly. And, she supposed, she had fooled herself long enough; he wasn't entirely to blame.

Why *didn't* she give him a reason? But she knew the answer better than the question. She couldn't bear to see the disbelief on his face. If those she had known and trusted for most of her life had thrown her explanations back at her like so much filth, why would she expect Derek to be any different? For once in her life, she wanted someone to believe in her because he *chose* to. She wanted trust based on nothing more than faith.

She wanted that person to be Derek.

*Derek?* Amber swallowed and pushed her rocking chair into motion, only to be disappointed when the familiar movement didn't relax her as it often did. *Why him?*

Uneasy possibilities occurred to her, refusing to be pushed away. What was happening to her? Why did Derek send her pulses racing, twist her thoughts into a jumble? And why now?

He drew her like no other man had, and it wasn't because he was finely made, handsome, strong or intelligent. He was, in fact, perhaps too intelligent. He was a man in pain—physical and, in some inexplicable way, emotional as well. The kind of pain that made a man clever at protecting himself and very effective at finding others' weaknesses. He had certainly found hers.

She let the rocker slow and gradually stop, then stood and moved to lean her hip against the veranda railing. He hadn't meant to, of that she was certain, but she was coming to see that Derek had revealed his own vulnerability. He had done his best to hide it, but he was human all the same.

She couldn't forget the fact that he could be hurt just like any other man—and he could die just as easily. The bullet through his shoulder proved it. A bullet had killed her father. Another had killed Richard.

Amber drew in a deep breath and turned to the house. Now, when it was doubtless too late, she must convince him to trust her.

"Are you awake?"

Derek turned, more than tired of staring out through the bedroom window. He'd done little else for two days, and his mind was weary of the frenzied thoughts that taunted him.

His spirits lifted when he discovered Amber standing in the doorway, but a burning annoyance followed immediately. Why the hell should he be happy to see her? *Are you awake?* was more than she'd said since storming out of the room.

He'd pushed her too far and gotten exactly what he wanted: to be left alone to wallow in his own selfish misery. Except he'd grown damned sick of his own company. The sight of his bedroom had begun to irritate him, the view beyond his window as well, and his thoughts had provided little comfort. No wonder he preferred to see a beautiful woman.

*That beautiful woman was your father's mistress.* His wandering thoughts ground to a halt. She had reportedly taken other lovers, as well. She hadn't tried to seduce him, though. Derek frowned. Why not?

"I'm awake. About time, too."

She raked a wary gaze over him, but he'd come to expect it. "You needed the sleep. Your body needed time to recover. I see you're able to sit up now."

"You call this sitting?" Derek looked down at himself. His chest remained bare, except for the bandage fastened at his shoulder, but at least he had on drawers again, thanks to Gideon's assistance. And because Derek had insisted he wouldn't lie flat for another moment, he now reclined against the headboard, covers puddled in his lap.

"You're the most impatient man I know."

"Impatient?" he sputtered, scowling. "I've spent two days confined here. Two days of sleeping, drinking that vile tea and eating nothing but sorry, weak broth. I've let you poke and prod and smear that soggy mess you call a poultice on me, and you think I'm *impatient?*"

She stepped into the room with obvious reluctance. "Your fever broke during the night," she said, her eyes distant, and yet her voice carried an unexpected reassurance that confused him. "After another day or two in bed, you should be able to get up. I'll see that you get back on solid food today. Can you move your shoulder?"

He held his tongue over her pronouncement of how much longer he should remain bedridden; it would gain him nothing to argue with her. He'd get out of bed when he wanted to, and she could do nothing to stop him.

In the meantime, he lifted his shoulder with slow caution. A sharp lance of pain darted through him, and he grunted. "I can move it."

"But it hurts?"

"Not like it did." And that was true. He couldn't move as much as he would like, but he *could* move. And while it hurt, it no longer felt like he was being seared by constant fire.

"That's good." She blinked and turned toward the dresser. "You heal quickly."

Derek watched curiously as she rearranged the basins, jars, bottles and other sickroom clutter that had migrated from the bedside table to the dresser. She plucked a crumpled towel from the floor and folded it with a haphazard twist of her hands.

What was she doing here, asking questions and behaving as though she had nowhere else to be?

"What's wrong?" The question was out before he could give it a second thought.

She spun around to stare at him. "What do you mean?"

He shrugged his good shoulder, ignoring the tug of pain from the other side. "You seem nervous, and since you've avoided me for two days, I reckon something must be wrong if you're here."

She looked down at her hands, clasped so tightly her knuckles were white, but her expression offered nothing.

"You're right, of course. It's…" She shook her head sharply. "I owe you an explanation."

His gut tightened. "An explanation?"

"I've been thinking—since the other day. It took awhile. I was angry about the things you said. I'm still angry about some of them." She shot him a dark look. "But you were right about something. There *are* things I should tell you."

Answers? At last? He shifted in an attempt to sit straighter. "What?" he asked, his voice harsh with impatience. "*What* should you have told me?"

"It's…complicated. I hardly know where to start, and I don't know if I can explain very well."

"Why don't you just start at the beginning, and I'll interrupt if I get confused."

"The beginning," she said with a sigh that sounded entirely resigned. "That would be Twigg. It's not a cheerful little village anxious for progress. You must realize that by now."

She paused long enough for Derek to nod. "Before the war, it may have been all that Frank Edwards would have you believe. But things haven't been that way in a very long time."

"And what does that mean for the Double F?"

"Maybe nothing. I told you, it's complicated."

He glared at her. "What is so complicated about a little town trying to hide the fact that rustlers are ruining the ranches in the area?"

"I don't know if that's all it is."

His gut tightened with the damned uneasiness he'd come to depend on. "You better tell me everything."

Her green eyes darted about the room like those of a cornered animal. "I…may know who did this to you."

"What?" The hushed deliberation of the word did not keep him from coming up off the bed.

"Derek, stop!" She rushed forward to press a hand against his chest, the other at his good shoulder. Carefully she nudged him down onto the bed. "Lie back. You'll hurt yourself again."

His left side throbbed with a wicked fury that mirrored the frustration whipping through the rest of him. He ignored it all. "What did you say?"

"I suppose I can't truly say I know who shot you—I can't give you a name. But there are things I should have told you."

He lay flat on the mattress, her hands heavy against him and his heart thudding angrily. Could she feel it? "What kind of *things* should you have told me? And what happened to your promise that you would never lie to me?"

She withdrew and sank to the edge of the bed. Her head dropped forward for a moment, but then she straightened and looked at him fully. "I didn't lie. Ever," she said inexorably. "But I have suspicions that I should not have kept to myself."

"This better be about more than *suspicions*, because this bullet—" he arched his shoulder up from the pillow "—told me there's a hell of a lot going on here."

Amber took an audible breath. Even so, her voice came softly. "You know that my father is dead. He was killed two years ago." Her fingers twined together, separated, then twisted again. "He owned the newspaper, the *Twigg Monitor*. Being a newspaperman was his calling, and he took the responsibility seriously. Some people appreciated it, some called him a crusader.

"His last crusade was over the growing violence in Texas. Law and order seemed hard to enforce by the end of the war, and cattle rustling became serious."

"The same rustling." It wasn't a question.

"Yes." She nodded but didn't look at him. "I didn't know until later, but Papa had been threatened—warned anonymously to give up his investigation or face the consequences. I don't believe he knew who was behind the threats, but he wouldn't have stopped if he had."

"He sounds like a brave man." Derek admired any man who followed his own strict moral code. Some of the finest men he'd ever met had died defending their convictions. Soldiers most had been, Federals and Confederates both, but that hadn't seemed so important after a while.

"Some would agree. I believe it. Others think he was stupid. You see, he was murdered because he tried to do the right thing."

"Murdered." A sharp breath forced its way from Derek's lungs. The people of Twigg had hinted as much. Hearing the truth of it, however, gave Derek a jolt of unexpected sympathy for Amber.

She nodded sadly. "The threats were more than warnings."

"But the murderers were arrested?" Clem and Twigg had said as much.

"Sheriff Gardner arrested two men with surprising speed. They never stood trial, however. They were killed in a prison fight in San Antonio, or so I was told."

Derek sharpened his gaze and stared at her. She didn't seem to notice. "And you don't believe it."

"Oh, I believe they're dead." She finally looked at him. "As for how they died...well, that goes back to my suspicions."

Amber took a deep breath, and her breasts rose under the concealment of her bodice. She wore her plain brown dress today, and he tried not to notice how well it accented her curves.

"Not long after that I realized I no longer belonged in Twigg," she continued, "so I moved here."

She shifted to face him directly, and at the same time raised her chin. "I may never be able to answer all your questions, Derek, but I must say that your uncle was a wonderful man. He was a good friend—and more—to my father and me, and he proved it unquestionably when I came to live at the ranch."

"Oh yes, he was a saint—right up there with Matthew, Mark, Luke and John, from all I hear."

"Not a saint." Amber shook her head with a peculiar, almost wistful little smile. "But he was a good man, loving and sensitive, and I couldn't have asked for anything more from him."

Derek held his tongue, although he couldn't eliminate a soft grunt of disapproval. It didn't take a genius to figure out why Richard would likely be so *sensitive*, especially with a beautiful young woman like Amber. Derek had his own sensitivity he could show her—and he'd do his damnedest to abolish any lingering thoughts she might have about his father.

If Amber noticed his reaction, she didn't show it. "Richard refused to discuss what he knew of my father's murder until I finally wore him down with my insistence. That's when I learned of the threats, and that Richard had his own suspicions."

"Such as?"

She leveled a grave look at Derek. "Sheriff Gardner insisted Papa's murder was nothing more than another act of meaningless violence after the war, but it wasn't. It was deliberate, meant to punish my father—and as a warning to others."

"I see." And he did. The pieces of the puzzle that he'd been carefully arranging in his mind locked into place.

"Restraint seemed gone after that. The rustling became worse, especially here. I thought perhaps it was because of me—Blair Laughton's daughter had moved to the ranch. Then I discovered Richard had been doing his own investigating. He'd gotten warnings—threats—of his own."

"So both men were murdered because of their questions? Because they were getting too close to the truth?"

Amber eyed him without blinking. "Your visit to Twigg didn't escape notice, I can assure you. Now *you've* been asking questions." She paused. "I can't say who did it, Derek, but I can tell you that it's no coincidence you were shot."

"Is that what this is all about?" The anticipation of finally getting his answers foundered.

"Yes."

He shook his head, battling back supreme disappointment. "Amber, I knew most of this the night I was shot—except about your father's death. I figured it out before I got back to the house."

# Chapter Nine

Amber set down a bowl of steaming fried potatoes, then stepped back to cast a critical eye over the rest of the table. A sparkling crystal vase, a treasured heirloom passed down from her mother, held the position of honor, displaying an arrangement of Amber's favorite pink sweetheart roses cut especially for the occasion.

The table was set for one.

Derek had announced this morning that he was ready for *real* food. It also marked his first full day on his feet since the shooting. It was not his first day out of bed, however.

He'd gotten up three days after he was shot and walked into the cookhouse completely dressed. His face was haggard, his eyes dull, but he stayed on his feet for three hours. Amber considered it a testament to pure determination on his part, and suspected the only reason he finally gave in to his exhaustion was because he didn't want to disgrace himself in front of the men.

Beau had fashioned Derek a sling after that first morning, and it had seemed to help; Derek managed to remain working until early afternoon on the second day. Yesterday—the third day—he had stayed up even longer. Today, he'd worked all day.

Amber checked the biscuits, tucked snugly under a cloth

napkin, then fussed with the silverware and plate. She repositioned the bowls of potatoes and black-eyed peas. She eyed the arrangement again and sighed. Why was she wasting her time tinkering with the table setting? Derek was unlikely to notice.

She had to admit that she *wanted* him to notice. She wanted him to recognize her worth as a housekeeper, to see her as an intelligent, competent woman. Not some fool who conjured up phantom dilemmas where there were none.

Like an overwrought ninny, she had agonized over her *suspicions,* her secrets. She had convinced herself to go to him, to forgive his crude accusations and tell him *the truth.* She had all but convinced herself that she may, in some small way, have deserved some of the blame for his being shot.

His response had shown that her gesture was for nothing.

A prickling sensation up her spine warned her of Derek's presence moments before he announced, "Beau said you were in here."

She turned to face him, a serious hitch in her breathing, and couldn't formulate an answer. She struggled to concentrate beyond the distraction of seeing him after a full day's work. His trousers were dirty, cotton shirt sweat-stained, and his dusty brown hat, shoved back on his head, revealed a furrowed brow creased with grime. His eyes were a faded blue, as though the day had almost done him in. Lines bracketed his mouth and his injured shoulder slumped in its dirt-streaked sling. Even dirty and exhausted, he looked entirely too appealing.

She cleared her throat and forced herself to speak. "I understand you'll be eating at the table tonight."

He flicked a disinterested gaze around the room and shrugged. "Wherever. It doesn't matter to me."

"The table's set, whenever you're ready." She tried for a polite, accommodating tone.

"All right. I'll wash up." He headed for the staircase directly across the hall, his movements deliberate, almost cautious. Was he in pain, fatigued—or both?

"Would it be easier to clean up in the cookhouse?" she called on impulse. "Or—my bedroom is near the stairs."

The offer slipped out before she could reconsider. He stopped, one foot on the bottom step, and turned to peer over his shoulder. Something hot and almost wild flashed in his eyes, but it disappeared with a blink.

"Thank you for the offer of your bedroom," he said in a flat voice as he turned away, "but I prefer my privacy."

"I…" Her voice trailed away, and she struggled to find new words—any words. What stupidity had possessed her?

"I'll have your beefsteak on the table by the time you're back," she croaked.

"Have you eaten?" He continued up the stairs.

"No."

"Then set a place for yourself. I want to talk to you."

Amber said nothing as Derek navigated the steps, merely watching his guarded movements until he disappeared.

A fist of dread lodged itself in the pit of her stomach, while an awful anticipation crawled along her nerves. *Whatever he wants, you don't have to do anything more than listen,* she told herself staunchly.

Turning to the handmade cabinet that held the fine dishes and collectibles Richard had accumulated over the years, Amber withdrew another place setting. She had added a few of her own belongings, like the vase, when she moved from Twigg, but nothing so fine as the precious china. She arranged it with care, directly across the table from the first one; that provided the farthest distance between them.

"Here's the main course." Beau entered behind her and placed a platter of beef on the table.

She flashed him a quick smile, relieved that it was not Derek—yet. And, as happened every time she watched Beau move, the way in which he adjusted to his handicap humbled her. He used his stump for balance and his good hand for everything else.

"It looks delicious. You fry a much better beefsteak than I've ever done."

"Thank you." His answering smile came slowly, as always. It pleased Amber to note the expression had at least begun to appear more natural on his face. Now and then she caught a glimpse of another man, perhaps a younger and more carefree Beau, that made her suspect he might have smiled and laughed often before the war had taken a part of his arm—and stolen his joy.

"You'll have to teach me your secret," she said softly.

He ducked his head and his cheeks flushed a dull pink, making her heart suddenly ache for this man, and all the others. Lord help them, but she was surrounded by fallen angels and wounded souls. They had all seen too much, lived too much. Lost too much: their belief in the world— and themselves.

"Beefsteak is a favorite of mine." Beau sounded almost shy. "After I burned a few and had to eat the disappointing results, I learned to do it right. This one is for Derek." He pointed at a huge slab of meat. "It's cooked rare, how he said he likes it. The other is for you."

"Me?" How had he known she would be eating in the dining room with Derek? "I—er, thank you."

"Derek said you would be ready shortly. Do you need anything else before then?"

"No, thank you."

"All right then." Beau turned toward the door. "I'll go check on that pie."

"Good." She smiled, thinking of the special dessert. "That's all of last year's peaches. It will have to satisfy us until the new crop comes in."

His expression turned wistful. "Peach pie was always my favorite. I haven't had it in a very long time."

"Then I'm glad I made it. Richard loved those peach

trees, and they've come to mean a lot to me, too. I used to come here as a child to help him when he first planted them. We worked very hard to get them started. But that was a long time ago.''

She blinked at the memory, then smiled. ''You be sure to get the first piece, you hear?''

''Yes, ma'am.'' He ducked his head. ''I'd better go. I don't want it to burn.''

Alone again, Amber conceded to the odd mixture of emotions that Beau's conversation had produced in her. Part of her reveled in a long-forgotten delight; how very wonderful it was to know that something as simple as peach pie could still give joy to another person. The war and the years since had robbed them all of so many innocent pleasures. Too often, life seemed little more than the most simple, basic survival.

How tragic, though, that another part of her must ache for the very same reasons. So few people—Derek among them—found little joy in life these days. Some days it seemed they had nothing to rejoice in.

His steady, measured stride alerted her to his approach. Her gaze jerked to the staircase. She hauled in a deep breath. *Don't let yourself forget,* she reminded herself sternly. *He can still change his mind about your suitability for this job.*

Life held no guarantees, and Derek had made no promises.

Derek took a bite of his steak and chewed slowly. His shoulder ached like the very devil, and he had only himself to blame. He'd spent the day on his feet, trying to maintain the pace he'd set before the shooting. The sling helped immobilize his arm, but it did nothing to repair the damage the bullet had done. Only time and Amber's faithful nursing could do that.

He rested his forearm on the edge of the table and allowed himself a small sigh. His arm had grown stiff from being held in the same position all day, so he'd left the sling in his bedroom. Now he regretted it. Why hadn't he realized how much effort it would take to cut his steak?

He ate a few more fried potatoes, at the same time glancing across the table through lowered lashes. At least he had made a respectable impact on his portion; Amber had mostly toyed with hers. She'd tried to disguise the fact by pushing the potatoes and peas around with her fork, but he'd noticed. He missed very little where she was concerned.

She appealed to him in a real physical sense. All right, he was damned attracted to her. Willingly or not, he'd been watching her since the day he arrived. Aside from that, however, he found he could almost *like* her. She couldn't have been a more devoted nurse, even as angry as she'd been. He couldn't fault her behavior: considerate, caring, responsible.

He blinked, sharpening his gaze in an effort to see her through different eyes. She wore blue calico today, a dress she rarely wore. The color seemed to sharpen the green of her eyes and somehow accent the auburn of her hair, the creamy paleness of her complexion. The bodice was cut tight, hugging the curve of her breasts and the slant of her waist with all the faithfulness of a lover.

*Oh, for chrissake. Stop it.* He snatched up his cup in irritation. *Can't you forget your lust for one minute?*

Amber flinched, and Derek swallowed another curse. He frowned, but allowed no other reaction to escape. He drank his coffee instead.

What the hell was wrong with her? She was as jumpy as a long-tailed cat in a roomful of rockers.

"I've been thinking." He deposited his cup on the table and sat back. "For a while, actually. Trying to remember."

"Yes. I expect you have." She looked up.

"I was alone that night, looking for a place to make

camp. They must have tracked me. I heard a noise—a long-horn or mustang, I thought. The sound and the shot seemed to come at almost the same time. I knew the instant I felt the bullet that it was connected to the rustling and Richard's death. I didn't factor in your father's murder, but knowing about it only reinforces my initial conclusions.''

''I...yes.''

''There's more to it, though, isn't there?''

''More?''

''More than a renegade band of outlaw rustlers stealing a few cattle and horses. And more than making an example of a couple of men who had every right to pry into an injustice. It's murder—but not just an all too common, violent occurrence at that. It's *personal.*''

His voice had hardened into sharp, cold steel, like that of the saber that had served him so well for four bloody years. It was the voice he'd learned to use in the heat of battle, when he could take no chance that his men would misunderstand. Acute satisfaction consoled him with the knowledge that he had not completely lost his edge.

''What do you mean?'' Her soft voice sounded breathless.

''I know the rest of it.''

Her fork slipped from her fingers, and she jumped as it clattered to her plate. ''What?'' The word was a harsh whisper, and her hands clenched into tight fists. ''What do you mean, *the rest of it?*''

''Micah told me how your father died.''

''What do you mean?'' she repeated breathlessly. ''*I* told you how he died! He was murdered.''

''You didn't say he was killed while trying to protect you. That the men who killed him attacked you first.''

The color drained from her face, and Derek cursed himself for being rough and thoughtless, but blunt was all he knew anymore. Jordan had seen to it that any gentle emotions were buried deeply, or beaten out of Derek, early on, and the war had taken care of any residue that might have remained. He had learned then how to make difficult choices—and how to avoid regrets because of them.

"Micah shouldn't have told you that." She averted her eyes.

"Why didn't you tell me?"

"It wasn't important."

"It wasn't important?" He stared at her. She'd been attacked—damn near raped, according to Micah. Derek's gut clenched anew with a fury he'd come to know very well since the beginning of the damned war. Had felt every time he'd faced the aftermath of battle, or when his men, drunk with alcohol and rage or victory, had thought to avail themselves of whatever female flesh they found nearby. Derek had seen first-hand, when he'd been too late to stop the brutality, what rowdy men could do to a woman.

Their animalistic behavior had sickened him, despite Jordan's persistent accusations that Derek was no better than a savage himself. But, by God, he had some decency. He'd had a mother...and even a fiancée—once. He'd court-martialed every goddamned one of those men.

"What happened to me doesn't matter." The dignity in her voice recaptured his attention. He watched and listened as she scooted back from the table. Tension radiated from her in waves. "I survived," she added tightly.

Derek pushed his own chair back and slanted an impatient gaze over her. "You seem to have forgotten something."

"And what is that?"

"You were attacked, and that makes you as involved in this as anyone else. It means that whoever is behind this isn't above harming—attacking, raping, even killing—a woman. Are they that desperate? Or that vicious?"

Her eyes widened as she stared at him. "I hadn't thought of that. I always assumed my part was a horrible accident."

"Amber." He used his saber voice again. "The problems here are far more serious than anyone has given them credit for, and it's dangerous to pretend otherwise. It goes beyond a decaying ranch or missing cattle, or even Richard's death. It's not random and it's not accidental. There's a deep savagery to all this, and my coming here has renewed it somehow. Until we discover who—or what—is behind it, no one at the Double F is safe.''

''You're…sure?''

He shot her a flat gaze. ''Absolutely.''

She nodded. ''I…you're right, of course. I suppose I haven't wanted to see the truth. Then again—'' her lips twitched ''—my father always said I lived in my own world of dreams.''

Derek eyed Amber curiously. A dreamer? No, he would never have described her that way. But realizing how much time and events had changed her saddened him. From young innocent to mistress for a man old enough to be her father.

A sudden image of her, naked and wrapped around a stocky, gray-haired version of himself, blazed through Derek's brain. His gut burned with the reminder, and he wished suddenly he hadn't eaten so much.

He forced his attention back to the topic at hand. ''Is there anyone in Twigg who might know something more?''

''Twigg?'' She sounded appalled. ''I have no idea. They could all know everything, and I would have no idea.''

''Is there anyone there you trust to ask?''

''I have no friends in Twigg. They consider me responsible for my father's death—and worse. They turned their backs on me. I would never humble myself to ask them for anything.''

''What about the Andrews brothers?''

The corners of her lips twitched. ''You've met them. They're…eccentric. What help could they give? A bet on how many cattle we've lost and when the rustlers will strike again?''

Derek couldn't resist answering with a smile. Clem and Twigg affected him that way. "I see your point."

"Are you ready for dessert?" Beau stepped into the room, carrying two small plates. "I don't want the pie to cool anymore. It's excellent, Amber. The best I've had since before the war." He served Amber first, then placed the remaining plate in front of Derek, who glanced down.

Curved, golden half-moon shapes of sliced fruit tumbled from underneath a flaky piecrust. The unmistakable scent tickled his nose.

*Peach pie! Oh, Jesus Christ, it was peach pie.*

Derek jerked to his feet and his chair skittered back behind him. A wave of nausea rolled over him, and he swallowed heavily. *Peach pie.*

For the love of God, he was going to be sick!

He took a step, two, then shoved past Beau and ran blindly from the room.

## Chapter Ten

"What happened?" Beau stayed where Derek had shoved him. He stared at Amber, wide-eyed and open-mouthed, looking from her to the empty hallway and back again.

"I don't know." She glanced around the room with matching distress. Derek had moved like a man possessed, the hounds of hell so hard on his heels he hadn't noticed when the chair pitched over behind him.

"Did I do something wrong? I thought you'd be ready for dessert by now. Maybe I—"

"No," Amber interrupted. "It's not your fault, Beau." She'd seen for herself what had happened—not that it made any more sense of Derek's reaction. "I don't understand it, either, but I'm sure you did nothing to provoke it."

"But why…?" Beau straightened. "I only brought dessert."

"I don't know." She shook her head. "He seemed fine until you set that pie in front of him."

"Do you suppose he doesn't like *pie?*"

Beau sounded shocked, as though he could not comprehend someone not favoring dessert. His tone tempted Amber to smile, but the impulse faded with the realization that the whimsy of it made more sense than Derek's behavior.

"No one reacts that way to something as simple and common as pie. Besides," she said thoughtfully, "he ate the pecan pie I made last week. It must be something more than that."

She stood and began to clear the table, having no more stomach for the fragrant peach pie than she'd had for the other food. Especially now. Beau righted the overturned chair and pitched in to help.

Her mind churned as they worked. What in God's name was going on? She trapped her bottom lip between her teeth as she tried to understand. Why would Derek race away like a man in torment? Where had he found the strength to charge from the room as he had?

"Beau." She dropped a fistful of silverware onto the table. "Can you finish alone? I need to find Derek."

"Of course. Go on. You just find Derek. He—" Beau's voice caught, a rough scrape of sound that demanded Amber's attention. A dark, haunted look had overtaken his features.

"Beau?"

He cleared his throat. "He needs you."

She scurried from the room and out the back door without another word, Beau's words ringing in her ears.

*He needs you.*

Derek had needed her before, when he was shot. At least he had needed her nursing skills. This was entirely different, but still…

An errant recollection, from just after Derek was wounded, whispered back to her. Why was it that everyone around her seemed so very wounded, and in so many different ways? she had wondered then. And how could she, of all people, help them?

The backyard was empty, as were the corral, the barn, the toolshed. Laughter sounded from the bunkhouse, but Amber doubted that Derek would seek out other company in his current mood. She glanced around with a quiet sigh. He could be anywhere.

Evening shadows shrouded the grounds, forcing her to move slowly and rely on the lantern she'd snatched from the barn as an afterthought. With a grateful glance skyward, counting herself lucky that the rising moon offered its own assistance, Amber scoured the area as best she could.

Eventually she found herself on the path to the ranch cemetery. Glancing up ahead, she saw a bulky shadow. She knew with uncanny certainty it was Derek. A picket fence enclosed the plot, and he sat on the ground next to it, his back against the fence. Two graves hallowed the ground: her father's and Richard's.

Richard's unexpected offer to bury her father at the ranch had touched Amber deeply. In the years since, she had become overwhelmingly grateful for his foresight. Having his grave so near had given her a comfort she had never expected to achieve after his death. She had often wondered, during the time she spent tending the small cemetery grounds, if Richard had experienced any premonition over his own death. He had joined her father there only a year later.

Now, she approached Derek slowly. He sat with his legs bent, head down and forehead resting on his knees. One arm was wrapped around his shins, while the other, his injured side, hung loose. He didn't move.

"Derek? Are you all right?"

He jerked as though her words struck him like physical blows. Slowly, so much so that she thought at first he wouldn't move, he raised his head and looked at her. She lost her breath and her heart broke at the sight of his face.

Lantern light warmed his fallen-angel features to a stark burnished gold. He always looked striking and beautiful to her, even when his expression was closed and distant, but now his face showed nothing but anguish. His eyes bore a bleak darkness made up of shattered emotion and torment, while deep lines of pain bracketed his mouth. Spent tears smudged his face, staggering Amber with a searing pain of her own.

"Derek!"

He didn't respond. He simply stared at her until she dropped to her knees next to him, heedless of the rocks and dirt. She hardly noticed as she set the lantern aside.

"Derek, what's wrong?" she demanded, growing steadily more afraid.

She had expected…something. She didn't know what, but not this. Derek routinely held all the world and its emotions at bay. Naively, she had been sure it was because he didn't care deeply enough.

She had been wrong, so very, very wrong. He cared… perhaps too much. He cared enough to *cry.*

"You ever see a man die?"

*"What?"* She reared back and stared at him. He didn't move, but the low, raspy question echoed between them. "Yes, I saw a man die," she whispered, forcing herself to answer, though she denied the memory of it. Tonight she couldn't afford the weakness it would bring.

"Your father." He glanced away. "I'm sorry."

"I know." She took his hand in hers and held it tightly, allowing nothing beyond comfort and understanding between them. His skin felt cold, unnaturally so, while his fingers were rough and callused. "Please, Derek. Tell me what happened."

He looked down to where she cradled his hand, as though he couldn't quite comprehend the meaning of her touch, then raised his eyes again. The awful desolation had not abated.

"First man I saw die stood right next to me. One minute he was shouting, 'Give 'em hell, boys.' The next he was dead, with a bright red hole in his chest."

The war. That goddamned war to end all wars. Her fingers tightened around his. "Derek, I'm so very sorry." It wasn't enough, but she couldn't think of anything more to say.

"Nathan and I used to play war. We fought Indians, the British, pirates. Anybody. We had sticks for guns, and we always won. The real thing, though—"

His voice broke. He blinked and cleared his throat before a long sigh shuddered through him. "Pittsburgh Landing was a quiet little place on the Tennessee River. They called the battle Shiloh. There was a little church near there with that name."

Amber shivered. She'd heard of Shiloh. Her father's face had been ashen as he explained what the battle meant to Texas, to the Union and the Confederacy. The South suffered a great blow that day in losing General Albert Sidney Johnston, and it was the first time she'd heard the names of those Northern generals, Grant and Sherman, who ultimately decided the outcome of the war.

"Yes, I remember it." She twined her fingers through his and held on tightly.

Derek didn't respond to her words or touch. He simply sat staring out into the darkness, hardly even breathing. The growing silence scraped against her nerves until she couldn't abide it another moment.

"I learned to take the war seriously after Shiloh," she said softly. "The casualties were appalling. Papa said the South couldn't win on pure bravado, and he was right. After that, people didn't claim one good Reb soldier was worth ten Yankees."

"A soldier is a soldier. And a bullet is a bullet."

"Yes." What more could she say?

"I didn't know better then. Not at Shiloh. It was my first battle. I was so damned patriotic—full of life. We'd whip them. *We had to.*" Derek's fingers flexed and tightened around hers almost painfully. "The war wasn't supposed to last. But I thought, that morning—that day—it would never end."

"Were you wounded?"

"I was *lucky*." His voice sliced the air with contempt. "I wasn't hit, while damn near every man around me was shot to pieces."

Amber sat abruptly as her knees gave out. She scooted closer until her hip met his. Her fingers, light and gentle, smoothed the hair back from his forehead, his cheek. She ached to do more but dared not.

Then Derek began speaking again, and it didn't seem to matter. "They called the center of the line the 'Hornets' Nest.' An apt description. The balls came fast and furious, all around us. It was like getting into the middle of a swarm of hornets, with no escape. They were everywhere. Men, shots, bayonets. I was on the left flank by...a peach orchard in full bloom. Nothing and no one could stand, not under that volley, so we lay there, firing and firing, and more of us kept dying. *And they just kept coming.* Coming and coming, firing back. Blossoms fell all around us, blanketing the ground. The living and the dead."

"Dear God." The soft words came out as a low whimper. *Peaches.* A peach orchard. He had been pinned down in a peach orchard, and she had baked him a *peach pie*.

"Derek." Her fingers trembled as she traced the arch of his brow, the high curve of his cheek. He didn't seem to notice.

"They say you can't really smell a peach tree in bloom—but you can. It's a scent like nothing else. Strong. Overpowering. It covered the stench of blood."

He looked at her then, but the guarded distance in his eyes told her he didn't see her; he wasn't even there with her. He was caught, trapped in the memories of a battle so horrendous that he could hardly comprehend it, even years later.

"I loathe peaches," he said in a hoarse, vicious voice. "The sight and the smell of them."

"I'm sorry." She rested her hand on his shoulder, near the column of his neck, stroking lightly. "I didn't know."

"It rained that night. Wounded men—*maimed* men—lay in the open, calling for help, for water. We couldn't get to them. The battle wasn't over, just the first day. No one had reckoned how to collect the wounded from the battlefield—not by the thousands—and they lay there in pain, dying. But God answered, some said, because it rained."

He brought his hand up to rest over hers, trapping it mercilessly against his shoulder. She tightened her fingers with a gentle squeeze.

"I saw them that night, when the lightning flashed." He continued in a still, hollow voice. "There were hogs on the battlefield. They...fed on the dead."

"Oh, God, Derek." Amber swallowed back a wave of nausea. Tears pooled in her eyes and she blinked until the moisture spilled over. With it went the last threads of her control.

She launched herself into his arms, her breasts flattened against his chest and her face tucked into the curve of his neck. Somehow she remembered to take care with his injured shoulder, but the need to touch him overwhelmed her.

Holding him didn't stop the tears, however, and Amber had no ability to check them. She cried for Derek, for all he had witnessed and all he'd been forced to do. She cried for the men who had fought so valiantly, for those who'd died—and those who survived and couldn't forget. And somehow, she cried for herself. For all she had lost, all she'd thrown away and all the mistakes she couldn't fix.

She never knew exactly how or when it happened, but she found herself wrapped in Derek's arms, cradled close against him. His heart beat against her with a heavy thud, and his breath stirred the loose hairs at her temples. He felt warm and safe and solid, as though his arms created a cocoon that would hold the world at bay. He didn't cry—now, at least.

She couldn't bring herself to release him, not even to wipe away the tears that streaked over her cheeks. Eventually she managed to haul in a deep, trembling breath and whispered, "I am so very, very sorry." Her lips moved softly against his throat.

His arms tightened around her, and he stroked surprisingly gentle hands over her back. Amber nestled closer, unwilling to accept any separation between them. He murmured something soft against her hair, near her ear, but she couldn't quite make out the words. She tilted her head back to look at him.

The intensity of his expression revealed little, and yet it prepared her for the moment when his lips met hers. Derek kissed her with a fierce tenderness that both excited and calmed her, beckoning her near while she settled in his arms. She sighed with the certain knowledge that she had never before belonged anywhere as surely as she did with him, at this moment.

He took advantage of the opportunity, and his tongue darted forward, testing the corners of her mouth, the fullness of her bottom lip. She held him to her, tenderly nurturing him with all the succor her arms could offer. She kissed him back, her lips moving delicately against his and her fingers tangling in the length of his soft, silky hair. His embrace tightened and he gathered her against his chest.

A deep groan rent the night, and he wrenched his mouth from hers.

"Derek?" Was that needful, breathless voice hers?

"My shoulder." A thread of pain underscored his voice.

"Oh!" Sanity returned and she jerked back—but Derek only allowed her to go so far. He anchored her body against him with his good arm, sprawled her across his lap. For a moment, at least, it seemed to be where she belonged.

"I'm sorry," she whispered.

He didn't answer, instead hauling in one deep breath after another. She worked to adjust her own breathing, and gradually the darkness and the silence calmed her enough to clear her head.

*Derek...the kiss.*

Instinct screamed at her to shove him away, but immediately on its heels came the need to hold him closer. She had never given herself to any man with such familiarity, and yet it somehow felt perfectly natural—right—to be in Derek's arms. If his wound hadn't pained him, where would it have led them?

What was happening to her?

"Nothing in my life has ever come close to Shiloh."

Amber flinched when Derek spoke. The dull sound of his voice subdued her panic, and confusion faded. He was a man in pain, emotionally and physically. She couldn't harden her heart against his suffering, hadn't the will to even try.

"Derek, the poultice I put on your shoulder was made of peach tree leaves."

He shuddered and sucked in a deep, harsh breath. "No."

"Shh." Immediately she stroked him, smoothing gentle, reassuring hands over his face, his neck, shoulders, arms. Wherever she could touch him and it wouldn't hurt. "It's all right," she crooned in a whisper. "I just wanted you to know that peaches can do good things, too. They can heal. They helped you. You'll be all right."

"They can't do a goddamned thing." He shook his head fiercely. "I'll never be right again. Nothing will be." His voice, in turns, sounded vicious, then wooden. "After Shiloh I didn't feel anything anymore. I still don't. And I've never been that scared again. Except maybe—"

His voice died abruptly. Tension filled the air, crackling between them. Amber looked up into his face and rediscovered the deep, age-old grief clouding his eyes.

"When, Derek? When else were you so scared?"

He didn't answer at first. He sat motionless, staring past her. Her heart began to pound.

"When—" he swallowed "—I found out Nathan was dead."

"Nathan? Your brother is dead?"

"Four years now."

She caught her breath and managed to hold it long enough to stave off new tears. It did nothing to cure the ache deep in her heart. For Derek and all that life had forced upon him. For Nathan and all he had lost. And perhaps even for Richard, who'd never had the chance to know his nephews.

"Derek, I…" She started to speak, but words came hard.

"He was always at the thick of things. He didn't lead men, he was one of them. He didn't survive Spotsylvania."

Derek's hand remained at the small of her back. His fingers twitched, and something hard pressed against her, as though he'd formed a fist. Did he blame himself?

"What could you have done for him?"

"I wasn't there in Virginia. I was…west. Later I talked to a man who was there and fought in all the major engagements since First Manassas." Derek fell silent for the length of a heartbeat. "He said Spotsylvania was the most terrible day he ever saw. I have my imagination to tell me what it was like."

She stroked her fingertips gently over his brow, pushing back a stray lock of hair that had fallen over his eyes. "I'm sure you and your family were devastated."

"My…father will never recover. And he will never forgive me."

"Forgive you?" Amber asked. Derek's words stole her breath and she inhaled deeply. "What could he possibly have to forgive you for?"

"I…you're right. I did what I had to do."

"It's grief, Derek." She gathered him close once more, taking care with his tender shoulder. "Your father was grief-stricken. When he recovers, he won't want to lose another son."

"Jordan Fontaine has no sons." Derek stiffened, pulling away with a soft groan she attributed to his wounded shoulder. He dropped his arms and shifted back. "I haven't seen him in three years, and I do not expect to see him ever again."

She held out her hand, but he ignored her.

"It's in the past. I shouldn't have spoken of it now. None of it."

"Derek?" She tried again.

"Come on." He grunted as he levered himself up with his good arm and stood. "It's late and it's dark. I'll see you back to the house."

Somewhat clumsily, he held out his hand to her. Amber could see no alternative but to accept his help. Perhaps if she put her hand in his, it would ease the awkwardness. Their unexpected and amazing closeness seemed to be evaporating like a pool of water on a sizzling summer day.

Derek released her and retrieved the lantern, holding it high to lead the way. She found herself walking on his injured side as he silently urged her forward.

She swallowed a frustrated groan. They had shared a closeness that all but shattered her, while his kiss—*his kiss!*—had somehow renewed her. Why did he have to spoil it? He didn't have to carry his pain alone; she could help him.

And perhaps he could help her.

They bumped shoulders over the uneven trail, and Derek sucked in a sharp breath. "I'm sorry," she whispered as their fingers brushed.

And then, quite astonishingly, his hand touched hers again. Deliberately. He linked their fingers and held on tightly. Amber squeezed back, and slowly, silently, they made their way to the house.

## Chapter Eleven

A whisper of sound, small and insignificant yet noticeably out of place, woke Derek from a light, fitful sleep. He lay quietly, listening for the noise to repeat itself, but the house remained still and silent.

Had it been a dream? He shifted, grumbling as he rolled onto his back. He heard nothing but the rustle of the covers twisted around his waist.

He cursed under his breath and tried to pull the sheet out from beneath him. The bedclothes became a tangled rat's nest that clung to his hips as he wrestled with them. They seemed alive, intent on foiling his every move. His shoulder ached with the effort of finding a comfortable position.

*You used to be able to fall sleep with no trouble.* He couldn't have survived the war without developing that particular talent. When had he lost it?

He sat up. *You're getting soft,* he told himself. Or maybe he'd spent too much time recuperating. Since he'd started back to his normal routine, he'd fallen into bed exhausted every night. Tonight it seemed to all catch up with him.

This morning he had gone directly to the barn and avoided the house at all costs. Shameful memories of what he had said, what Amber had witnessed, destroyed his appetite, and there had been no other reason to return before nightfall. He had worked steadily and deliberately, exhausting himself again, and the day had passed. But now, tonight, he didn't feel tired in the usual way.

He hauled in a deep breath and glanced around him, at the heavy shadows that identified the room's furniture: the armoire, the dresser, the washstand, the chair. It all seemed familiar, so very ordinary, and yet he felt so very different.

How could he have said what he did, revealed the things he had shown? He swallowed. Amber must have been disgusted to find him sitting next to the cemetery, blubbering like a baby. He had revealed some of the most painful, private moments of his life—moments no one else knew of. Moments he *wanted* to keep private.

Derek closed his eyes against the blackness of the night. He had reasons, and damn good ones, for trapping those things in the depths of his soul. Civilians could never understand the war from his perspective. Veterans like Gideon and Beau might be an exception, he supposed, but who wanted to relive such memories?

*There are other reasons, more serious than that,* a firm, self-protective voice pointed out relentlessly. *They are the reasons you don't speak of it. What would those fine Confederate soldiers think if they knew how you spent the war?*

Derek grimaced, a bitter clenching of his teeth that would never pass for a smile. His upbringing as Jordan Fontaine's son, of the *Charleston Fontaines,* left him with little doubt about what they would think. And *that* was why he could never share his memories with anyone.

How had Amber gotten past his guard?

He swung his legs over the side of the bed, grunting as he used his stronger arm to sit and maneuver. Amber had done one hell of a lot more than simply *get past his guard.* He had kissed her—and she'd kissed him back. Her lips were soft, and she tasted so very sweet, like the finest clover honey. He could still feel her breasts press against his chest, her breath tickle his throat, her arms around him, tender and comforting.

What the hell had he been thinking? Derek swallowed. He could no longer pretend he was not physically attracted to her. He had been from the instant he saw her. But that didn't—couldn't—matter. He should never have touched her, kissed her. Not last night, not ever. Not when his father had held her, kissed her, the same way. And not when Derek himself was who he was and had done what he'd done. If she knew everything about him…she would never forgive him.

No one would.

*What ghost do you want to fight first?* The demand came to mind with harsh strength. *The ghost of your father and what he meant to Amber, or the ghost of yourself and the reasons she can never be yours?*

The reasons she would never *want* to be his.

He stood, more abruptly than he'd meant, and his shoulder pulled with a deep ache. He accepted the pain with an abbreviated groan and stalked to the window, where he stood inspecting the long shadows cast by the bright, late-night moon. The serenity called to him, intrigued him as nothing he'd ever known.

He closed his eyes and dropped his head forward, rubbing a hand over the back of his neck. No, he had known little serenity and tranquility in his life. Jordan was not a peaceful kind of man, and he had no tolerance for such weak emotions in his sons. Particularly not in the son he'd never wanted.

Later, when the war and battles like Shiloh were all Derek could remember of life, his education had been complete. Still, he could never completely overcome the regret that life offered nothing better.

Was it just Derek himself, or had Nathan experienced his own insecurities, fears and anger—even pain? Sadness hollowed out a deep emptiness in Derek's gut. Not a day went by that he didn't wonder about his brother and the choices they had made. Had Nathan experienced his own Shiloh, his own peach orchard?

Why couldn't he forget? Derek wondered. Why did the memories seem suddenly so strong, forcing him to relive the battles over and over in his mind? He thought he had put it all behind him after Appomattox.

Derek sighed and glanced longingly toward the bed. If he laid back down, maybe he could sleep. If he could just—

A shrill, bloodcurdling scream rent the night. Derek bolted across the room and out the door without another thought. He skidded down the hall toward the stairs as another sharp cry was cut off abruptly. This time he made out one word.

"No!" The voice was Amber's, and she was terrified.

*Thunder rumbled, and a shard of lightning issued an eerie glow over the darkening interior of the newspaper office. Amber glanced out the window and frowned. Dark, roiling clouds scudded across the afternoon sky.*

*"Papa?"*

*"What is it?"*

*She headed into the back room, where her father was busy sorting type from yesterday's edition of the* Twigg Monitor. *"I think I'll go on home. It's nearly time to start supper. It looks like rain, and I don't want to get caught in the storm."*

*Blair nodded. "All right. You go on. I'm almost finished here myself. We can have supper after I get home. Unless young Mr. Jeff Buchanan is going to stop by this evening?"*

*Heat flooded Amber's face, and she put her hands to her cheeks. "Papa! Jeff isn't some callow youth. He's twenty-five and a veteran. He fought with John Bell Hood at Gettysburg."*

*Blair set down his type case with a low sigh. "Amber, honey. I understand what you're saying. Those things are important to Jeff. He fought—and valiantly—with one of the best units in the Confederacy. But the war is over. It has been for a year. Life goes on, and Jeff must do the same. It will only cause you both pain to dwell on the past. It's over and can't be changed.''*

*Amber sighed. Understanding and guilt warred within her, a familiar struggle that had plagued her since the early days of the War for Southern Independence. She understood her father's views and shared many of his opinions. But she had grown from childhood to maturity amid the politics and emotionalism that led the country to war, and couldn't escape a nagging guilt that her patriotism was somehow lacking.*

*''I know, Papa. I know.'' She sighed. ''Jeff doesn't seem ready to give up on the Confederacy, but I know in my heart the Cause is lost. I'm trying to help him see it can't be our future.''*

*Blair opened his mouth as if to say more, but Amber raised her hand to stop him. ''I know, Papa,'' she repeated. ''But it doesn't matter. Jeff isn't coming by tonight.''*

*Blair's eyebrows shot up with a surprise Amber expected; Jeff had taken to spending most evenings with them. Then her father blinked and merely said, ''I think I'll invite Micah to eat with us. His rheumatism has made this a difficult week, and he's been drinking again.''*

*Another shard of lightning crackled outside, and Amber jumped. She laughed, a sheepish little sound. ''That would be nice. I planned chicken and dumplings, and that's one of his favorites.''*

*Blair strode across the room and caught her up in a quick embrace. She returned the hug and earned an extra squeeze. Was it a thank-you for thinking of Micah, an apology for his concerns about Jeff or momentary reassurance because of the lightning? Any of the reasons would do, she decided with a smile, and tightened her hold. All of them told her he cared.*

*She started to turn away, but at the last moment he caught her arm. Curiously, she looked back at him. "What, Papa?"*

*He gave her a tender smile. "You are so beautiful, honey. Inside and out. When did you become such a lovely young woman?"*

*Heat flooded her cheeks for a second time. "Oh, Papa." She stood on her tiptoes and brushed a quick kiss across his cheek. "I didn't do anything special. Whatever I am is because of you and Mama."*

*"I must have done something right then, even without your mama, because you are special, my girl. I don't know how I managed it without her, but we did all right with just each other, didn't we, honey?"*

*The thunder rumbled again, and Amber did her best to ignore it. "We've done just fine, Papa."*

*Blair's smile softened. "I think of them at times, your mother and Foster."*

*She nodded. "So do I. More often than you might think. There are times I wish I knew what Mama would have done in my place."*

*"You're doing just fine. She would be very proud of you."*

*"I've always hoped so." Amber sighed with soft wistfulness. "Sometimes I wonder what Foster would have grown up to be like. He would have been exactly the right age to fight."*

*Blair closed his eyes. "I know. And he was such a hothead, even at twelve. It's the only reason not to regret his death."*

*A roll of thunder boomed, quickly followed by another sharp crack of lightning. An odd moment of melancholy struck her, and Amber couldn't hold back a short laugh. "That could be Foster now. He was unpredictable, just like lightning."*

*Her father shared the laugh. "Does that mean your mother's temper was like the thunder?"*

*Amber's eyes widened as she realized the implication. "That's not very flattering, is it? She could scare the dickens out of me when I was little, though."*

*Blair laughed with delight. "Your mama would be tickled to hear that. It hurt her worse than it did you when she had to punish you children. That stern face was all for effect."*

*"I'll remember that when I have children."* Privately, Amber hoped Jeff would declare his intentions soon, and then she might have a baby of her own to love in a year or so.

*"I'll be there to remind you, don't you worry about that."*

She grinned at the glint of mischief in her father's eyes. *"You're incorrigible, Papa. I'll see you at the house."*

He turned back to sorting the type. *"I'll stop at the boardinghouse on my way home and invite Micah to supper."*

*"All right. I love you, Papa."* Amber offered her customary goodbye as she moved into the front office. With the printing house fire that had killed her mother and older brother, she had learned never to take anything for granted. Since their deaths, she never left her father without telling him she loved him.

She swept up her shawl and left the building, hurrying down the boardwalk toward home. The wind danced around her, pulling tendrils of hair from her braid and fluttering the hem of her skirt. She pulled the shawl tight around her shoulders and glanced about, only to spy Eliza Bates coming in her direction. A perpetual scowl, the only expression Amber had ever seen on the woman, was fixed firmly in place.

Mrs. Bates was the last person she wanted to see. The woman was rude and bossy, she liked to gossip, and her daughter, Melinda, had set her cap for Jeff. Mrs. Bates never lost an opportunity to remind Amber of the fact.

A streak of lightning caught Mrs. Bates's attention, and she looked to the sky. Amber took advantage of the moment, searching around her desperately—and then spotted Dr. Harris's office and the house next door. A small pathway ran between the buildings, and Amber headed straight for it. She slipped down the passageway and came out in the alley behind the row of buildings, her father's office included.

"Well, what do we have here?"

Amber jerked her head up. A tall, thin man, unshaved and dirty, sidled up next to her, his outstretched hand filthy.

She stepped back. "What do you want?" she snapped, doing her best to imitate her mother's "thunder voice."

"We don't want nuthin'." The man grinned, showing brown and broken teeth. He jerked his head toward a smaller man she belatedly noticed. The second man was similarly dirty and rough-looking. "We wuz just admirin' a purty girl."

A chill raced up her spine, a shiver that owed nothing to the increasing wind that grasped at her skirts and forced her to clutch her shawl tightly around her. The leering, predatory way they looked at her made her feel as dirty as they appeared, as though she hadn't bathed in weeks.

"Yes, well…thank you, but I have to go," she announced with prim bravery, instinct turning her away from the direction she'd been headed. Her father's office was closer, and she would be safe there.

"We don't rightly care what you want, girlie." The tall man grabbed her arm and jerked her to a stop before she'd gone a step. "We got us a job to do, but we got a little time a'fore that. How about we spend it with you?"

Amber's heart began to pound, and she thought for a moment the men could hear it, too. It was only the drumming of the thunder, a grim accompaniment to the deep-

*seated fear blossoming in her chest. She had seen men like these before, from a distance; her father had warned her of the things they would do. Men like these languished in saloons and houses of ill repute. They would kill each other over a hand of cards or a soiled dove. They would rape a good woman without conscience.*

*They were not welcome in this part of town—and yet here they were, one of them with a tight, punishing grip on her arm.*

*"I..." Her voice wavered, and she drew a quick breath. "My father is expecting me." She tried to back away, tugging at her arm as she did so.*

*"We ain't ready fer you to go yet, girlie." He pulled her close with a sharp jerk. "Me an' Ned, we wanna kiss."*

*"A...k-kiss?"*

*The man grinned, and she was close enough that his rank, fetid breath washed over her like a foul breeze. She started to gag, but swallowed, forcing it back.*

*"That's right, girlie," he said, bending closer. "A kiss."*

*"Let me go!" She had remained calm as long as she could. Reason was not something these men appeared to understand, and the longer she remained with them, the more vulnerable she became. She twisted, struggling in earnest to free herself, but the man held tighter the more she moved.*

*"We got us a wildcat here, Ned!" He laughed and wrapped his arms around her, binding her until her lungs seemed ready to explode from lack of air. Her efforts to free herself became weaker, and then she couldn't breathe at all as the man fastened his lips over hers and shoved his tongue into her mouth.*

*She did gag this time and instinctively bit down. Hard. The man howled and jerked his head back. Amber didn't think, but took advantage of the few precious seconds of air to fill her lungs and let out a piercing scream.*

*"Bitch!" he raged, and slapped her with brutal force. It*

*stunned her for a moment, but it loosened his hold on her enough that she was able to shake free of him.*

*"Help!" she shouted as she raced for the newspaper office. The first drops of rain splattered around her.*

*"Grab her, Ned!" Pounding footsteps accompanied the words.*

*Her feet flew out from under her, and Amber went down hard. The fall knocked the wind from her and left her gasping. Her knees and elbows burned, but something pulled at her ankle before she had time to assess her injuries. Amber spared a glance behind her to where bony fingers clutched her leg.*

*"I got 'er, Earl."*

*"Hold her, then. I'm gonna teach that bitch a lesson."*

*Earl stalked up to them, his face dark with rage. He jerked her up from the ground, and she gasped with pain as her arm felt like it was being pulled from the socket.*

*"No!" she screamed. "Help me, please!"*

*"Shut up, bitch!" He slapped her again and hauled her against him, pinning her arms behind her back. "Get a rope, Ned, and tie her up."*

*"Stop it! Please!" Amber renewed her struggles, but an odd lethargy seemed to overtake her senses. It was almost as though she had stepped back to watch a heinous attack on another woman, someone she might empathize with but no one she knew.*

*She began to notice other things: the force of the wind, the low growl of approaching thunder, the wetness of raindrops on her cheeks—or were they tears? Then a new sound—different from all the rest—intruded. She glanced around, inexplicably and suddenly frantic, and saw him then. The back door to her father's office opened, and he stepped into the alley.*

*"Papa!" she screamed.*

*"Get the sheriff," Blair shouted—to whom? Anyone?*

*He ran to her and tossed the smaller man aside like so much garbage.*

*"Take your hands off my daughter," he snarled at the other man. The strange languor Amber felt made everything slow like time at half speed.*

*Earl laughed, his voice a low, unnatural hiss. "Now ain't that cozy?" He shoved her away, and she fell to her knees. The burning started anew, but she struggled to her feet. "Get her, Ned," the man snapped before she could do anything more.*

*"Are you okay, honey?" her father asked, without sparing a glance in her direction. He sounded odd, fierce and yet tender at the same time.*

*"I—Papa!" she gasped. Horrified, she could do nothing but watch as Earl snatched his pistol from its holster. Ned crawled close and grabbed her leg once more, but Amber hardly noticed.*

*This couldn't be happening! Not right in the middle of Twigg, to her or her father.*

*Blair raised his arms. "You don't want to do this," he said in a hard, deliberate voice.*

*Earl laughed, an ugly, guttural sound. "You shoulda listened when certain folks told you to keep yer mouth shut." He pointed the gun at Blair.*

*"No!" Amber screamed, and she lunged toward her father just as the gun went off.*

# *Chapter Twelve*

Derek threw the door wide, heedless of caution or propriety, and bounded into Amber's bedroom. His eyes darted to each shadowed corner, searching quickly, methodically, but finding no threat hiding in the room.

"Papa." The whimper came from the bed. "No. Please."

His heart pounded, and he realized his fingers had begun to tremble. He clenched them into fists and stepped into the room, taking a second, closer look. Nothing. An austere, nondescript room, it contained hardly enough furniture to cast a shadow, let alone hide some sinister assailant.

He approached the bed. "Amber?" he called softly.

"Papa? Oh, no. No. Please!"

Moonlight trickled in through the window, enough that Derek could make out her form. She had one arm outstretched as though reaching for something—someone—but then she recoiled, and the last of the bedcovers fell to the floor in a heap. Her prim white nightgown rode to midthigh, revealing shapely, tempting legs he'd never expected to see.

*Don't notice!* He knew where those thoughts could lead....

"Amber." He cleared his throat and forced himself to

speak louder than the whisper that seemed most natural. "Wake up, angel. You're having a bad dream."

Her head rolled sharply, and her shoulders arched up from the bed. It was more than a bad dream, and he knew it. *Damn.*

Derek blew out a caustic breath and plowed one hand through his hair, waiting—hoping—that Amber would work her way to true wakefulness. He couldn't just leave her to it, though. He dropped his hand and rounded the bed, sinking down onto the edge of the mattress. The sketchy moonlight didn't allow him to make out her features.

He reached for her with a sigh. "Come on, angel." He swept his fingertips lightly against her forehead, smoothing back sweat-dampened tendrils of hair with reluctant care.

Amber whimpered and tried to push him away, but he insisted. He cupped her cheek and found himself muttering unintelligible little noises deep in his throat. He meant them as comfort, reassurance, but from him they sounded desperate and foreign.

"Amber, it's Derek. It's time to wake up, honey. You're having a dream."

She heaved a deep breath and a sob of heart-wrenching pain. Derek swallowed a faint curse. What the hell was he supposed to do next? But he knew. He'd always known.

"Ah, now, come here, angel. It's all over." He scooped her up into his arms, grunting softly as pain stabbed his shoulder.

"They killed him," she whispered through her tears, sounding utterly heartbroken, and she threw her arms around him as though his touch was all that saved her from drowning. At one time in his life Derek might have known what to do for her, but he no longer understood such softness. Now he could only cradle her close and murmur odd little noises that seemed to console her.

Amber shifted in his arms and he tightened his embrace. He held her securely against his chest, and at the same time wished to hell she'd stop moving. His unruly body noticed every damn twitch.

He knew he should release her and walk out of the room, simply let her cry out her grief in the privacy of the night, but her tears kept him where he was. She hiccupped, then took a deep breath, and somehow Derek found himself touching his lips to her forehead in a light, ephemeral kiss.

"It's over." She whispered the words with a soft, sobbing sigh, and he kissed her once more. Surely she was waking, and it was not his touch that soothed her so.

"That's right." He brushed a hand over her hair, and his fingers tangled in the riot of loose waves that tumbled over her shoulders. "It's all over."

She shifted, snugging the rounded curve of her hip against the sharper angle of his lap. He tried not to notice how well she fit him, nor the press of her breasts against his chest, but he couldn't ignore every movement she made against that lively, masculine part of him. Or the shape and feel of her nipples as they poked against his chest through her thin nightgown.

It had been so long since he'd held a woman, lost himself in the scent and taste and textures that were uniquely feminine. And Amber felt so damn good in his arms, tucked against him.

She released a shuddering sigh that held more emotion than actual tears. Her lips tickled the slope of his neck, and a shiver marched down his spine. He swallowed, hard. His hands seemed to move of their own accord, one trailing leisurely down her back to the curve of her hip and then up again. Her nightgown felt soft against his work-roughened skin, and his weathered fingertips caught at the material.

His other hand, meanwhile, dallied at her cheek, smoothing errant tendrils of hair from her face. How fine her skin felt! Living in south Texas as she did, toiling in the garden under the blistering sun, how did she keep her skin so soft and supple? He could well imagine the sweet sensitivity of the rest of her, hidden so carefully beneath the protective layers of cotton.

Oh, sweet Jesus. His body hardened, and he shifted to accommodate the reaction. His mind saw the folly of indulging in such thoughts, but the rest of him disregarded such wisdom. Instead he tightened his hold a fraction and murmured silly, unintelligible noises against the downy silk of her hair.

"Shh, baby. You're all right. You're safe here, with me."

"Safe?" The tears all but gone, she sighed, nestling her head against the crook of his neck. "I wish it were true."

He meant to do nothing more than hold her, but her softness mingled sweetly with the fresh scent of vanilla, luring his good sense to abandon him. He pressed his lips to her forehead with butterfly softness, and Amber nuzzled closer. He tightened his arms around her, and her head fell back, draping a thick curtain of hair across his chest and over his arm. Plea or not, Derek took it as such, and he couldn't help but answer.

His lips caught hers lightly. Gently. They clung without heat, exposing a tenderness that stunned him into immobility. Such emotions could not come from within him—could they?

Before he could think past the pounding of his heart, Amber opened her mouth and her lips softened beneath his. Ahh…the taste of her. He had been too distressed to fully appreciate her kiss that night by the cemetery, but now he settled his mouth over hers with an instinctive need. He lost his breath and stole hers—and whatever else she would give. His tongue slipped past her lips and stroked deeply into the recesses of her mouth. She tasted fresh and sweet, and he groaned with the need for more.

Amber reached for him. Her fingers tangled in the hair at his shoulders, then curled around the column of his neck.

Did she mean to hold him close? Derek deepened the kiss with a sweep of his tongue; he wasn't going anywhere.

He brought his hand up, dragging it over the soft cotton with a heavy stroke that marked her from hip to shoulder. Her tongue danced with his, and she made soft, breathy little noises. He tested the fullness of her bottom lip, tempting her to taste him, and she arched against him, her tongue darting forward.

He cupped his fingers around her breast, delighting in its plump weight and the saucy poke of her nipple into his palm. He stroked his thumb over the crest, announcing his desire with a deep, almost guttural groan that would not be stifled.

He swept his tongue forward again, meaning to take possession of her mouth as he teased her nipples to aching hardness...and noticed a sudden difference. She felt stiff and awkward in his arms; no longer did she snuggle trustingly against him or offer a response to his kiss.

He pulled back cautiously, sucking in a heavy breath. Gradually the sensuous haze began to fade. Amber wriggled against him, her movements sharp and jerky. He blinked, and squinted to see through the shadows.

"Derek?" Her breathless voice cracked.

"Yes."

"Derek!" Full realization seemed to strike her, and she flung herself from his arms. She scrambled to the other side of the bed. "You—I...*what are you doing here?*"

"You were having a nightmare."

"A...*nightmare?*"

"Yes."

"But I—we...you're *naked!*"

He glanced down at himself—at his bare chest, relieved by a white splash of bandage at his shoulder, and the dark shadow that perhaps disguised his full erection from her. Then again, she'd snuggled her bottom so sweetly against the unmistakable hard ridge, he couldn't have concealed it if he wanted to. He looked back at her. "It didn't seem important when I heard you scream!"

"I screamed?" she asked, sounding altogether breathless. She seemed to keep her eyes fastened on his, but he couldn't be sure in the feeble moonlight.

"I'm surprised they didn't hear you at the bunkhouse."

And that was a matter Derek would deal with in the morning. The need to post guards hadn't occurred to him until this moment, but the necessity of it seemed suddenly plain.

"I…oh, God." Her shoulders drooped as she wilted before him. "The dream. It was about my father's murder."

"I gathered as much."

"I'm sorry. I haven't had that dream in a very long time."

He shrugged. "I have nightmares of my own." Why try to hide it? Amber had already seen him at his worst. Well, not his *worst;* he had far more sordid secrets than anything she'd seen, but she'd seen enough. Anything more and she would hate him forever. "They never seem to go away entirely."

"No. They leave you in peace just long enough for you to think you're safe. Then, when you least expect it…" Her voice grew thicker with each word until it trailed off completely.

"Something happens to bring it back up."

"Yes."

"Will you be all right here alone?"

"All right?" Amber sighed. "I suppose so. The dream hasn't changed once in two years. It's always the same— exactly as it happened. I remember every detail. How could I forget?"

"I know."

"Do you? Do you really?" Her voice sharpened from simple contemplation to fierce resentment. "What is it you think you know? Did they tell you all about it in Twigg?

How Amber Laughton lured two filthy, no-account drifters away from the whores, and how her daddy was murdered when he caught them together?''

Her harsh words echoed, invading the dark, empty night. A whole group of people suddenly seemed to have crowded into the room: the gossips from Twigg, the ghost of her father, the men who had killed him.

A familiar rage flared deep in Amber's chest, an anger she had learned to tamp down as far as she could, as often as she needed to. It had been necessary, but each time the bitterness reignited, it burned that much fiercer, brighter.

"There was talk. I didn't listen."

"Didn't you?" She scoffed in disbelief, swallowing as she struggled to get the upper hand on her emotions. "You listened well enough to accuse me of being your uncle's mistress."

He didn't answer, nor did he move or otherwise give her any indication of what he might be thinking. The dappled moonlight shed only enough illumination to cast long, deep shadows that teased more than they revealed.

"It doesn't matter," she announced, abruptly impatient with his seeming indifference. "You want answers to your questions? Well, let me tell you the truth about my father and how he died. Not the truth Eliza Bates and Frank Edwards would have you believe, but the truth my dreams force on me endlessly. The truth nobody else wants to hear."

"All right." Derek sounded uncertain, as though he didn't quite trust her offer, but his willingness to listen dissolved some of the fight in her.

She took a breath for strength and began to recite the events of that day. Doing her best to pretend it was someone else of whom she spoke, she pronounced the words with a stark formality. But as she spoke, a familiar tightness in her chest began to work itself loose for the first time in two years.

"I was saved from rape, but not the pain or the lies," she concluded. "Oh, the physical pain meant little— scraped skin and bruises gave me something to think about. What hurt was the pain of losing my father and having people I knew and trusted suddenly look at me as though I had killed him."

She leaned forward, searching for more than Derek's shadow in the darkness. "I knew people would listen when Mrs. Bates told and retold the details of my scrapes and bruises, my torn dress, my cries. I just never expected them to *believe* her."

The mattress shifted as Derek rose, a dark specter that stopped near the foot of the bed. "She's very forceful."

Amber might have smiled under other circumstances. "Yes, and I imagine you received the sharp side of her tongue when you met her." The thought of it made her weary, but Eliza Bates always had that impact on her. It took tremendous energy to face the woman. "No doubt she was quick to point out my shortcomings. Did she predict dire consequences if you kept me on here?"

"She tried." His voice carried a hard edge that surprised her. "I believe she found my answer less than gracious."

"She was only trying to save you from a wicked hussy with no conscience."

"I'm sure she thinks so."

"And I'm sure it's more my fault than yours."

"I gathered that, as well."

Amber's small reserve of emotional strength began to fade as she imagined the scene with Mrs. Bates. "Have you ever been tired, Derek? So tired you think of running away—hiding—where no one will ever find you? So tired you almost wish…"

"For what? Death?"

"I don't know. That's a sin."

She thought he shrugged. "I've sinned worse."

"Yes. I suppose I have, too."

He didn't answer, and she wondered if he was thinking about the sins he'd committed. She thought of her own often enough: the times she'd wished she could kill the men who had murdered her father—or prayed they would burn in hell. The horrible things she'd thought of those who had been so quick to condemn her; refusing to tell the truth to those who willfully believed the worst about her. The way she had turned her back on Twigg and never looked back.

What were Derek's sins? It was all but certain he'd killed during the war, but in the name of the Confederacy. Killing for your country wasn't the same as wantonly breaking the commandment—was it?

A young, wealthy man in Charleston, he had no doubt led a wild, carefree life before the war. She'd overheard Richard and her father talk of their own rakehell days of liquor, gambling and women. Derek, too, must have enjoyed his share of women.

How many had he held, just as he'd held her? How many had he kissed, just as he'd kissed her? And—more. He'd wanted more from her; the way he'd held her and touched her told her so. And, God help her, she'd wanted to give it to him. She *would* have given it to him if she hadn't been startled to awareness by the increasing intimacy of his hands and the low, hoarse sound that came from deep in his throat.

*Desire.*

She was no green girl who knew nothing of the ways of life. Life in a ranching community and time at the Double F had given her a basic education of that sort. Her father, bless him, had offered a somewhat awkward explanation of *physical matters,* he'd called them, when the demands of her young girl's changing body had required it. And after the attack, old Doc Harris and his wife had taken seriously the task of completing her education in the ways of nature.

Now Derek stood only a scant few feet from her, naked and seductive, every bit a man—and completely unreachable. He tantalized everything that made her a woman, and intuitively she knew nothing could be more dangerous to her.

"I'm very tired," she said softly, earnestly. "I think I'll try to sleep again."

"Will you be all right?"

"Yes. I'll be fine. I've always managed before."

She sensed movement and the floorboard creaked. In a moment, he was at the door. "Good night, then. I'll see you in the morning."

"Good night. And, Derek?"

"Yes?"

"Thank you."

He closed the door behind him, leaving her alone in the darkness. Silence settled over the room, but her thoughts withheld a similar peace from her. Gradually at least one truth coalesced from the obscurity of night: she desired Derek.

Powerfully. Irresistibly.

He might think he desired her, too, but only because she was convenient. Or...because he was like all the others.

*No.* She shook her head. He wasn't like Frank Edwards or Jeff Buchanan. Two years ago Jeff—and others—had seen to it that there would be no husband for her, no family or future. She had learned then, irrevocably, what the people of Twigg deemed appropriate for her. Kissing, touching—wanton *nakedness*—were part of that sordid life. Going from man to man, doing private, intimate things, pleasuring them without conscience—*that* was the behavior anticipated from her.

Derek hadn't used his position at the ranch to coerce her into his bed or force her into an illicit encounter. Nor had he taken advantage of her vulnerability tonight. He had too much integrity for that.

If she had learned anything about Derek, it was that he

had a particular brand of unwavering *honor*. It might not be what another man would do in his place, and he did his best to conceal its very existence. But all the same, his decency remained.

# Chapter Thirteen

Amber remained in bed the next morning until after she heard Derek leave the house. *Coward,* she berated herself, but the accusation came without heat. Coward she might be, but it was best for them both.

She rolled onto her side and glanced out of the bedroom's lone window. It faced the river and her beloved garden, opposite where Derek would be headed. The sun had just crested the horizon, creating a new day at the Double F. Time for those at the ranch to be up and about, and Amber in particular—despite any awkwardness of the night before.

With a soft sigh, she sat up and massaged her forehead with her fingers. She had slept fitfully at best. Somewhere in the long hours of wakefulness, she had come to accept that memories of her nightmare were easier to bear than thoughts of Derek and his kisses. Such an admission had not arrived with ease.

The intimacy with Derek had all but shattered her. It might not have done so if she'd ever been held and comforted like that in the past. But she hadn't been. Amber had faced her nightmares alone, until finally they dwindled to a rarity. Eventually she had learned that events like hearing of Derek's horror at Shiloh would bring the old pain to the surface. Still, she didn't regret for a moment that she had heard his confession and offered the best comfort she could.

He had done the same for her.

But...then it had become more. He had been naked. He had cradled her on his lap, and his maleness had pressed firmly against her. He had kissed her, and she had kissed him back. She'd opened her mouth for him and pressed her body against his with wanton abandon.

Amber put her palms to her cheeks and found them hot with shame. She had behaved exactly as people in Twigg had always accused her of doing.

*Stop it, my girl. Sitting here and feeling sorry for yourself won't solve a thing.*

The words might have come from her father; he had offered similar advice whenever she'd been tempted to indulge in a fit of childish sulking. He had been right: self-pity bred contempt. But when her "friends" had turned their backs on her after his murder, it had become difficult not to brood.

Difficult perhaps, but not impossible. Amber squared her shoulders and fell into the soothing familiarity of her morning routine, washing and dressing.

Anticipating the comfort that awaited, she went directly to the garden. She weeded for a time, filling and dumping the wooden bucket more than once. When her back began to ache, she turned to hoeing between the garden rows. Eventually her shoulders grew stiff, her grip weak, and she began the arduous task of watering. Careful to waste not a drop of precious water, she toted bucketfuls from the creek. Finally she harvested a few spring crops, some lettuce and onions and a few green tomatoes, perfect for frying.

She stretched, standing straight, and twisted from side to side. The stiffness and aching muscles felt oddly pleasant, well earned from her physical labor and without the heavy weight of added emotional pain. She blew out a soft breath and glanced around at all she'd accomplished.

"Why, it must be nearly noon," she muttered, realizing the sun blazed high overhead. She had kept her mind and body occupied through the entire morning. She smiled.

"Riders comin'."

Amber turned, resting the back of one hand against her forehead and planting the other on her hip. Micah stood at the edge of the garden.

"Riders?" Her smile died slowly, and a breathlessness stole over her.

"It's the Andrews brothers, or at least one a' them. And somebody else."

"Where's Derek?" Amber asked.

"Down at the barn. He rode in just a little while ago."

"You better go get him."

"You gonna go meet them?"

"No, it's Derek's place to do that now."

Micah eyed her curiously. "Well…all right." He sounded disgruntled, as though he considered her somehow uncooperative. "But you go out there an' keep an eye on them. At least till I get back with Derek."

"Micah—"

"I'm serious, Amber-girl. With all that's been goin' on around these parts, you don't know what's gonna happen. I ain't feelin' all that trustin' these days."

He had a point. Derek had warned her of the same thing the other night. She had created enough confusion by not being candid with him about the things she knew. While it may have been difficult—even painful—to answer some of his questions, it had never been worth the price of his being shot.

She would never take such chances again.

She wiped her hands on her apron, pushed back a few errant strands of hair from her forehead and headed for the house. She rounded the corner nearest the driveway just as Clem rode up.

"Bring the wagon 'round this way, Twigg," he called over his shoulder.

"Hello, Clem."

He swung around and squinted in her direction. "Mornin' there, Amber. Me and Twigg got some comp'ny fer ya."

"Company?" Her eyes grew wide and she glanced around his horse. Twigg was driving a wagon loaded with trunks and boxes—and two women. Strangers. Amber looked back at Clem. "We weren't expecting anyone. At least..." she paused as a new apprehension shifted through her "...I don't think so."

Clem grinned, a funny, monkeylike expression that never failed to produce a smile from her. "Nope. I don't think nobody here's expectin' these folks. Looks like things could get a might lively."

"Lively?" *We've had enough liveliness already,* Amber thought, but kept the observation to herself. If she said anything, the old men wouldn't rest until she explained herself fully. "What do you mean by that?"

The wagon rolled to a stop before he had a chance to answer, and Twigg waved his hat in the air. "Howdy there, Amber-girl. Yer lookin' like a pretty daisy today."

"Thank you, Twigg." She offered him a distracted half smile as she got her first good look at the women.

They perched stiffly on the wooden seat next to Twigg. A mother and daughter, perhaps? The older woman looked to be past fifty, with sharp features tightened to an austere expression. The younger woman appeared to be only a few years older than Amber herself—and stunningly beautiful, though no happier than her companion. Both had dark hair, the elder's shot through with silver, and were dressed in elaborate traveling gowns.

Amber forced herself to remain calm. Fussing with her disheveled coiffure, pinching color into her cheeks or cast-

ing off her worn, stained apron would make no difference;
she could never measure up to the beauty in the wagon.

At a loss, she took a deep breath. "May I help you?"

The younger woman glanced briefly at her companion,
then back in Amber's direction without allowing their eyes
to meet. "We're here to see Richard Fontaine," she said
tightly. "We'll wait for him."

"Ri-Richard?" Amber dragged her gaze to Twigg, but
he studiously ignored her and fiddled with the leather reins
in his hands. She turned her attention to his brother.
"Clem?"

He smiled at her with deceptive vagueness and swung
down from his horse. "Where's Fontaine?" he demanded.

She narrowed her eyes. The women evidently knew
nothing of Richard's death, and these two rascals obviously
had not seen fit to enlighten them. Nor, apparently, did the
old men have any intentions of doing so, and she wasn't
sure it was something she should attempt, either.

"He's coming," she finally answered. "Micah went to
get him. What's going on here?"

"We'll wait for Richard," the older woman answered
loftily.

"Ma'am," Amber began carefully, pausing as she considered exactly what to say.

"Hello, Mother. Mariah."

All heads swung around as Derek approached from the
barn. "Derek!" The women spoke simultaneously.

"Where's Jordan?" he asked, an edge to his voice that
Amber had never heard before. "And what brings you to
the Double F?"

"Derek?" the older woman repeated in a faint voice.

Amber stared. *Mother,* he had called her. She was Derek's mother? Amber glanced from one to the other. She
didn't see much physical likeness, but then he bore such a
stunning resemblance to Richard.

"Surprise," Derek drawled. He sounded...bored, but

Amber saw the icy glint in his eyes and the tightness around his mouth.

The younger woman—Mariah, he had called her—slipped one arm around his mother in a gesture of comfort. "Derek, where is Richard?" she asked stiffly.

"Gone."

"What do you mean, *gone?* When will he be back?"

Derek didn't hesitate. "He's dead," he said flatly, his blue eyes positively frigid.

"Dead!" His mother gasped and her eyes grew wide, then she all but crumpled in her seat. "No, not Richard, too."

"Shh, Carolyn. Everything will be all right. I promise." Mariah spoke softly, soothing the older woman and ignoring the rest of them.

"Can I assume Jordan has departed the land of the living as well, since the two of you are here alone?"

"Yes," Mariah snapped, glancing up through the fan of her lashes. "Last fall."

"Richard, too. Gone. I can't believe it. After all this time, I've finally—" Mrs. Fontaine broke off whatever she had meant to say. Then she looked directly at Derek.

He stared back, his gaze never wavering. Sympathy for the woman stirred within Amber; she had been on the receiving end of that glare herself. "When?" Mrs. Fontaine asked in a small voice. "How?"

Derek remained silent, continuing to stare until Amber felt a sharp rawness to her own nerves. She stepped forward.

"It was a year ago, ma'am." She spoke in a gentle tone. "He was looking for strays and...something happened. I don't know what." She turned to Derek, to encourage him to speak up, but he merely stared back with that unrelenting expression that she knew hid bleakness. "He was found the next day."

Mrs. Fontaine slowly lifted her head. She glanced from Amber to Derek. "Who is this?"

"Mother, Mariah, this is Amber Laughton, my house-keeper. She worked for Richard, as well. Amber, my mother, Carolyn Fontaine, and my sister-in-law, Mariah."

Amber offered a soft greeting, unacknowledged by either woman. Both pursed their lips into tight little pouts and inspected her as though she was some distasteful creature of whom they disapproved. Highly.

"I'm sure this has been a shock to you after a long, difficult journey. Would you like to come inside and freshen up? Or perhaps relax for a bit?" Amber made the offer with all the polite dignity she could muster, ignoring Derek and the other men, and concentrating solely on the women.

"I..." began Carolyn, but her voice faded away.

"Thank you." Mariah picked up where her mother-in-law had left off, though she sounded neither grateful nor gracious. She looked toward Twigg. "If you will let us down, sir."

The old man scampered from his seat and helped first Mariah, then Carolyn from the wagon. How odd, Amber thought, that Derek stood back and watched the proceedings with his damned blank eyes, his good arm at his side and the recently injured one held at an angle against his belly. Did his wound still pain him enough that he wished not to risk it, or reveal too much by helping the women? Or did he simply object to their arrival?

She would not understand it now; past encounters with him had taught her that much. She accepted it with resignation and stepped forward. "This way, ladies," she said, and led the way into the house.

Derek stalked to one corner of his study and poured himself a shot of whiskey. Richard had kept a crystal decanter and glasses there, and for the first time since his arrival,

Derek made use of them. The liquor went down smooth and sweet—obviously good stuff, not some cheap rotgut distilled out behind the bunkhouse. Alcohol had never been his favorite vice, not after witnessing years of Jordan's growing dependence on it. Today, however, Derek needed the burn in his throat and the sharp punch to his gut that the first swallow of whiskey always provided.

His mother and Mariah. Their arrival had shocked the hell out of him. He hadn't seen anyone from his family since the last year of the war, when Charleston had been burning all around them. Derek had learned the awful truth about Nathan's death in the brutal Wilderness Campaign then, and Jordon had revealed the truth of Derek's birth. Finally—gloriously!—he'd understood so very much.

While he rarely thought of those days any longer, the stunning clarity of Jordon's furious words would be forever with him. For one startling instant Derek had even welcomed the knowledge. There were *reasons* he had never been accepted as a member of the only family he'd ever known.

But now his *family* had come to the Double F, of all places. And Jordan was dead. Derek ought to feel something, he supposed; he'd thought of the man as his father for most of his life. But the news stirred not a shard of emotion within him. His only regret, Derek ruefully acknowledged, was that he was left as the last surviving Fontaine male.

Why were they here, his mother and sister-in-law? Why hadn't they stayed in Charleston, at Palmetto? Jesus, he'd gone through hell to save the plantation for them and future generations of Fontaines, though it had begun to seem unlikely there would be any. Who was there now, overseeing it?

"Derek?"

He turned. Mariah stood in the doorway, tentative as she glanced about the room. She had changed from her traveling gown into a lavender dress that surprised him with its plainness, considering the elaborate wardrobe he'd seen her wear in the past. But, he supposed, the war had changed that, as well.

"Hello, Mariah."

"Your mother will be down soon. This has been difficult for her."

"The trip here is not for the faint of heart."

"That's not what I meant—though you are correct. It was a grueling journey from Charleston."

Derek sipped from his glass and relished the slight burning in his throat. "The Andrews brothers said you arrived with a group of settlers."

"Yes." She trained her eyes somewhere behind him. "We met up with them along the way, in—"

"Mariah, why are you here?"

"What?" Her gaze snapped to his.

"I know what it takes—physically, emotionally, financially—to get here. You didn't come all this way for a short visit or on a whim. So why are you here?"

"We should wait for your mother."

He tilted his head to one side and considered his brother's widow. She appeared more distressed than he'd ever seen her—and she had reason to be. She and his mother had dropped themselves on his doorstep without warning. It had been a double-edged surprise, however; they'd had no idea it was *his* doorstep. They had expected Richard. And that made their arrival all the more intriguing.

They wanted something—but what? And would they want it from Derek, as well?

"Mariah?"

He heard his mother's voice from the hall and answered before his sister-in-law could. "In here."

Carolyn Fontaine entered the room with as much uncertainty as her daughter-in-law had. "Derek."

"Mother." He angled his head in her direction. "Please, sit down."

The women glanced at one another, but they sat. Matching chairs faced the large mahogany desk that dominated the room, and each perched on the edge of one. With a sigh, Derek refilled his glass and took his position behind the desk.

"All right, tell me," he said. "Why are you here?"

"Oh, Derek," his mother began with a soft, forlorn sigh he had heard countless times in his life. Whenever she wanted something of Jordan or her sons, something she expected they would decline, given any choice. "It's lovely here. We've never ventured so far across the country, and with…well, Mariah—we thought…I'd hoped—"

"Carolyn." Mariah's voice held a low warning that Derek didn't miss. He saluted her perceptiveness with a nod.

"The truth, Mother. Whatever it is, you can't avoid it." He pinned her with a stern gaze. "My patience is limited."

Carolyn looked at him, and her eyes filled with tears. He had seen them often enough in the past, as well.

"Derek," she said softly, and he would have liked to believe the underlying sadness in her voice. He didn't.

He fastened a steady gaze on his sister-in-law. "Mariah, you tell me. No lies, no games."

"We came here because we have nowhere else to go."

"Nowhere to go?" A certain nausea churned to life low in his stomach. "What about Palmetto? I risked—well, you know what I did to save that place for Jordan—for you. What happened?"

Mariah squared her shoulders and took in a deep breath before she spoke. Gathering her courage, it seemed, and Derek couldn't ignore a growing glimmer of admiration for the strength she displayed. She wasn't the same immature girl who'd married his brother seven years ago. She had been young and naive—and she'd gone through so very much since then. But so had they all, and nothing was the same.

"We lost it," she finally answered.

*"You lost it?"*

"We lost everything except what we brought in the wagon."

Derek stared at her while his brain examined the entirety of her statement. "Go on," he said tightly.

Mariah glanced at Carolyn, who appeared far more fascinated with pleating the fabric of her skirt between her fingers. Eventually his sister-in-law shrugged and looked back at him. "Jordan found it difficult to cope when the war turned against us. When we got word of Nathan's death—well, you saw him after that. And you know what he was like at the best of times."

"Yes."

"His grip on reality dwindled each day, and once General Lee surrendered, it went completely. I had no choice but to begin making the decisions. Your mother had her hands full taking care of your—of Jordan."

She paused, her navy-blue eyes probing Derek's. Gauging his reaction, he guessed. Mariah had always been far shrewder than Jordan—or Nathan, for that matter—had ever recognized. Unfortunately, her intelligence had never made any difference for any of them.

She sniffed, perhaps with a touch of disapproval, and continued. "It didn't seem to matter all that much what we did—it was too late already. My inheritance was gone by then—Jordan assumed control after my father was killed at Sharpsburg—and little remained of your family's fortune."

"No, I imagine most of that went to the Confederacy."

"And we were all glad to give it." She shot him a fierce, accusing frown. "Anything that kept Nathan alive was worth it."

Carolyn reacted to the whiplike sound of Mariah's voice with a frown. "Mariah!"

"It's true." She scowled at Carolyn, but the expression carried a certain tenderness. "We can no longer afford the considerations we may have made in the past. You know that. We've talked about it."

"Yes." His mother sighed, her gaze flickering between Derek and his sister-in-law. "I just thought everything would be all right once we got here to Richard. But now—"

"Now you found only me." Derek refused to allow the least emotion to find life within him. He turned his gaze to Mariah. "You were saying…"

She stiffened, if it were possible. "I held on as long as I could, selling whatever we had to keep us alive. The prices were never fair. No one had money except the Yankees."

"You're very resourceful. You…surprise me."

"The will to survive does remarkable things for people."

"But you finally ran out of things to sell?"

She shrugged. "Yes. But mostly it was the carpetbaggers and their damn taxes. We didn't have money for the taxes and no way to get it. They foreclosed and took Palmetto, and we were forced to rely on the goodwill of friends. It's what killed Jordan, in the end."

"I find it hard to believe he died of a broken heart." Derek made no attempt to conceal his skepticism.

"No, he died of rage. Rage at…all of us."

"And his youngest son in particular?" Derek's question came out a harsh scrape of sound. "Oh—that's right. I'm not his son, am I? I was never his son. I was just an embarrassment. The bastard result of an affair between his wife and his brother."

## Chapter Fourteen

Could Derek's words be true? The tray in Amber's hands wavered, and before she could stop it, the teapot and matching china cups tumbled to the hall floor with a crash. She sank to her knees with a gasp.

"What was that?" asked one of the women, her voice tentative and tear-filled. Derek's mother.

The sound of footsteps thudded closer, and Amber grabbed for the nearest shard of what had once been the spout of the teapot. The study door swung wide.

"Amber?"

She dropped the jagged piece of china onto the tray as though it had suddenly become a blazing-hot poker, and jerked her head back. Derek towered over her, framed by the gaping doorway. His icy blue eyes took in the scene with one sweeping glance.

"I'm sorry. I thought your—the ladies would like some refreshments." She looked down at the pool of tea seeping across the wooden plank floor and the shattered tea service strewn about her. "I don't know what happened. I—"

"Derek?" A stronger, younger voice. Mariah. "Is everything all right?"

"Fine," he barked, and crouched down, stretching to collect whatever china fragments had skidded within his reach. "Just a slight accident," he called over his shoulder. "I'll be right back." He plucked several small shards from the floor, while Amber blindly gathered the rest.

Neither said anything more as they collected the debris that had once been Richard's prized tea set. Amber swallowed the admission that she had overheard Derek's bitter words, and he refrained from questioning her clumsiness. He knew she had heard—she saw it in his eyes. But now was not the time to mention it.

"Be careful, or you'll cut yourself."

"Oh!" As though his words were prophecy, a tiny sliver poked into her finger. Amber raised her eyes and glared at him in accusation.

"I told you to be careful." He snatched her hand in his and turned it over, inspecting her finger with keen eyes that missed little.

His own fingers were strong and insistent as he probed the small wound, his skin warm—hot—against hers. An odd excitement welled up deep within her, until she could hardly catch her breath and her fingers trembled.

"Ouch!" A jab of pain deflated her agitation, and she blew out a soft breath, grateful to have at least a portion of her concentration back. What was happening to her? Lord, she felt much like she had last night, perched on Derek's lap and pressed against his solid maleness.

*Oh, God.* Her hand jerked of its own accord.

"Hold still and let me see. I think there's a little piece of glass in there."

Somehow she did. His touch unsettled her to the point that it put a hitch in her breathing, and yet she seemed able to do little besides kneel there and watch him, her hand gripped securely in his.

Derek bent his head low as he worked, and his blond hair tumbled over his shoulder, concealing his face from her. She ached to reach for him, to smooth his hair back and feel its silken weight thread through her fingers as she revealed his features to her burning gaze.

*No...please. He may have kissed you, but you can't give in to this wantonness.* She curled the fingers of her free hand into her palm and kept her arm safely at her side.

"Almost...there." His warm breath bathed her skin, and she closed her eyes in reluctant reaction. "That's it." He sounded triumphant, and she raised her eyelids to find him watching her.

"I..." She tried to speak, but her voice didn't cooperate and she could only look at him. He stared back, his eyes narrowed as though he was focusing every speck of his attention on her. Had his face carried that same heavy intensity last night when he'd held her and kissed her? When she'd perched on his naked lap and all but wrapped herself around him?

His fingers tightened around hers and she jumped, yanking her hand from his. He blinked, and then all outward reaction disappeared from his face. The bleak mask returned as though it had never been gone.

He released her hand and stood. "Are you all right?"

"Yes." She swallowed and tried to think. "Of course." She forced herself to stand as well, glancing around, feeling oddly as though she had just come out of a daze. She looked at her wounded finger, at the blood welling up on its tip, then to the mess on the floor. Finally, when she could delay no longer, she looked at Derek and answered in a thin, polite voice. "I'm perfectly fine. Thank you." And she stuck her finger in her mouth to staunch the trickle of blood.

Derek's eyes flared anew, and he inhaled a sharply audible breath. She stared at him, wondering at his reaction, and pulled her finger from her mouth. "I'll finish cleaning up this mess and bring you another tray."

He blinked. "That won't be necessary. We're nearly

done.'' His voice sounded husky, as though he needed to clear his throat.

''If you're sure…''

''Just ask Beau to serve the noon meal when he's ready.''

''Yes, of course.'' She collected the tray from the floor and carefully skirted the puddle of tea. ''I'll be back to finish cleaning up.''

Derek nodded and turned toward the study. He hesitated, then squared his shoulders and headed back into the room.

Amber frowned and set off down the hall. Derek had seemed to pause, as though gathering his strength—but she must be mistaken. He had strength to spare, or so it often seemed. But enough to add his mother and sister-in-law to his already full list of responsibilities?

Amber stopped at the back door and stared at the broken china in her hands. Naturally the women would mean more to Derek than the others at the ranch; they were *family*. They carried with them his past…and his secrets. Or some of them.

Richard was Derek's *father*? He'd had an affair with a married woman—*his brother's wife*—then left her behind when he ran off to Texas? Had he loved Carolyn, or had it been the kind of sordid thing of which Amber had been accused? And why hadn't Richard told her of his son? Certainly Derek had known since before he'd come here; why hadn't he said anything?

The myriad questions created a dull throbbing in her head. A part of her shied away from speculation; she had never been one to tolerate gossip, even before she became the topic of so much debate. Such thoughts of Richard now gave her a sick, petty feeling. His memory deserved better.

But something within her wondered still. Not so much for Richard's sake, but for Derek's. Strong and capable he might be, but he was vulnerable, too. Physically *and* emotionally. The bullet in his shoulder had proved it.

Who would watch out for him if Amber didn't?

She swallowed and closed her eyes. Thinking that way was nothing but dangerous. The growing physical attraction between them had already proved itself; putting herself in the role of Derek's guardian angel was the riskiest thing she could do.

Opening her eyes, she took a deep breath and squared her shoulders. She was nothing more than the housekeeper; it was none of her business.

And it must stay that way.

Amber came awake with a start and found herself half sitting up in bed before she quite realized it. She blinked and peered through the darkness, looking and listening for anything that seemed out of place. The inky blackness revealed little, nor did any sound identify itself to relieve her mind.

Had her imagination brought her out of a sound sleep? She rubbed her eyes and tried to think if she had been dreaming, but no fleeting dream images came to mind. On the other hand, both Derek and Micah had warned her of untold dangers at the ranch. Suppose a new and different threat existed, and she was the only one aware of it?

The question brought her wide awake and utterly alert. She crept from her bed carefully so as not to warn anyone of her presence. Neither slippers nor robe were handy, and she couldn't be certain to be quiet enough to find them without a light. Rather, she made her way from her bedroom, around the staircase and into the front hall in her prim white nightgown.

The front door stood open. She swallowed back a sudden whimper of fear. No doubt she should have awakened Derek first, but she hadn't wanted to face him again. Not alone and in his bedroom. So, instead, here she was, unarmed, alone and confronting…what?

*If it turns out poorly and they find you dead, murdered in the yard, you'll have only yourself to blame.*

*Oh, stop it!* She shook her head in disgust. She was sounding completely overwrought.

She held her breath and stepped onto the veranda. The night air carried a soft breeze that danced over her skin and tugged at the hem of her nightgown. A low chuckle sent her reeling.

"Come out to join me, have you, angel?"

"Arrgh!" She whirled and glared into the darkness. "Derek?"

"Were you expecting someone else?"

"What are you doing out here?" she snapped in an irritable whisper, moving closer to where he sat in her favorite rocking chair. No point in shouting and waking everyone else.

"Minding my own business. What are you doing?"

"I heard a noise. I thought…well, I don't know what I thought. You and Micah warned me no one was safe, so I—"

"Came to investigate? How noble."

"Derek, what are you doing?" she repeated impatiently. "It's after midnight."

"Celebrating. Have you come to join me?"

"I didn't hear you come in. You missed supper. Are you hungry? I could fix you something."

"Ever the good little housekeeper, eh? I stopped by the cookhouse on my way in. Beau left me a plate."

"Oh." She thought for a moment. "What are you celebrating?"

"The arrival of my dear mother and my poor brother's widow, of course," he answered immediately. "Would you like a drink?"

The shadows around him shifted as he raised his arm and offered her something. A bottle? "What is that?"

"Mescal."

Mescal? What was he doing with a bottle of Mexican tequila? As if guessing the question, he added, "I got it from Carlos."

"Are you drunk?" Her voice sounded more tremulous than she would have liked, and she took a half step back. She had learned to be wary of men who drank. The animals who'd attacked her—she never thought of them by name— had been drunk. She would never forget the sour alcohol smell.

Derek gave a low grunt. "Not even close." He sounded disappointed.

How did one reply to such a statement? Amber had little other experience with drunks, or those who wished to be drunk. She merely waited silently, hesitantly.

"I've seen you in your nightgown as much as I've seen you in your dresses."

"*What?*" She wrapped her arms around herself as though to prevent him from seeing more than was absolutely necessary.

"Your nightgown is white. It shines bright as a flare in the darkness. It made me think of the times I've seen you this way...as opposed to other women, I suppose."

"Don't tell you've never seen another woman in her nightclothes," she snapped without thinking.

"No. Most women I might have seen in their nightgowns were wearing nothing at all."

She gasped as a vivid, unwelcome image flooded her mind's eye. Derek and a woman—nameless and faceless, though undoubtedly very beautiful—with their arms wrapped around each other in a heavy, torrid embrace. They were naked, and they kissed and touched and writhed together in wonderful ecstasy.

A deep-seated longing swelled in Amber's heart, sending a blazing heat to burn through her, razing any question about the woman's identity. It was *she* who wanted to be held in his arms, she who wanted to kiss him. *She* who wanted to learn the shape and texture of his naked body, imprinting it against her own.

*Please, don't.* She condemned herself with an inner plea. *How can you even think such things? He doesn't believe in the most important things about you. Wanting a man who doesn't trust you makes you into the kind of person you're accused of being.*

She clenched her hands into tight fists, but restrained other outward reactions to a mere swallow. "You shouldn't say such things," she murmured breathlessly.

"No," he agreed. "I probably shouldn't."

His voice carried an unaccustomed tone of resignation that eased the edge of her panic and hooked her attention to new considerations. "Derek? What's wrong?"

"What could be wrong?"

*The bastard result of an affair between his wife and his brother.* The words came back as clearly as if he had just proclaimed them.

She chose her response carefully. "I don't know. But I've never seen you drink before."

"You haven't been around at the right time."

She heard the slosh of liquid, and her eyes had adjusted to the darkness well enough that she could see his head tilt back as he took a long drink. Something about the action seemed so very desperate, and Amber found she couldn't turn away from him. Moving closer didn't seem like any better of an idea, so she sat down on the top porch step.

The night fell quiet, more so than earlier, and the air seemed to somehow grow almost oppressive. Derek said nothing, and Amber cast through the recesses of her mind for some stray thought to relieve the tension. She settled for the truth.

"I didn't mean to eavesdrop earlier today, but I heard what you said about Richard." She stared straight ahead; the darkness prevented her from seeing Derek's expression in any case.

"I know."

"It's true, then?"

"Yep. Richard was my 'real' father and I was raised as his brother's son."

"And your mother—Carolyn..." Words failed her as Amber searched for a polite way in which to phrase the question.

"Carolyn is my mother. She had an affair with her husband's brother."

"Are you sure? Could it be a mistake? That is—"

"I'm sure."

The rocker squeaked as he suddenly put it into motion, and she heard another slosh of liquid as he took another drink of mescal—or so she decided when he said nothing more.

She couldn't just let him sit here in the dark and drink. She turned toward him. "Do you want to talk about it?" she asked gingerly.

"Curious?" He gave a rough laugh heavy with cynicism. "Well, what the hell? I suppose you deserve to know the caliber of man your lover was."

A sharp lance of pain stole her breath, and Amber gasped. She hadn't imagined that they'd moved past the issue, but she hadn't anticipated the attack, either.

"You cannot understand the kind of relationship I had with your unc—with Richard. You don't *want* to understand." If the words sounded accusatory, so be it. She let them stand.

"What is there to understand? You haven't told me enough to *make* me understand."

She shrugged, even if he couldn't see her. "Why waste the time? It doesn't matter. Richard is dead, as you've pointed out more than once. You don't care about the truth." She threw the words at him with blunt bitterness. "You've already made up your mind about things and only want to change the subject."

"What is it you want? The whole sordid story?"

He got up, or so Amber assumed from the clatter of the rocker. She knew for sure when a dark shape separated itself from the shadows. His presence reached across the distance as though he'd touched her.

"My family held some shipping interests then. That was how the Fontaines made their money. Jordan traveled extensively to look after the business, and left Richard to cope with Palmetto. Egotist that he was, Jordan was sure no one could manage the business as well as he. I don't know what he thought his brother was doing at the plantation—though certainly not carrying on an affair with his wife."

Amber blinked, peering through the darkness, but she could see nothing more than shadows. How she wished for the sight of Derek's face! He sounded so distant, so speculative, and she knew better. He was talking about his life—his very conception. He must feel something.

"Jordan was often gone for several months at a time, more on occasion. After one of his longer trips he came home to find his wife three months into a pregnancy he couldn't possibly have participated in. So it seems I've long been a surprise to everyone."

Amber ignored his last remark for the moment; what could she possibly say to discount it? Little else could have created a greater scandal. "And Richard left?"

"After a fashion. Over the years I picked up some gossip, and Jordan said enough for me to assume he was forced out. Jordan was very good at threats. And carrying them out."

"Richard was never a coward. Perhaps he left for your mother's sake."

"Anything's possible." Derek's voice pulsed with the sting of disbelief. "He sure as hell didn't do it for *my* sake."

"He left you the Double F, didn't he?"

"Always his champion, aren't you? I suppose that's what

lovers should do. Well, let me tell you, leaving me to be raised by a man who resented my very life was no favor. Ever.''

She could not defend Richard against the accusation; every indication proved it to be true. What kind of childhood had Derek endured? It took no imagination to see that he still carried the scars of a young boy who hadn't been wanted.

''Have you always known?''

''Jordan told me during the war. After Nathan was killed and when he disowned me.''

Her heart ached for him. ''That sounds very cruel.''

''Jordan wasn't known for his kindnesses. Especially not to the son who was forced upon him. The son who reminded him every single day that he'd been cuckolded. He never let me forget it, though at the time I didn't understand why.''

''I wouldn't have liked him.''

''Not many people did.''

''Are you glad he's dead?''

The silence stretched out so long, Amber began to believe Derek wouldn't answer. Slowly, finally, he said, ''No. I never wished him dead. I don't feel *anything*.''

He sounded…curious. Perhaps disappointed, as though he wished he *did* feel some emotion for Jordan. Even hatred?

''It's sad—ironic,'' Derek continued. ''He's dead, and all the things that were important to him during his life are gone. All that's left are an unfaithful wife and the son he was forced to claim as his own.''

'''Whatever a man sows, this he will also reap,''' Amber quoted, sounding utterly pious. She didn't particularly like her tone of voice, or even the Bible verse itself, but she didn't recant. Everything she was learning about Jordan Fontaine put her on edge, and perhaps Derek, of all people, would understand.

"Will your mother and Mariah be staying on here?" she asked.

"I suppose so. I don't see any other choice."

"Of course not. You're very gracious to offer them a home."

"They don't want my hospitality. They came to Richard for salvation. Another of my surprises to the world, it seems."

"Of course they want your hospitality!" Amber stood abruptly. The idea of Derek remaining unwanted in his own family, even now, produced some fierce, untested emotion within her. "They're lucky you're here and the kind of man you are."

Why did she feel this protectiveness toward him? Hadn't he proved he could take excellent care of himself, and damn the rest of them? Hadn't he been crude and unfeeling, readily believing the worst of her at every turn?

Perhaps. But he had been wounded, a man in pain when he'd said some of those things. And later, a man in emotional turmoil. She had cared for him; he had depended on her. And later, he had offered comfort when she needed it. That alone changed things between them. Forever.

She stepped up onto the porch, but her purpose flew out of her head when she discovered that Derek stood not an inch away, radiating the heat she'd come to associate with him. He carried the same distinctive scent, as well—pure masculine cleanliness, she supposed. But there was something else, perhaps the sharp smell of mescal. Odd, but it wasn't at all the unpleasant, sour odor that she associated with the murderers.

Then it was too late. Too late for thought, too late for safety. She knew it the minute she heard his low, husky voice.

"What kind of man am I, Amber Laughton?"

She swallowed, her throat suddenly parched. "You aren't the unfeeling rogue you want people to believe."

"And why would you say that?"

"I..." She couldn't think, not with him so near. She could only hear the sound of his breathing, all but feel his solid presence, despite the distance between them.

"What kind of man do you think I am?" he demanded again. "This kind?" Then she was in his arms, his mouth on hers.

There was a crash in the distance and something wet splashed over her bare toes, but it hardly signified in her mind. All she knew were Derek's arms around her, his lips on hers.

His mouth was soft, persuasive. He teased her with a delicate bite at her bottom lip, again and again. Finally, when she moaned a soft protest, he took advantage of the moment and his tongue slipped past the barrier of her teeth to twine itself around hers.

She kissed him back, in a way she hadn't before. Her tongue became the aggressor, tasting him, seeking the mysteries of his mouth. She'd never kissed a man this way, hadn't known such wonder existed—and perhaps it didn't without Derek. All she knew, all she wanted, was to offer him everything within her that marked her as a woman.

His chest pressed against her with a hard, wonderful pressure that flattened her breasts, yet her nipples ached with the need for something more. She sagged in his arms, her knees threatening to give out.

He wrenched his mouth from hers with a billowing breath. "Jesus." The curse tore through the night air.

"Derek?" Her voice cracked, an agonized whisper.

"Yeah."

"What—"

"Go inside." He shoved her away, toward the open doorway.

She stumbled and caught herself against the wall. "What?" she repeated in a labored voice.

"Go inside, Amber. Get the hell out of here. Now."

"But—"

"Now!" His voice was a whiplash. "If you want to make it through the night in the same condition Richard left you in, then get the hell out of here."

She took him at his word and fled into the house. But his words scored her with angry talons of frustration—and need. Need...?

Derek *needed* her, and as a woman—but any woman would do just as well. And she? *She* needed something more.

# Chapter Fifteen

A week later, Derek approached Twigg without the trepidation that had marked his first visit. The town appeared exactly as he remembered, the tumbledown old house greeting him first. He'd expected one of the new families might move into the place, but none had as yet.

It reassured him somehow that the town hadn't changed; everything else in his life seemed to be spinning out of control. It wasn't the first time the world had gone upside down on him, but dare he venture the slightest hope that things would be different this time? That the results would not carry the same disastrous consequences?

He sighed, tussling with the discouragement that had begun to plague him of late. The emotional struggle exhausted him, and yet he could never quite give in to the hopelessness that always loomed just behind him. Life seemed destined to provide him with nothing better than certain disappointment, and yet lately he'd been surprised—and more than once.

His arrival on Main Street ground Derek's thoughts to a halt. The imposing edifice of the bank loomed first, and he identified other businesses farther down the street: the barber, the dressmaker, the livery, the doctor, and the newspaper that had once belonged to Amber's father.

"You lookin' to see if we got us a saloon, young Fontaine? Well, we do. At the far end a' town, where it won't bother the ladies none."

Derek glanced across the street and recognized the Andrews brothers sprawled on a wooden bench just outside the mercantile. He guided Charlic in their direction.

"Clem, Twigg." He greeted them as he swung to the ground and tethered his horse to the hitching post.

"What you doin' in town today?" Derek guessed it was Twigg who asked the question. "You come to git away from the wimmen? Three wimmen livin' in the same house could be two too many iffen they don't see eye to eye."

"You know...I might be persuaded to take one a' them off yer hands." Clem attempted an expression Derek guessed was meant to look innocent, but it resembled more of an embarrassed grin.

"Oh?" He did his best to adopt a distantly curious expression. "Which one?"

"Why, yer ma, a' course!" Clem straightened, as though the occasion called for it. "She's a fine lookin' woman. I seen her a coupla times now. Could be she's lookin' fer another man."

Derek bit the inside of his lip to suppress a smile. Smile? Hell, he wanted to laugh like he hadn't done in years! Clem Andrews and Carolyn Fontaine?

"I doubt if my mother is looking to remarry anytime soon, Clem," he managed to answer in a mild voice. "She's still in mourning."

The old man's eyes bugged wide, and he shot a look of full-fledged panic from his brother to Derek. "Who said anything about *marryin'*? I was talkin' 'bout—well, you know, keepin' company. I ain't never gettin' married."

"Me, neither," stated Twigg, as though Clem needed a consenting opinion.

"My mistake." Derek avoided looking at either of them. "I...misunderstood."

"So, d'you think she'd be interested if I come to call on her?" Clem demanded, sounding more hopeful than imperious.

"Hmm, I'm not sure," Derek temporized. "She hasn't been here long. She may need some time to settle in after the trip."

"Yeah, wimmen set a big store on settlin' into a place." Clem nodded wisely. "That's 'zactly what she said."

"When they arrived in Twigg?"

"Nah, when they come to town a coupla days ago. That one-armed feller brought them in the wagon. He got some supplies from Billy." Twigg waved a hand toward the store. "Mostly, though, he waited while they poked around town."

"You gettin' fergitful, or havin' trouble keepin' up with the goins-on 'round yer place there, son?"

Any remaining amusement fled under Clem's chastisement. "I was out with the herd for a couple of days." The compulsion to explain gnawed at Derek with a familiar bite. He had learned the futility of making excuses years ago, when he was still in short pants and facing Jordan's disapproval. But something about these old men commandeered his respect.

Both nodded, and Clem spoke up. "An' you stayed out with them critters overnight, I bet. Don't blame you fer that. Iffen it was me, I'd be spendin' my time away from the house, too. That's what I was sayin'! Wimmen're dangerous that way."

Warmth heated Derek's neck. It took all his concentration to merely stare at the identically curious faces with a bland expression of his own. The Andrews brothers continued to amaze him; despite their eccentricities, they perceived the truth with remarkable insight. Derek *had* been avoiding the house at every opportunity. And the women, too.

He had his reasons, as many of them as there were

women, but mostly it had to do with Amber. Derek blinked and tugged at the brim of his hat, as though the sunlight had suddenly become too bright. Things were changing between them, and he couldn't seem to understand it, let alone stop it.

He no longer thought of her as his *housekeeper*. She was a woman, and she had shared some of the darkest secrets of his soul.

More troublesome, she was a woman as complicated and difficult to understand as the mysteries of the universe. A woman who elicited emotions from him he'd thought long dead, if they'd ever existed at all. Emotions he didn't want. Emotions that seemed to thrive with a life of their own.

*If she knew how you felt, then what?* Derek felt a familiar tension rise within him. Sharing his reactions with her would mean sharing other parts of himself as well—and that was something he could *never* do. His family, his friends, his fiancée, none had ever understood him and his choices; why should Amber, a woman he hardly knew, react any differently? And she'd been lovers with his father, for God's sake!

Even knowing that, Derek had held her, kissed her—lain awake nights wanting her! His body reacted as fast and hot and hard as a young boy with his first woman. He'd have done damn near anything to take her that night on the porch, until some notable semblance of control had surged from the depths of his conscience to save them both.

Desire, red-hot and crushing, gnawed at him, refused to leave him in peace. And only Amber could satisfy it.

"Damn, there, Fontaine, you're as peculiar as yer uncle."

Derek started, blinking, and blew out a soft breath as he refocused his gaze. "I beg your pardon?"

"You been standin' there just starin' at us—thinkin' about somethin'. Richard used to do that, too, and it were damn spooky. Never could figger what kind a' powerful thinkin' he had to do, right in the middle a' anythin' and ever'thin' else.''

''I…'' Derek couldn't conjure up a response. How could he have been so stupid? Considering the trouble at the ranch, giving in to such useless preoccupation was a damned dangerous thing to do. He frowned, torn between embarrassment and irritation.

''It's the women,'' he finally said, without giving any more of an explanation. And it was true enough—as long as it explained things from the Andrews brothers' perspective.

The men nodded sagely, and Twigg said, ''Ain't it always?''

Clem squinted suddenly, as though a powerful thought struck him. ''Wonder if Richard's problem was that he didn't have no woman—least not till Amber moved out there.''

''Don't you start talkin' 'bout Amber, old man,'' Twigg snapped before Derek could say a word.

''I ain't sayin' nothin' *bad.* I didn't say him an' Amber was *doin'* anything.''

''Well, young Fontaine's got plenty a' wimmen. What about Miz Mariah?'' Twigg asked. ''You think she's ready fer a new man?''

Derek's eyes widened. ''Are you thinking of…courting Mariah?''

Clem lost his scowl and burst into a great guffaw. ''That'd be good.''

''I ain't!'' Twigg insisted, his brows wrinkled, and did a determined job of ignoring his brother. ''I was thinkin' 'bout you, Fontaine.''

''Me?''

''Maybe you need a woman.''

''What about our Amber-girl?'' demanded Clem with a ferocious frown. ''She's just as good as some widderwoman from back East. Maybe he wants her.''

Damn right he wanted Amber. In his bed, naked and ready and waiting for him. Her arms wide, her legs spread, her mouth open under his. He could all but feel her move with him.

His body reacted with a sudden surge, and he swallowed a groan. *Oh, no you don't. Not here and not now.* If he meant to lust after Amber, it would be in the privacy of his own bedroom.

"Are you two matchmaking?"

"Matchmakin'? Us?" they cried in unison. Their eyes widened, though neither looked particularly innocent.

Derek shook his head. If anyone else said such outrageous things to him, he would have stopped the discussion damn quick or simply walked away. The Andrews brothers had somehow made themselves exceptions to his rules, perhaps because they were equally audacious with everyone. They made a man feel like they only meddled because they cared.

Derek's good mood had become a thing of the distant past by the time he rode back to the ranch. Instead, a provoked frown was etched firmly on his face. Clem's and Twigg's antics had proved the only bright moments of the trip.

Bill Andrews had been helpful enough, Derek supposed, willingly detailing the supplies Beau had acquired a few days earlier. But the man always acted so fretful, he put Derek's nerves on edge. Frank Edwards, meanwhile, had been jovial and friendly as he'd outlined the status of Derek's accounts, but he'd been *too* jovial and friendly for Derek's peace of mind. Then, of all the luck, he'd met up with Eliza Bates. Her disposition hadn't improved. She'd been all too eager to recount her meeting with his mother and Mariah.

God only knew what that could mean.

Derek grunted as the ranch house emerged in the distance, a welcome silhouette rising up from the prairie grass ruffled by the breeze. He frowned as the fading afternoon sun cast a friendly glow over the cluster of buildings. *Welcome* and *friendly* were hardly words he'd ever meant to use in describing the ranch. It was only supposed to be…there.

He led Charlie into the empty barn, settling the horse with an efficiency borne of years of practice. He skirted the garden and cookhouse, heading for the front veranda; chances were better than good that Amber would be out back.

"I do not understand this!" He slowed as his mother's voice issued from the house, her tone sharp and incensed. "What do you *do* with yourself all day, Miss Laughton? I told you this morning I wanted the silver polished, the floors waxed and those hideous rag rugs burned! I meant for you to start laundering my wardrobe tomorrow, but you haven't even finished the chores I assigned you today."

Tension stiffened Derek's spine. He had learned as a child to hate that particular tone of his mother's voice. It always signaled injustice, an unfairness that was never explained. He suspected now that Jordan had often been involved—but the man was dead. So what was this all about?

"I'm sorry you're unhappy, ma'am." Amber sounded calm—but at a price. Her voice carried an edge he recognized from their own disagreements. "I meant to do those things but—"

"No excuses! I want results." Derek recognized the beginning of a long and bitter tirade as his mother's always thin patience snapped. "And I—"

"Mother, stop this." He pushed open the door.

"Derek!" Carolyn spun to face him, while Amber remained in place, eyes downcast and her face carefully devoid of expression.

"What is going on here?" he asked.

"Nothing. I am just trying to get…*this woman* to do her

job.'' His mother sniffed and rolled her eyes before looking back at him. ''Richard was apparently too lenient with her, and it seems you have done no better. I suppose that's to be expected when men— Well, it's a disgrace.''

Derek did not miss his mother's innuendo, nor did Amber, it seemed. A shock of pain widened her eyes, but she quickly blinked, and the familiar detachment returned. He might have missed the reaction weeks ago, before he'd seen past the surface facade she used so desperately to protect herself, but he *had* seen past her defenses. His mother had hurt her—and deeply.

It occurred to him then, in a moment of unexpected simplicity, how very vulnerable Amber had become. She had cut herself off from others, erected barriers, avoided town— whatever she deemed necessary to protect herself. His arrival had changed all that, and his questions had reopened her secrets to new scrutiny.

''Derek?'' His mother's impatient question drew his attention back to her. ''What is it? I am trying to make a point here.''

''I have a point of my own, Mother, and I am going to make it now so there will be no misunderstandings.'' Amber showed no reaction, while Carolyn tightened her lips in obvious irritation.

He forged ahead. ''Amber is not your servant, Mother, nor your personal maid. This is a working ranch, and she keeps the house up—the only one to do much of the work. She also helps Beau in the kitchen and tends the garden— which is sizable, as you may have noticed. That garden puts a good share of food on our table. She knows when polishing silver and waxing floors can be done. Frankly, I hardly consider them priorities.''

Amber's gaze shot to his, eyes wide and darkened to a deep, lush green. His mother, meanwhile, gaped at him, her mouth open like a fish out of water. ''Well, I never!'' She snapped it shut and blinked furiously.

"If you want those things done, you are welcome to do them yourself. Or Mariah can help you. Things aren't the same as they were before the war, Mother. You know that. You knew it in Charleston, long before you came here."

"Thanks to *you*."

He tightened his jaw. "Why are you here then?"

"I thought Richard—"

"Why did you *stay* once you discovered Richard was gone?"

"I…" Her voice faded, and she shook her head.

"I don't have a bevy of maids at your beck and call. Richard never had them, and I surely can't afford them. It shouldn't be such a hardship. You haven't had that kind of luxury in years."

Carolyn glared at him, her expression dark with an unlikely mixture of emotions: anger, utter frustration and an odd uncertainty she'd always reserved just for him.

"Amber has run this household for years." Derek refrained from looking at her, continuing to face his mother instead. As it was, he could feel Amber's presence as keenly as if she stood hip to hip, shoulder to shoulder with him. "If you would like to help, I'd appreciate it. If not, then I'll thank you not to make any more work for her than she already has."

"I see." A sudden sheen glazed his mother's eyes, a warning of tears to come, and prompted Derek to take refuge in the icy detachment that had seen him through so much. He'd witnessed the same reaction dozens of times and in a myriad of circumstances, always designed to earn his mother the most sympathy. Any chance of remorse disappeared from within him.

"You're taking her side over mine?" Her voice softened with the exact quiver he expected.

"There are no sides, Mother. There is only the ranch, its needs and what I am capable of providing. We aren't exactly prospering at the moment. This is the best I can do."

"Is it? Or are you just protecting your whore?"

"*Mother!*" The word erupted from him, but it was too late. The vicious accusation lingered like the roar of a cannon, and the destruction was just as terrible. *This* was what Eliza Bates's gossip had wrought.

Carolyn turned on her heel and stormed toward the stairs, making a wide sweep around Amber that left no doubt of the intended insult. All color bleached from her face, Amber remained as still as a statue, staring straight ahead as though nothing could penetrate her consciousness.

Mariah appeared at the top of the stairs, missing all but Carolyn's dramatic departure. She stopped halfway down, intercepting his mother, while at the same time shooting Derek a look of weary anger. "There now, Carolyn." She turned to help the older woman up to their rooms. "Everything will be fine."

Derek dismissed the women with the ease of knowing the confrontation had been simply another in a long line of disappointments between his mother and him. Whenever she didn't get her way, their disputes ended like this. He turned back to Amber. She held herself with brittle care, as though she might shatter if she moved. And yet, when he extended his hand to reach for her, she stepped away from him.

The silence stretched out until he could endure it no longer. "I'm sorry," he said, his voice oddly hoarse. He cleared his throat with unaccustomed self-consciousness.

She collected herself with a dignity that pained him to watch, even as he admired her for it. She breathed deeply, and her breasts rose and fell with each movement. He noticed everything until her gaze caught his.

"For what? You feel the same way."

"No, I don't. I never called you a—"

"Whore? Yes. You did."

He'd never meant to say it, hadn't realized how ugly it would sound until it was too late. Or maybe he'd meant it at the time and only regretted it now for the way the word haunted him. In any case, it had been cruel, and Amber deserved better.

"I was wrong. You're not...like that. I'm sure you had your reasons for whatever you did."

God, he hated admitting such a failing. *You might as well tell her you're no better than any of the rest of them, lusting after her yourself. You want to take Richard's place,* he thought.

He would never say it, however. He couldn't, any more than he could simply walk away and leave her like this. He didn't like it, didn't understand it, but he couldn't escape it.

She nodded slowly. "I'm not without the sin, just allowed an excuse for it." Her low voice held an ache he had never heard before.

"Amber—"

"It's nothing new." She shook her head. "At least you've given me more credit than most." Her eyes, suspiciously moist, flickered toward the stairs.

"Mother and Mariah went to Twigg the other day."

"Yes."

"They met Eliza Bates. But you knew that."

"Yes."

"Why didn't you tell me?"

"What should I have said? They wanted to go, so Beau took them. We needed some supplies." Her voice sounded stronger.

"I'll talk to them and explain things."

Amber shot him a fierce look that relieved him as much as it surprised him. Her spirit—something he'd grudgingly come to admire—was returning. "And what will you tell them?" she demanded. "That I became Richard's mistress after two men attacked me and killed my father? That people in Twigg don't understand—but you do and they should?"

"Don't," he snapped, stepping closer. "It isn't like that, and you know it."

"It *is* like that—and *you* know it."

"I have no intention of discussing your personal life with them," he said stiffly. "It's none of their business. I will simply remind them that you answer to *me*. They are perfectly capable of managing for themselves. I meant what I said, and I'll see that they understand that."

"All right. If that's what you want."

"What else can I do?"

She shook her head. "Nothing."

She'd given as much as she intended to. He could see it in the taut set of her shoulders, the firm purse of her lips. But there was much she hadn't said; he knew it as well as he knew all the things that *he* chose to keep to himself. Which of them, he was beginning to wonder, carried the more serious—the more damning—secrets?

# Chapter Sixteen

Amber slipped into the house through the front door. Derek and his family were settled in for the evening meal in the dining room, one of the few concessions he'd made to the women's arrival. At least on occasion.

Amber had taken to using the time for chores, such as lighting the lamps in the parlor and study. She worked quickly whenever the other women were nearby, not wishing to invite the least comment, although Derek's presence seemed to ease a fraction of the awkwardness.

In the month since he had defended her against his mother, Amber had arranged her schedule carefully, avoiding Carolyn and Mariah as much as possible. It hadn't been difficult; they seemed much of the same mind. In fact, Carolyn had refused to speak to her since then. Hadn't said a single word.

While Derek ate his evening meal with the women several times a week, he spent virtually no other time with them. Amber saw little more of him herself.

At first she had been relieved by the time alone, humiliated as she'd been by the confrontation with Carolyn. Derek's mother could not think worse of Amber—and Derek had witnessed her animosity. Not only that, but he had come to Amber's defense. She hadn't needed *rescuing* in a very long time, and that Derek had been compelled to do so didn't settle well with her.

And yet at night, when she was alone in the dark privacy of her bedroom and the house grew quiet, a certain heartfelt amazement would steal over her. Derek had defended her— *her!*—and offered at least a modicum of respect. He might not approve of her, but he appreciated her.

At least her worth to the Double F. Could it be possible *he* would be the one? The one to believe in her, against all odds?

And if that was the case, she owed him something. An explanation. In all honesty, she owed him the truth about Richard and her, no matter what. But it wasn't an account she could give quickly or easily, with no thought to the words or the consequences. Not now, after she'd held her silence for so long. And not when she saw Derek only in passing.

Then when?

Amber hurried into Derek's study rather than indulge in that line of thinking. She lit the lamps, then moved across the hall to the front parlor. Located next to the dining room, it was where Carolyn and Mariah most often spent their evenings.

One of the lamps had been temperamental of late, and tonight it gave Amber more trouble than usual. Impatiently she fussed with it, stopping only when Mariah's voice carried from the next room.

"Derek, your mother and I have been talking. We think we should have a party."

"A party?"

Derek's question echoed in Amber's mind like a discordant groan, and her heart began to pound. What kind of party?

"Nothing elaborate, of course. We *are* still in mourning." Carolyn emphasized the words as though only she had lost a loved one. Or perhaps that she was the only one to show the proper respect.

"Then it would seem any celebration would be inappropriate." Derek's voice carried a cautious dismissal that reassured Amber of his distaste for the idea.

"Perhaps at one time that would have been true," his mother admitted. "But as everyone keeps reminding me, times have changed since then. We are no longer in Charleston."

"Your mother and I feel it would be good for us to get to know your neighbors—our neighbors now. We plan to invite those from Twigg's society—if they can boast such a thing. If not—"

"I will not invite Twigg *society* into my home."

Derek's low voice, filled with absolute, utter aversion, made the hair on Amber's neck stand on end. Did the other women realize the strength of his conviction?

She glanced down, scowling at the lamp, and tried to light it once more out of pure desperation. It caught this time, and she uttered a small "thank you" as she hurried to the door with quiet caution.

"Derek, I don't understand why," said Mariah. "Mr. Edwards at the bank seems like a perfectly nice man. Dr. Harris and his wife have been very cordial, as well. And Mrs. Bates is quite friendly. Her daughter and son-in-law…"

Amber lost whatever else Mariah might have said because of a sudden wave of nausea that sent her stomach roiling. *Oh God, no.*

Of all things she had endured, *that* would be too much. It would be all but impossible to face those people in this house—the only place she had to call home any longer. She would need every bit of her strength to pretend a civility toward them that she could never feel—and they didn't deserve. But to witness the happily wedded bliss of

Jeff and Melinda Buchanan? Amber could hardly contemplate the idea.

"No!" Derek's voice issued down the hall with barely suppressed fury, effectively disrupting her frenzied thoughts.

Amber caught her breath. The silence strung out until it became untenable. "I told you before, this is a *cattle ranch*." Derek enunciated each word with utter clarity. "It sat virtually unworked for a year. I do not have the time or the resources to establish your vision of society here. Even if I did, I wouldn't agree to it. Frank Edwards and Eliza Bates have not impressed me as people I would like to count among my friends, and I refuse to invite them here."

The sound of wood scraping against wood—a chair being pushed back from the table?—charged Amber into action. She stole from the house as silently as a thief and raced toward the cookhouse. Whatever else Derek might have to say didn't matter; she, at least, took his point clearly enough.

Swallowing, she took a deep breath, arranged her features into a bland smile and strolled into the kitchen. "They're still at the table," she informed Beau in a casual voice. "Why don't we eat before clearing the dishes?"

He looked up from where he was cutting large squares of fragrant buttermilk cake and stared at her. "What's wrong?"

"What do you mean?"

"I know that look. And that voice." Beau offered what she had come to recognize as his attempt at a crooked half grin, and he brushed a lock of sandy brown hair back from his forehead. "You can't fool me. You'd make a terrible poker player."

She snorted and shot him a frown. "I don't know why you say that. You're the only one who does."

His smile turned genuine, then wilted with a hint of sad-

ness. "I knew someone like you once...a long time ago."
He blinked and shook his head. "Now what happened?"

"I don't want to go back in there just yet.
They're...talking. Mariah and Mrs. Fontaine want to have
a party."

"A party?" Beau dropped the knife to the table and
stared at her. "Why?"

Amber shrugged. "To establish Twigg as the hub of
western society."

Beau grinned for real this time. "And she's going to do
that with the women from Twigg? Eliza Bates and her
friends?"

"You've met them?"

"Unfortunately. On one of my many trips to town."

He'd been the one who most often had to take Carolyn
and Mariah to Twigg. Amber had thought little of it at the
time, other than commiserating with him over the chore.
Now she realized exactly what his chaperoning duties had
meant. He would have heard Eliza Bates's gossip, if not
from her, then from its retelling on the way home. And that
meant—

"Then you have..." How could Amber say it?

"Figured out the woman's a self-righteous old biddy?
Yep, I saw that right quick."

"But...that is, you didn't say—"

"Amber, don't." He planted his hand on the table and
leaned forward. "It doesn't make a damn bit of difference
to me what people like Eliza Bates say. I know you and
your kindness. You and Derek have treated me like family—better than I deserve. You've become a friend, and I
haven't had many of them in the last few years. I'm not
going to repay you by listening to tales from jealous old
women."

"Beau..." She tried to swallow past the lump in her
throat, at the same time blinking furiously to chase away
the tears that prickled behind her eyelids. No one had ever

said anything so kind to her. She had no words to thank him; she could only give him a gently tender embrace, the kind that no one seemed to remember anymore.

"Thank you," she whispered after a moment.

Beau pulled away, smiling at her shyly until his gaze darted past her. "Derek!" he said with some surprise, and perhaps a bit of awkwardness, as well. "Can I—we—help you?"

Amber spun around. Derek stood in the doorway, the force of his presence emanating across the room as his shoulders filled the opening. His remote expression was nothing if not impenetrable.

"Derek?" Why didn't he speak? "I'm sorry if you were waiting. Are you ready for dessert?"

"We won't be eating dessert tonight. Mother and Mariah have retired."

"What about you?" Beau gestured toward the table. "We have fresh buttermilk cake."

"Thank you, no." Derek spun on his heel and walked away.

Amber sighed and closed her eyes. Lord, what next? The clash over the party had likely put Derek on edge, and she could fully empathize with him over that. But it didn't take any stretch of her imagination to guess at other reasons behind his surly mood.

He'd seen her with Beau. Did he suspect something between *them* now? That she was intent on seducing her way through the ranch hands? Could he have so little faith in her?

Her hands fisted. *You don't have any idea what he's thinking. Don't borrow trouble.*

But it was possible. The distant look on his face—the icy-cold expression—told her it was entirely probable. He wore the same expression whenever he spoke of her relationship with Richard.

*Richard.* The topic she had avoided at every turn, refusing all Derek's attempts to understand the bond between her and his father. The time was coming—and soon—when she would have to swallow her pride and this useless need for unconditional acceptance. Derek deserved to know the truth.

But first, she couldn't let him think badly of Beau. This job had given Beau a new start, a chance to work and regain his self-confidence. She saw it every day in his changed attitude, his tentative smiles, the mere fact that he had learned to meet her eyes when they spoke. She couldn't take that away from him.

Nor, it seemed, was she willing to allow Derek to continue thinking badly of her. His opinion had begun to matter—more than was healthy perhaps, but there it was.

She gave her head a small shake. It had happened so gradually as he charmed her with small, ordinary discoveries. His efforts to learn about the ranch and its operations, his understanding of the limitations of others, the sweet tooth he tried to hide. And then there were the bigger, more memorable things: the shooting, the night by the cemetery, her nightmare.

And now? Where had her emotions settled now?

Derek pulled a ledger book from the top of the pile and flipped it open on the desk before him. Richard had kept meticulous records of ranch production and growth, and the information was turning out to be immensely useful. Once he had a chance to study the figures in detail, Derek hoped to understand his father's reasoning and perhaps discover any patterns behind the man's decision making.

Tonight, however, the words and numbers ran together in a blur. All he could see was Amber standing so sweetly in the arms of another man. Not just any man, but Beau Montgomery. Someone Derek had begun to trust. Someone he liked.

The memory sharpened in his mind's eye, detailing the

likeness with all the faithfulness of those remarkable new photographs he had seen on occasion during the war. Amber's arms had been wrapped around Beau's back, while he had held her close in much the same way. His good arm had rested high, his hand splayed wide over the middle of her back. His other arm—his stump—had settled near her waist.

Dammit! How could Derek fight a man like that for her?

He slammed the ledger shut and sat back, rubbing his fingers over the middle of his forehead, where a dull throbbing had settled. What the hell was he thinking?

Fight for Amber? Why would he?

*Don't be a damn fool.* An impatient voice spoke up from the recesses of his mind. *You'd fight for her without a second thought, and it wouldn't matter who you had to face or what you had to do. You want her—and only her—so bad you shake with it.*

So maybe he did want her. Bad enough to shake with it. But bad enough to take on Beau for her? It didn't seem fair somehow; Beau had lost so much.

And what if Derek was wrong about the whole thing? What if he'd somehow misunderstood what he saw? Discounting the old rumors he knew were half lies, Amber had given him little reason to question her behavior as his housekeeper—or a woman. Nor, for that matter, had Beau been anything but trustworthy.

But what if he *hadn't* misunderstood? His uncertainty persisted. Beau could make her smile—laugh—like no one else. And she seemed more at ease with him than anyone, except perhaps Micah or Six. More than a year had passed since Richard's death; Amber's grief must surely be waning. What if she was ready for a new protector? What if she was in love?

Derek grunted, his mind immediately rejecting the question. *He* was the man who'd held her, kissed her—and she had kissed him back. She would have given him more, had he asked for it. If he hadn't come to his senses that night on the porch, he could have had her in his bed and himself buried deep inside her, easing the ache that plagued them both. She couldn't have held him, touched him, kissed him, as she had, and still turn to Beau now.

"Derek?"

He jerked his gaze to the doorway. Amber stood waiting, more in the hall than the room.

"What?" Guilt made him snap.

"I'm sorry to bother you, but…"

"What?"

"May I come in?"

He gestured her forward. "What is it?"

She moved with a smooth elegance he didn't recall noticing in any other woman. Back straight, head high, she walked with a flowing grace that gave her a decided dignity. Her breasts rose and fell with each breath.

She stopped before the desk and swallowed. "I…this is a bit awkward, but I was in the parlor when you were at dinner. I overheard Mariah mention a party—and your response."

He scowled. She wanted to talk about that stupid society party Mariah and his mother had thought up?

Amber continued before he could respond, perhaps because of his frown. "I wasn't eavesdropping, I was lighting the lamps and couldn't help overhearing. I understand why you refused—and you must guess that I'm relieved you feel that way. But have you considered another kind of party?"

"Such as?" he asked blandly, grappling to make sense of where this was heading.

"A party for everyone at the Double F. A celebration of your taking over the ranch—a chance to relax and for the new hands you've been hiring to become acquainted. And…a way for Mariah and your mother to see the kind of life we live here. Maybe…"

The strange tightness in his chest began to relax. A party.

She was here to talk about his mother's silly party. "A way to pacify them. To give them the entertainment they crave."

"Yes."

He eyed her curiously. "Do you want to plan it for them?"

"Oh, no!" Her eyes widened with obvious dismay. "No, you should mention it to them as though it was your idea, and let them plan it. It would be better that way."

"That's very generous of you. I know my mother, and I doubt she or Mariah have been very gracious with you."

Amber shook her head, and her gaze slipped from his. "I can understand some of what they must be feeling, having their lives upset this way."

"The idea is excellent." He chose not to force the point. "It may smooth over some of their disappointment."

She nodded eagerly. "I'm glad you agree."

"I'll mention it to them tomorrow."

She nodded again without comment, but made no move to leave.

"Was there something else?"

She turned to the window without responding. Night had fallen long ago, and only shadows lingered beyond the glass.

"Amber? Was that all?"

Slowly she turned back to him. "No," she said quietly. "That was the excuse I invented to come in here."

"The excuse..." He trapped her gaze with his. "What is the *real* reason, then?"

"I..." She wet her lips. "I wanted to explain about Beau."

Everything in Derek stiffened, from the set of his shoulders and the clench of his jaw to the angle of his brows. And lower, that most masculine part of him hardened from nothing more than the sight of Amber's tongue as she wet her lips.

"It's none of my business."

Her eyes widened. "That's not what you said before. You said everything that happens at the ranch is your business."

Dammit! Why did she insist on talking about this now? He wasn't ready to hear his words come back to haunt him.

"Yes."

"Then I've come to explain."

Derek blinked, but allowed no other reaction. "All right."

"I was thanking him."

"How nice."

She sniffed in clear irritation. "He said some very nice things—about both of us. He said we treated him like family."

"He's had it rough."

"Yes, he has. And it's a shame, because he's a wonderful man. But his difficulties have made him a better person. He doesn't listen to gossip, for one thing. He heard the things Eliza Bates told your mother and Mariah about me, and he chose to ignore them."

Derek stood and rounded his desk. He settled against the edge of the desktop and leaned back, an arm on either side of him. His injured shoulder ached with a dull throb.

*Amber and Beau…she'd been thanking him?*

"Beau has treated me with the same courtesy since the day I met him," she continued after a moment. "He's like a brother. It's very special to me that he looked past the rumors and saw just *me*. No one has done that in a very long time, and I wanted to thank him for it."

Yes, Derek could see that she would. Apparently Beau had asked no questions nor made any accusations. He simply accepted the woman he had come to know. Not like Derek himself.

But…a brother? Did she really see him that way? And could Beau possibly see Amber as a *sister*?

"I didn't like seeing you in his arms."

The words startled him, slipping out before he could think about them. He frowned, pinning her with his stare.

"It didn't mean anything." She sounded quite earnest, with worry lines scoring her brow. "Just an innocent hug between friends."

He moved close to her, stopping only when he couldn't take another step forward. Vanilla teased his nostrils, a faint, fresh scent. Amber's head arched back and she peered up at him, her eyes darkened to a shade of green that looked almost black.

"Derek?" It was a soft, breathy question.

"An innocent hug between friends?"

She nodded. "Beau meant nothing more by it, and neither did I." Her throat rippled as she swallowed. "You asked for my promise that I would never lie to you—and for answers to your questions. You haven't always gotten those answers, but in this case you deserve to know the truth."

Without quite meaning to, he reached for her, smoothing a loose tendril of hair back from her cheek with one not-quite-steady finger. "The truth?"

"Yes."

She stepped back, away from him, and he followed. The windowsill brought her up short.

"You and Beau are just friends. You were thanking him."

"Don't believe me then." She frowned crossly, but her voice came out a bit thin.

"Who said I don't believe you?"

"You're baiting me. I can tell."

Did she have any clue how desirable the tilt of her chin and flash of her eyes made her? He almost smiled. "Why do you think that?"

She took a deep breath—or was she trying to back out through the window? Satisfaction, purely male and completely improper, coursed through him. Good; he made her nervous. She sure as hell played havoc with *his* senses.

"Derek." She glanced down. Her hands were clasped at her waist—all the room there was between them. She looked back up, but kept her gaze shuttered. "I've been thinking. For a while."

"About what?"

"A lot has happened lately. To you—me. Us."

*"To us?"*

"That afternoon in the hall. You defended me against your mother."

A distinct uneasiness began to creep up his spine. "She was being unfair. I've seen her behave that way before, and no one ever benefited from it."

"Still, you didn't have to do it. I didn't expect you to."

Somehow, her words stung. "Is that what you think of me and my honor? That I could just ignore her arrogance?" He'd fought some damn long, hard battles to prove how important justice was to him. He'd thought Amber would understand after that night by the cemetery. But perhaps he'd been wrong.

"It's not you. It's me." She sounded a bit desperate. "No one has willingly come to my defense in a very long time. Well, except the Andrews brothers—but you know they're peculiar. As much as I care for them, it's not the same. I simply…wasn't expecting it. Not from anyone."

Her admission didn't exactly come as news to him, and yet hearing the words from her pained him in some odd, fleeting way. It occurred to him with succinct simplicity that she had never done anything so very *wrong*. She had witnessed her father's murder and found a way to survive it. Why did he—why did anyone—find that so difficult to forgive?

Derek found himself reaching for her, his fingers jittery as they traced lightly around the oval of her face. He couldn't stop himself from resting his palm against her cheek. "Richard was your champion, wasn't he? Now he's gone, almost a year, and you haven't had anyone since. Have you?"

The words sounded overloud, abrasive, carrying a double meaning Derek hadn't meant. *Fool!* he chastised himself. His thoughtlessness would ruin her attempt at peace between them.

"No, there's been no one." She angled her head, leaning into his hand.

She didn't take offense? Perhaps she hadn't noticed his double entendre. Regret turned to relief. Perhaps he hadn't destroyed the fragile understanding she seemed to be trying to build. Could she really be that naive, after everything?

"Have you been lonely?" he asked softly.

She closed her eyes for a heartbeat, two. Eventually she tilted her head back and looked at him—really looked. He stood quietly, allowing her to do as she pleased.

"Yes." The word was hardly audible. "At times. But then, that's life in Texas. I suppose it's also made me...vulnerable to a man like you."

"A man like me?" The question came out a little rough, due mostly to the husky voice he almost didn't recognize as his own. He seemed to have lost the ability to think, his body intent on reacting. Perhaps the image he couldn't quite forget, that of Amber standing so sweetly in another man's arms, prodded him to do things he normally wouldn't. Or it may have been nothing more than desperation, the result of knowing how unworthy of her attention he truly was.

Amber's eyes grew to dark, round circles, her breathing sketchy. She brought her hand up to cover his, still curved at her cheek.

"We're very much alike, you and I." She tried to smile, but couldn't quite manage it. "Even when it causes us no end of trouble, we demand honesty and decency from those around us—and ourselves—despite our own secrets, private places we try to avoid. Still, there's something between us—something neither of us seems able to ignore.''

Derek stared, noticing everything about Amber as though he'd never seen her before. Her auburn hair in its prim coiffure tempted him, his mind's eye offering a saucy reminder of how it looked at night, falling around her shoulders and down her back. Her neck arched gracefully above the very appropriate high collar of her dress. Dove-gray cotton covered the rest of her quite properly, and yet it displayed her curves and angles to their best advantage.

He smiled—a bit primitively, gauging by the emotions teeming through him—and indulged in the memory of holding her in his arms. The taste of her mouth, the press of her breasts at his chest. He wanted her that way again— but naked, and she would be desperate to be a part of him.

He slipped one hand behind her neck and rested the other at her waist. She dropped her arms to her sides and swallowed.

''I don't seem able to ignore you, Amber Laughton,'' Derek whispered, pulling her close. The juncture of her thighs pressed against the unmistakable ridge of his erection. ''And now I know you can't ignore me, either.''

''Derek, I—''

He caught her mouth with his, and her lips parted with little coaxing. His tongue swept forward, dancing through the recesses of her mouth and teasing hers to life. She clung to him until slowly, and with an uncertainty that both surprised and delighted him, she took up the dance, following his lead and acquainting herself with his mouth in much the same way.

He swallowed a guttural groan and cupped her breast. He swallowed her small cry as well, and she arched her back, pressing her fullness into his palm.

''You've thought about it, haven't you?'' he demanded against her mouth. ''Remembered our kisses? Remembered how you felt in my arms, the way your heart pounded.''

"I—"

He devoured her response with another kiss, this one longer and deeper, leaving her no chance to withhold anything of herself. She seemed to share his need, tangling her fingers though his hair with one hand and clutching the back of his shirt with the other.

"You want me. As much as I want you." His voice came out much like a breathless wheeze. "Don't you?"

She held fast to him, her hands clutching his shoulders, and blinked, as though her eyes wouldn't focus. "Don't you?" he repeated, trailing the tip of his tongue along the fullness of her bottom lip. "You want me every damn bit as bad as I want you."

She blinked again, but answered with a low huskiness that shot a new surge of desire through him. "Yes...I'm shaking." She lifted one hand from his shoulder, staring at her fingers as though she'd never seen them before.

He held up his own trembling hand. "I want you the same way."

She inhaled, a deep breath that tormented him with the rise of her breasts and increased the pressure of her pelvis against his. He flexed his hips in response. Jesus, did she have any idea what she did to him? He couldn't get any harder.

He dipped his head and took her mouth in another kiss, crushing her against him and engaging her tongue in a sudden, desperate assault. Amber hesitated, perhaps shocked by his ardor, but only for a moment. Soon her fingers kneaded his shoulders before slipping up to snarl in his hair. Her head fell back, her mouth widened, leaving Derek to wonder faintly where he ended and she began.

"Derek, are you—"

The words exploded in the room. He jerked his head back, blinking owlishly as his breath wheezed into oxygen-starved lungs. His arms tightened around Amber when she would have pulled away.

"What?"

"I'm sorry!" Mariah stood poised in the doorway, her eyes wide as saucers. "I didn't realize…" She hesitated, her voice trailing away.

Amber, meanwhile, took a long, shuddering breath that only served to renew Derek's desire for her. He gave her little choice but to remain pressed against him, her face tucked against his chest as she, too, struggled for equilibrium. He felt each little movement she made.

"What is it, Mariah?" His voice was a gruff demand.

Her eyes narrowed. "I can see you're…busy. I apologize for interrupting, but I wanted to talk to you."

"I see." He struggled for an even tone. "Is it possible that this discussion could wait until later?"

"No, you should talk now." Amber straightened and stepped back, insisting when Derek would have held her close. She kept her eyes downcast, looking at neither him nor Mariah. She sounded entirely breathless.

"Wait." He reached for her arm.

"No, really. I should go." She darted a quick glance in his direction that begged him to cooperate.

Mariah, meanwhile, conceded nothing. She waited calmly, silently, with all the patience of a bird of prey. In that instant Derek saw a woman determined to have her way—whatever the cost—while next to him stood a woman who had already paid the ultimate price.

"All right." He let Amber go with a lingering sweep of his fingers and half turned toward his sister-in-law. He needn't flaunt the evidence of his arousal. "This had better be good," he added, watching Amber rush from the room as though she couldn't escape quickly enough.

# Chapter Seventeen

Seated on the front veranda, Amber settled back in the rocking chair and looked at the bounty spread out before her. Tables were arranged in a convenient U-shape, designed to invite partaking of roasted beef, wild turkey, breads and rolls, salads and vegetables. A separate table, placed off to one side, was laden with pies, cakes and cookies for those with a sweet tooth.

The men of the Double F had begun to assemble thirty minutes earlier, dressed in their finest. Or, she amended with a fond half smile, at least they had bathed and put on clean clothes.

All except Derek. He had yet to make an appearance.

Amber caught her bottom lip between her teeth and watched indifferently as Mariah circled the men and tables with an elegance that she, Amber, would never learn. It didn't matter; nothing did. She shouldn't have expected Derek to attend the party, having seen so little of him since their disastrous embrace in his study.

What a paltry description of what had passed between them that night! But now was not the time to give in to the memories, nor was it fair to label the encounter a disaster. More to the point, it had *ended* dreadfully, with Mariah's haughty interruption.

When Amber had gone to Derek, she had not expected he would feel a physical need that surpassed hers. And though Mariah's intrusion had come as a distinct shock, when Amber had collected her scattered wits, she'd come to view it with marked relief. It had been remarkably easy to avoid them all since then. Carolyn and Mariah had immediately begun party preparations, and Derek had just as quickly rendered himself absent this past week.

Now the first hint of evening was beginning to bathe the grounds with blue-tinged shadows, and the party moved at a lively pace. Six had brought out his fiddle, and a new hand whose name Amber couldn't remember joined in with a harmonica.

Though she knew better, she searched the crowd again for Derek. He wasn't there.

Her stomach clenched with shy restlessness, a queer feeling she'd fought since she'd begun to dress for the party. In her heart of hearts, she had anticipated this evening as much as Carolyn and Mariah had. It would give her a chance to see Derek in a setting unlike anything the two of them had encountered before. Amber pressed one hand to her abdomen and pushed the rocker into motion with her foot, as though movement would soothe her queasiness. It didn't.

She hadn't suffered such nervousness in years, not since she'd been in the throes of first love with Jeff Buchanan. What an odd sensation, dreading a man's arrival and yet fearing that he *wouldn't* come, and how extraordinary that Derek Fontaine would bring such emotions to her life again. She had been so sure her capacity for tender feelings had long since died.

Why, oh, why had she ever discovered Derek for the fraud he was? She would never have cared what he thought of her or his father if she hadn't realized his distant facade and clipped manner hid a certain kindhearted caring that went as deep as his soul. A man like that deserved the truth of her past—all of it—no matter what that meant for her.

"Good evening, Amber."

She jumped, stopping the rocker in her surprise. "Gideon."

He came up the front steps, and she conjured up a belated smile to soften her response. A second man—the first Negro Amber could recall ever having seen at the ranch—ascended the stairs just behind him.

"Amber, meet Simon Harrison, our newest hand," said Gideon.

She stood and smoothed her skirts, exchanging polite words with the man. Simon's keen brown eyes flickered warily, taking in the details around him in a reaction that seemed common since the war. Satisfied, he met her gaze frankly and spoke with a courteous assurance that earned her approval.

"Are you enjoying the party?" she asked as Six fiddled his way into the opening of "Home Sweet Home."

"It's quite a spread." Gideon turned and looked out over the crowd. "It's good for the men."

Was it her imagination, or did his good eye crinkle as his lips tilted upward at the corners? Amber's eyebrows rose.

"And you, Simon? Have you met everyone?"

"Most," he said with a nod, but a disturbing hardness flickered through the depths of his eyes. He spared a glance at the crowd, but his gaze settled on the distant horizon.

"Gideon?" Amber gazed from one man to the other. "What's wrong?"

His mouth tightened and his eye narrowed. "Nothing worth mentioning."

"Gideon." She dragged out his name and slanted him a firm look. "You know I don't like to be deceived about things."

He let out a long breath and shot her a glance of obvious

frustration—and perhaps a twinge of admiration? "It's just Whitley being Whitley."

"What now?"

"He'd rather not work with a man of color," Simon observed.

"I see." She searched until she found Whitley in the crowd, loitering near the dessert table. He stuffed whole cookies into his mouth and washed them down with long swallows of ale. She sighed. "Please don't worry, Simon. There won't be any problems, I'm sure."

"No, ma'am." The confidence in Simon's voice left her with little doubt that he would deal with any situation, whenever it became necessary.

"You're right, it will not be a problem."

The voice came from just below them. The men turned and Amber glimpsed a figure beyond them. She needn't see more to know it was Derek who spoke; the sound of his husky baritone seemed etched on her soul.

"Derek." Gideon offered the greeting. "I wondered when we'd see you."

"I thought I'd let the men have a little fun on their own, before the boss showed up."

"And when does the boss relax and have fun?" asked Gideon softly.

Derek didn't respond, but started up the stairs instead. "It will be dark soon. Would you see that the lamps are lit?"

"Of course." Gideon nodded in Amber's direction.

"It was a pleasure meeting you, ma'am." Simon followed Gideon down the steps.

"Thank you, gentlemen." Amber waved. "Enjoy yourselves."

An abrupt silence descended over the veranda until Amber's ears rang with it, somehow echoing louder than Six's fiddling or the conversations that eddied around them. She could not seem to convince herself to move, but stood there and stared at Derek.

He stared back.

"I've hardly seen you this week." The words came from nowhere, before she realized it.

"I've been busy." His gaze, shuttered as usual, didn't release her.

"Yes. We all have been."

"You've done a fine job. The party's a success."

She shook her head. "I'm hardly responsible. Your mother and Mariah did most of it. I only helped out where I was needed."

"Where they would let you, don't you mean?"

She shrugged. "The party means a great deal to them."

He nodded and glanced over the crowd. "That it does."

"Beau needed my help, in any case."

Derek looked back at her, a sharpness in his blue eyes that hadn't been there a moment ago. She cursed herself silently. Why had she mentioned Beau? She had explained about the embrace, but Derek had never gotten around to responding.

"Derek," she began, but a whoop from the crowd interrupted.

Micah waved from where he stood next to Six. "Howdy there, boss! Whaddaya say? Let's get us some real dancin' started. You bring Amber-girl down here an' show them how it's done."

A chorus of cheers rose up from the men, and a few started to clap their hands in rhythm. All eyes seemed trained upon them—including the scowling ones of Carolyn Fontaine.

Six grinned and swung into the first strains of "Lorena." Amber's heart sank. The song was much favored since the war, and it made the possibility of escaping Micah's suggestion far more difficult. But how could she allow herself to step into Derek's arms here, in front of everyone at the ranch? They would all see...and know she was falling in love with him.

*Falling in love with him?* Oh, God.

She swallowed, trapping a soft moan in her throat. An anxious look in Derek's direction provided no relief; he continued to stare at her with an intensity that even the deepening shadows didn't hide.

The catcalls grew louder, more insistent, and Derek's shoulders shifted as he pulled in a long breath. He held out his hand. "Dance with me."

"D-dance?" She stared at his hand, knowing with absolute certainty that if she took it, things would be forever changed between them.

The corner of his mouth lifted, giving her a glimpse of the man he worked so carefully to disguise. She could almost believe that his attempt at a smile carried the same uncertainties she felt.

He took her hand without another word and led her down the steps to the area that had been cleared for dancing. The cheers grew. Then she was in his arms, and outside burdens ceased to matter.

His arms enfolded her with a strength that offered comfort, safety, reassurance, and yet she could not forget the differences between them. He was hard where she was soft, firm and muscular where she possessed the roundness of gentle curves. His skin felt rough where their palms touched, and the splay of his hand at her lower back burned through her all-too-thin cotton dress.

*No, don't notice.* She stared at a place on his shirt, just below his shoulder, where her gaze fell naturally. *Not his touch, his scent, the sound of his breathing. Don't think at all!* Her thoughts rang with an alarming touch of desperation.

It was instinctive, this awareness she had of him. Equally automatic was the knowledge that she must not give in to it—him. And yet, close to Derek, with the heat of him coiling around her to bind her ever closer, she wanted nothing more than to press against him and stay there forever.

But not here. Or now. Not in front of the others.

"You're an excellent dancer," she murmured. Her voice sounded oddly hoarse, but at least she managed to speak.

"My mother made certain her sons were suitably equipped for our social obligations."

Amber dropped her head back and searched his face for clues to what he *wasn't* saying, but, predictably, there was nothing. "I'm sure you were very much in demand at parties and balls."

"No more so than any other young man from a wealthy family. Certainly not like Nathan."

"Why not?"

"He was more at home with Charleston aristocracy. He was the eldest son—the heir."

"You sound so cynical."

He shrugged. "The courting rituals never much impressed me. It was always about money and power. Breeding, like a stable filled with studs and fillies to be paired off."

The comparison prompted a faint heat to crawl up her neck. "But you weren't *paired off?*"

He slanted her a look and waltzed her away from where Carlos and his wife, proving more enthusiastic than accomplished, had joined in the dancing. Derek seemed to weigh his words carefully before he said, "I was engaged once, but we never married, if that's what you're asking."

A hollow disappointment settled low in her stomach. *Engaged.* He had once cared for a woman enough to ask her to be his wife. Had he loved her? Most certainly he had held her as he now held Amber, kissed her as he had kissed Amber. But they hadn't married.

"Why not?" she asked.

He anchored his hand more firmly at the base of her spine, exerting a subtle pressure that brought their lower bodies together with a stunning intimacy. She didn't mistake the significance of his action—or what she felt pressed against her.

"Derek?" She tried again, though her voice shuddered, sounding winded. She cleared her throat. "Why not?"

He gave her a shrewd look. "The war."

The war. Always the war. A weary resignation settled over her. Time and again the war provided the answer for a variety of changes that otherwise made little sense. After a while, a person had to stop asking *why*.

One question wouldn't be stifled, however. "Why didn't you marry her after the war?"

"She was already married."

"What—"

"Shh." He bent his head and whispered in her ear. "No more about the past and Mariah—"

"*Mariah!*" Amber reared back and would have kept going if his arms hadn't stopped her. Her eyes felt too wide to blink, and an odd roaring in her ears drowned out the waning strains of "Lorena."

"Amber, dammit."

She ignored his fierce tone of voice and the scowl that pulled his brows into a deep V. "You were engaged to Mariah?"

"It was a long time ago. She married my brother."

"But what about now? Your brother is—"

"No."

Amber didn't realize the music had stopped until she heard Derek's voice, firm and uncompromising without any background accompaniment. Other voices died, and the sound carried, gathering attention from all around them.

Derek jerked his head—as a signal? A moment later the first notes of "When This Cruel War Is Over" filtered through the air, and he pulled her tightly against him, so close she could feel the buttons of his shirt press against her breasts.

"Don't say another word," he hissed into her ear. "Not about Nathan and not about Mariah."

"But I—"

"Not another word. Maybe someday I'll tell you about it, but not tonight."

She accepted his pronouncement, but only because she had no other choice. Aside from their very public exposure, it took most of her concentration to keep in step with him. Their legs were tangled together, his thigh pressed familiarly between hers, and she all but straddled his leg.

Gradually Amber settled into this new, intimate stance. It almost became comfortable until a shout, loud and piercing, much like a genuine Rebel yell, diverted her. She stumbled and Derek slowed his pace.

"Lookee here!" Whitley yelled. "Gideon's got Miz Mariah up an' dancin'!"

And so he had. Gideon led Mariah into the cleared area and picked up the rhythm of the song with the smoothness of long practice. Fallen angels who danced as though they had invented the steps at God's bidding. What else could she expect from these men?

Did it matter? *Does anything really matter,* she found herself wondering, *as long as Derek continues to hold you?*

"I can feel your heart pounding against me."

The words were soft, Derek's lips moving at her temple. With aching slowness, she tilted her head back to look at him. His hair fell over his forehead, his shoulders, and provided an effective shadow for his eyes. Her fingers itched to brush the blond length back from his face, or perhaps test the softness of his beard, but she knew better. She wouldn't stop until she had pulled his head down far enough that his lips would touch hers.

She wasn't *falling* in love with him; it was already too late.

"What about you?" she whispered. "Is your heart pounding?"

He didn't answer. Instead he tucked her head under his chin and tempted her to rest her cheek against him. Gently he stroked his hand over her hair.

The song went on and on, and yet it ended much too soon. The men started up with a chorus of cheers and whistles that left her with little choice but to pull away from Derek, desperately leaving behind the intimacy of his touch.

"Thank you," she murmured quietly, her gaze darting almost anywhere but at him. If he looked into her eyes, he would see everything.

"Amber." He raised her head, using two fingers under her chin and giving her little choice but to look up into his face. His lips curved with a blatant sensuality, and he seemed to be leaning closer, his eyelids drifting downward.

"Boss?"

Amber hardly noticed Micah's interruption.

"What?" Derek stopped moving, but he didn't look away.

"Somebody's comin'. I dunno who—he's alone."

Derek looked up then, releasing Amber from his spell. She blinked and glanced around, noticing with abrupt discomfort that all eyes seemed to be upon them. All but Gideon's and Mariah's; they appeared intent only upon each other.

"Who's on watch tonight?" Derek demanded. Any softness she might have imagined earlier no longer existed.

"Whitley," Micah answered immediately. "But he didn't wanna miss none of the fun, so we're all kinda keepin' an eye out fer trouble."

"Whitley!"

Derek's tone left no doubt that he expected his summons to be answered—immediately. Fortunately, Whitley had the good sense to comply. "Yeah?"

"You had the watch tonight."

"Yes." He drew the word out as he narrowed his gaze.

"Did you understand there are no exceptions for this duty?"

"Yeah." The younger man's features settled into the familiar sullen expression that made him look like a pouting child. His voice, equal parts angry and whining, did nothing to relieve the effect. "But I—"

"No exceptions."

"I…yes."

"Fine. Now get out there and see who's coming. We'll discuss it later."

"Yes. *Boss.*" Whitley stalked away.

Amber gasped. His deliberate emphasis of Derek's title made his disrespect more than clear.

Micah shook his head. "Yer gonna have to do somethin' about that boy."

"I know." Derek sighed and ran a hand through his hair. Amber wished again that she had the privilege of touching him that way. "He's had enough chances."

Gideon approached with Mariah on his arm. "What's wrong?"

"Whitley," Derek answered, watching him ride out to meet the approaching stranger. "He missed watch, and someone's coming."

No one else spoke, which suited Amber just fine. It gave her the chance to look at Mariah through the cover of lowered lashes.

She had once been engaged to Derek. Had agreed to be *his wife*. But they hadn't married. She had married his brother instead. Why? Did she regret it? And, more importantly, with Nathan gone, did she want Derek to be hers again?

The possibilities chased around inside Amber's head with the fury of a windstorm, always ending with the same agonizing question: did Mariah want Derek to be hers again? And if she did, what could Amber do about it? Mariah had the better claim, having once been his fiancée—

and she wasn't saddled with the reputation of being the local soiled dove.

Mariah didn't seem to exhibit any particular jealousy, just a general dislike of Amber. And yet there had been moments such as her interrupting them in Derek's study. Had she entered the room deliberately?

So many questions, all without answers and leaving Amber distinctly uneasy. It came as a relief when Whitley rode up, jerking his horse to a stop. The stranger followed a few paces behind.

"Here he is, *boss*." Whitley scowled, snapping out the words with the same insolence, and waved behind him with a carelessness that suggested strangers were everyday arrivals. Then he wheeled his horse around and rode back the way he'd come, presumably to keep watch as he'd been assigned.

The stranger rode to the very edge of the light.

"Hello, little brother. Looks like you've done damn fine for yourself, Yankee or not."

## Chapter Eighteen

"Nate?" Derek peered through the shadows, desperately trying to identify the features of the brother he'd grown up with. The boy whose understanding and sympathy and sense of humor had seen them through their formative years as Jordan's sons. A man who, like many others, had gone through years of hell. A man who was—dead.

"Nathan, my God, is it you?"

Derek turned to look behind him. Mariah stared straight ahead, her mouth slack, and all that kept her standing was Gideon's arm around her shoulders.

"Derek." Amber whispered his name, and her fingers curled over his forearm. If she meant to reassure him, he appreciated the gesture, but her touch was ice cold and she trembled.

"*Nathan,* my God!"

The belated screech came from Carolyn, and she slumped in her seat beneath the cottonwood tree. Beau was there to tend her. Thank God.

Nathan, meanwhile, remained on horseback, observing them. No one spoke, and the silence became progressively heavy until it seemed to resound as loud as any cannon fire Derek had ever heard. When he could stand it no longer, he offered the only greeting that occurred to him.

"Welcome to the Double F."

The words effected a liberation of sorts. Amber released his arm and scooted closer to his side, while Mariah roused herself from Gideon's grip and stepped forward. "We thought you were dead!" She held out one hand to her husband, moving with uncharacteristic awkwardness. "They told us you were dead! They sent us your things."

Nathan shrugged. "I guess they didn't expect me to make it, but I surprised them. I surprised a lot of folks. Especially the guards in that Yankee prison camp." His gaze burned into Derek like the singe of a torch held too close.

"Where?" The crack of Derek's voice made it a demand.

"Prison camp!" Mariah sounded much like Derek. "You were in a prison camp?"

"In Illinois. Camp Douglas by name. A sorrier hell I've never seen—but that's the Yankees for you."

Derek forced back the images and swallowed the words that immediately came to mind. He knew how prisoners of war were treated on both sides; he'd seen his share of horrors on and off the battlefield. But his personal sorrow and regret would hardly be welcomed.

Even so, there were other things he could say. Places he could mention such as Libby Prison in Richmond, Camp Davidson on the edge of Savannah—and Andersonville. The notorious Confederate prison camp in Georgia had carried a reputation that outstripped all others, so vile that the commandant had been hanged for treason. Now didn't seem the best time for debate, however; it would only belittle Nathan's suffering. Nor did it seem particularly wise to advance reminders of how much he and Nathan differed in their general outlooks on life and politics.

"I'll see to your horse, if you like, sir, while you get reacquainted with your family." Gideon made the sudden offer as he stepped forward.

Thank God. Someone could think—act—beyond the incredulous *reactions* that weighed Derek down. And as if in confirmation, a small feminine noise whispered softly through the night. Derek glanced around. Mariah stood squarely between Nathan and Gideon, a most peculiar mixture of expressions bathing her face: shock, dismay—horror?

Nathan laughed, but it was an ugly sound that carried little humor. It effectively redirected all attention toward him. "Why not?" He slid from the horse and grabbed his saddlebags. Gideon led the animal away, leaving Nathan to face the group. "Coming out on the winning side of the war seems to have set you up right nice," he commented to Derek.

Any lingering doubts about his brother disappeared as Derek stared at the man who stood defiantly before him. Nathan Fontaine was, indeed, alive and well and here at the Double F. The men were of a similar height, and their features resembled each other enough that their brotherhood could never be doubted. *Half* brotherhood, at least.

"Nate…"

"What?" He dropped the saddlebags to the ground and swaggered to a stop before Derek. "What exactly could you have to say? Do you want to tell me how sorry you are? How bad you feel that we lost everything—country, home and family? Or do you want to remind me that you were right and I was wrong? That I backed the wrong side, you picked the winner, and this is what happens when you lose?"

The bitterness in Nathan lowered his voice to a snarl, his face a mask of fury. It energized the air all around them with a certain tense anxiety. No one responded, not with a sound, but why would they? The words were meant for Derek and no one else.

Amber fumbled for his hand. He couldn't acknowledge her touch, and yet he found himself clinging to her fingers.

Somehow it helped him focus on the accusations Nathan had thrust at him. The words were all wrong; too much remained unsaid. Lost was the closeness they'd known in childhood, growing up united against an irate father and ineffective mother. Lost like everything else since that goddamned war.

"No." Derek shook his head. "I didn't want to say any of those things. I wanted to say how glad I am you're alive."

"Now why don't I believe that? Didn't you do everything you could to see just the opposite?"

"No. I didn't."

"You enlisted in the goddamn Union army, for chrissake! You spent four years trying to kill me, or any of the men and boys we grew up with who crossed your path. Are you telling me that whole sorry time meant nothing? That it was for my own good?"

"It wasn't like that, Nathan, and you know it."

"What *was* it like, then? How the hell did you get yourself set up here with your own little empire, while Palmetto and all the rest of it is gone? Tossed aside like it meant nothing. But then, that never really belonged to you, did it?"

Amber took an odd, wheezing breath, but that was the only sound. Derek jerked his hand from hers.

"You knew?" He fixed a fierce gaze on his brother.

"Hell, yes, I knew. I've known since the day you went off to join your Yankee friends. Father told me, and I understood a lot of things after that."

Understood, when Derek had struggled with it endlessly. Struggled with it still. "You had the advantage then. I didn't find out until the end of the war. But if you know so much, then understand *this*. There are days when I thank God I'm not the son of Jordan Fontaine."

Derek's heart pounded, and the blood seemed to race through his body. It almost exhilarated him to say the words, as though the bonds of the past *could* be severed. As though he didn't have to pretend that the day he'd arrived at the Double F was the day he'd been born. As though all the things left unsaid and undone in his life could somehow be righted.

"This ranch was left to me by *my father*," he declared in a deliberate voice. "It offers a future to us all. Mother and Mariah are welcome here—and you can have a home here, too."

Amber laid a gentle hand on his arm and squeezed lightly. "Perhaps you should go inside and finish this discussion." She gestured behind her. Most of the ranch hands had gathered as close as they dared, listening avidly. Beau, meanwhile, had managed to see that Carolyn regained a measure of her composure.

"I'll stay out here and get things cleaned up," Amber added after a moment, when no one else spoke. "Beau will help me."

"And who do we have here?" Nathan demanded, as though just noticing Amber's presence. He nodded toward her with heavy insolence. "You got a woman here to see to your comfort, in addition to *my wife?*"

"That's unfair," Mariah gasped.

Derek glanced from her to Amber. Torchlight revealed equally pale faces. "There is nothing between Mariah and me. There hasn't been since her father broke our engagement the day I told him of my plans to head North."

"You think I believe that?" Nathan glared at them all.

"Derek...inside," Amber urged again.

"No, by God." He glared at Nathan, and a profusion of unaccustomed words crowded at the back of his throat. "We'll say what needs to be said, and we'll say it here and now. What is it you think—that Jordan bravely hung on while the rest of the world deserted him? He didn't. He went mad—over that edge of sanity we joked about as boys. And do you know who held things together until the bitter end?''

"My selfless little brother," Nathan drawled.

"No," Derek snapped. "Your wife. I'd done my part already. I damn near got myself killed trying to save Palmetto during the war. For you. I didn't know you'd been reported dead, or that no one considered me part of this family. No one ever had."

"You expect me to feel sorry for you? You *betrayed* us."

"I don't expect a damn thing except for you to *listen* to me. You think it was so easy during the war? When days and weeks—years—went by without a letter? Not one damn letter. Did you know I was with Sherman? Did you hear a lot about his troops having it so *easy?*"

"No. I heard they were butchers and rapists and thieves."

Derek's gut clenched as if he'd taken a body blow, and he stepped back. He sucked in a long, harsh breath, grappling for composure, and finally managing to speak from sheer strength of will. "I was with him from the beginning. It seemed like a good idea at first, to go west, away from Georgia and South Carolina. Then came the march, and I was there through the whole of it. When we headed for Charleston, I lied and all but deserted to get to Palmetto. I pretended I was on Sherman's staff, that troops couldn't ransack and burn the place because he was going to use it as his headquarters."

Derek sucked in a sharp half breath. "The old man told me the truth then and disowned me. He thought you were dead, and he was eaten up with bitterness and rage."

"How very touching. You expect me to feel sorry for you?" Nathan repeated the bitter question. "I don't. Why should I? You didn't have it so bad—and here you are now, with everything, while I have nothing."

"What is it that you think I have, Nathan? I have a piece

of ground. My family? They'll take my protection and my money, but they tolerate me at best. Friends? I haven't had one in six years. The *Yankees* didn't trust a Southerner, and the Rebs sure as hell weren't going to trust a Southern Yankee. So just what is it you think I have that you want?''

"You have—"

Gunfire cut off whatever Nathan had meant to say.

Derek took off without hesitating, emptying his mind of all but the concentration he needed for the next crisis. The useful trick he'd learned from his father's tyranny, and employed so effectively during the war and beyond, had never let him down.

He headed for the corral, where the shots had come from. Amber called his name, but he didn't slow down.

"Stay here," he shouted over his shoulder without looking back. "Beau, get the women in the house."

Dammit! He should have known better than to let his guard down. Why had he ever agreed to this party? And when he discovered Whitley wasn't doing his job, Derek should have fired him on the spot and taken the guard duty himself. Now, because of his own lack of foresight, the rustlers—murderers—might have made it all the way to the house.

A shadow separated itself from the far side of the corral, the movement punctuated by a sharp grunt. Derek recognized the voice and skidded to a halt just shy of the bunkhouse. "Gideon?" he called softly.

"Yep."

"What happened?" He set a more moderate pace.

"Our shooter's back—alone, I think—but he's gone now."

"You all right?"

"Will be. Bullet grazed my arm, but everything works fine. Stings like holy hell, but a little whiskey ought to take care of that."

"Derek!" Amber ran up behind him, followed by Nathan and Mariah. Beau brought up the rear with a lantern.

Derek turned to glare at them all. "I thought I told you to get the women into the house."

"You ever tried to make these ladies do anything they didn't want to?" Beau's resignation might have been comical under better circumstances. "Best I could do was get your mama inside. Micah's staying with her."

"All right." Derek couldn't argue with Beau's decision. And he knew better than to think he could keep the truth from any of them—now. "Gideon's been shot."

Amber immediately stepped forward. "Come with me. I'll fix you up."

"I'm fine." Gideon moved back. "It's just a scratch."

"Maybe so. But a scratch can turn into something worse if you don't take care of it."

"This won't—"

"Gideon, you know better than to argue with her. I'll take care of things here."

"There, you see?" She took Gideon's uninjured arm and steered him toward the cookhouse. "Everything will be fine."

Derek watched Amber lead Gideon away, staring into the darkness even when he could no longer see them. It struck him how willingly she came to his aid, helped him, supported him. Emotionally and physically. It wasn't the first time.

In more years than he wanted to count—since before the war, at the very least—he had been alone. So alone he no longer knew how to let anyone close. Not even a beautiful, desirable woman like Amber.

She, however, didn't seem to need his permission for intimacy. Nathan thought Derek had *everything?* He didn't, but it seemed he had more than he'd thought. He had Amber.

He blinked, so startled by the thought that he shot an

irritated glance at those around him. Most of the hands had slowly gathered. "Where's Whitley?"

"Ain't seen him." A voice came from the darkness. "Guess he rode out a bit fur to check on things."

"Someone get him."

"I'll go." Simon stepped forward.

"Fine." Derek nodded sharply. "The rest of you grab a lantern and spread out. With all this commotion, I doubt if we'll find anything, but we might get lucky."

The soft mutterings sounded like indignant irritation, but slowly the men began to move. Derek didn't waste time wondering about the uncharacteristic response; the answers were clear enough. Not only had his command effectively ended the party, but the knowledge of his wartime choices was bound to cause something of a ruckus.

He swallowed a weary sigh. He could only deal with one crisis at a time. The questions surrounding his service in the Union army would have to wait until tomorrow.

Derek stood at the window of his darkened study, a shot of whiskey in his hand. It was going on midnight, and a sliver of moon did little to stave off the desolate blackness that stared back at him. He looked out over Amber's garden, or where it would be visible in the light of day. For the moment, it was enough simply to know it was there.

Not everything changed. Crops still grew, requiring hard work and care, and tomorrow he would see Amber out there, tending to her chores. The rest of his world might be whirling out of control, but that, at least, remained the same.

Nathan was alive. *Alive!* The arrival of his brother had both astounded and exhilarated Derek as nothing before. And, in the end, nothing had ever hurt more.

*Yankee.* Nathan had said the word with such bitterness that it bordered on hatred. He had glared at Derek as though he'd deliberately betrayed him.

Derek raised the shot glass and tossed back the whiskey. "I didn't do a damn thing but survive."

And Nathan had done the same. Thank God.

"Derek?"

Amber's voice drifted through the darkness and sent a shiver of reaction up his spine. He straightened and half turned from the window.

"It's late. You should be in bed."

"I couldn't sleep."

"No, I don't suppose you could."

"Did you find anything?"

"Nope. He got away clean."

She didn't reply, and he turned back to the window. Sounds from behind him pinpointed her movements, but it was the faint scent of vanilla that warned him when she came up behind him.

"Is it true?" she asked in a small voice.

He didn't move or wonder what she was asking. "Yes."

"You served in the Union army?"

"Yes."

"And that story you told me about Shiloh?"

"True."

"You never said you fought for the North."

"It didn't matter. Death and horror were no less for the North—or South."

"You could have told me the truth." Hurt curled in her voice like a shadow. "You could have trusted me."

He shrugged. "When you've spent as many years as I have on the fringe of trust, you forget how to recognize it."

"I thought…things might have been different with me."

"You're right…." The words, though they came from his own lips, astonished him with the ache that lay beneath them. She *was* right. "Things should have been different. You deserve better."

"Shh." She touched his shoulder gently, seeming to accept his apology. "Never mind now. We'll sort it out later."

"Amber, why are you here?"

"I watched you tonight. Nathan was so angry, he didn't care what he said or how he hurt you. You didn't try to hurt him back. You tried to explain instead."

Derek made a rough noise, disputing her words. At the time, he'd wanted to say all the things he'd thought he'd never have the chance to say.

"It's not your fault that he's still blind after all these years."

He dropped the shot glass and turned, reaching for her and pulling her close. Her hips met his, and he dropped his arm to her waist. They stood like that for long enough that she gradually began to relax against him. She rested her cheek against his shoulder, fitting as naturally as though they had touched that way for most of their lives.

"How is it that you understand?" he finally asked, unable to ignore the question any longer. "Why would you want to? I haven't given you much reason."

She looked up at him, turning just enough so he could pull her around and pin her between his body and the wall. She didn't protest.

"My father wasn't much of a Confederate supporter." She tilted her head back, resting it against the window frame. The moon shed enough light that he could just make out her features. "We came here from St. Louis after my mother and brother died in a fire, but my parents were raised in Massachusetts. Papa didn't believe in slavery, but he wasn't certain that giving the Federal government absolute power over states' rights was a wise thing, either. I don't know if he ever completely reconciled the issue in himself."

"And he survived the war that way?"

"He struggled. I've always believed it contributed to his being killed. If he'd been a stronger Southerner, the rustlers might have tried another method of warning him. As it was, they must have felt murder was justified.''

Derek couldn't keep from touching her. She stood so close, with that delicious scent and warmth that drew him. Taking a small step, all that separated them, he arched his hips against hers. He brought one hand up to rest his fingertips against her cheek.

"Why are you telling me this?" He stroked the softness of her skin.

He felt her smile more than saw it. "I wanted you to understand that I never considered myself the staunch Southern patriot that others expected me to be. There was guilt in that. And as men formed regiments and left to fight, I got caught up some in the fervor of secession. It seemed exciting, daring…romantic. But when the fighting started, I understood the realities of war even from a distance, and any zealousness disappeared. War became only man's insanity, and no one seemed to notice a woman's sacrifice or worry. So many men didn't come home, and those who came home had changed.''

Something within him tightened. "Someone special?"

"Yes."

Derek's hand stilled, and Amber continued. "After Jeff came home, he described himself as having fought at Gettysburg with John Bell Hood. For him, that said it all. He had a terrible bitterness that ate away at him. I struggled to understand the hatred and anger. I thought, with time and my love, he would get past it and see how destructive that thinking was.''

"But that didn't happen?"

"Not while we were close, and now I'll never know. After my father was killed, Jeff wouldn't see me again."

"He—what?"

She brought one hand up to Derek's, covering his fingers with hers. "It's all right. We weren't engaged, though I had hoped we would marry. I should have known I was no match for Eliza Bates.'' Amber smiled—crookedly, Derek thought.

"What did she have to do with it?"

"She'd always coveted him as a son-in-law. After my father's death, Jeff married her daughter, Melinda.''

"Your—Jeff is Eliza Bates's son-in-law?'' Guilt kicked Derek in the gut as he recalled accusations he'd made. *Are you saying...you didn't try to seduce Eliza Bates's son-in-law?*

"Yes, but that doesn't matter anymore.'' She straightened, and the movement pressed her body against the length of him. She didn't shift away, even when his body hardened blatantly with an immediate response. ''What matters is you and me.''

"Us?'' Something about the word warmed him. It sounded like he belonged somewhere, to someone.

"We've both suffered. We've made mistakes. Even recent ones. But we've done some things right, too.''

"What have we done that's so right?'' He wrapped his arms around her and pulled her close enough to ease—and torment— his erection.

"This.'' She slid her arms around his neck and urged his head down. And then her lips found his.

# Chapter Nineteen

Amber lost control of the kiss in only moments. For a heartbeat, Derek's mouth cushioned hers softly, then he parted his lips and his tongue swept forward. He teased her with a confident, dangerous expertise, the promise of untold delight just beyond the horizon, until she opened her mouth for him.

She tilted her head back quite instinctively, never questioning the need to give him greater access to her mouth. Her breasts flattened against the muscled hardness of his chest, delighting and exciting her. A soft moan originated somewhere deep within her. Her heart pounded with a heavy beat, so loud she thought they must hear it as far away as the bunkhouse.

"You taste good," Derek muttered against her mouth.

"Mmm." She could offer nothing more. His words put an idea into her head, and she could think of nothing save *tasting him.*

Her tongue darted forward with a will of its own, testing the fullness of his bottom lip before she retreated. It was over too quickly, hardly satisfying her, and giving rise to an unaccustomed longing. It made her brave enough to dare the kiss again, and with a greater degree of boldness.

Derek seemed to approve; he parted his lips and gave

her generous access to the warm cavern of his mouth. She took her time, learning each curve and ridge with delighted fascination.

"You taste like whiskey." The breathless words came later, when she had to either break the kiss or faint.

"Do you like it?"

"Very much."

He kissed her again, thoroughly, wresting command of the moment—and her—until her senses sizzled with life. Her fingers trembled as she traced them up the column of his neck to tangle in the silken strands of his hair. Meanwhile her tongue traded forays with his, playing a heady game of hide and seek that stripped her of the ability to breathe. His hips flexed against hers, outlining the hard ridge of his manhood against her belly. Shockingly, she found herself duplicating the movement.

Derek groaned from deep in his chest, and the kiss intensified, if such a thing were possible. His hands came up to cradle her head, his fingers digging into her hair and destroying the hairstyle she had created especially for the evening. Her mother's treasured heirloom combs clattered to the floor, but she hardly noticed. Nothing mattered but Derek.

Dear Lord, he was dangerous! The thought occurred to her with a fleeting awareness that heightened her sensibilities. Dangerous and wild and heady and elemental.

She kissed him—or he kissed her—until she had no breath left, save what they shared between them. She tore her mouth from his and dropped her forehead to his chest, welcoming that first gulp of air. Why, she wondered through a haze, was it necessary to waste time breathing when they could be *kissing?*

Derek arched closer, and she spread her legs for balance. He took advantage of the moment, tucking one leg between her thighs and pressing against her most intimately.

*"Derek."*

"I want you, Amber." He said the words softly, fiercely, against the curve of her ear. He stroked his tongue around the oval contour, nipping at her earlobe. "I've wanted you for weeks. You must know that."

"Yes." She could hardly answer over the cacophony in her head. The exultation, the hesitation, the rightness…the knowledge that they had been headed for this from perhaps the moment they met. And yet, how could it be destined when she had left unanswered the one vital question that meant so much to him?

"Derek, I need to tell you…about Richard."

"Richard?" He growled the name. "I don't want to talk about him. Ever. He doesn't matter. Your past with him doesn't matter. He's gone and we're here. I want you and you want me."

"Yes." She swallowed and wet her lips. "But—"

She gasped as Derek swept her up in his arms. As though she weighed no more than a feather, he carried her through the darkness with the assurance of a man who knew what he wanted. His trademark boldness took them down the hall, past the staircase and into her bedroom, where he shut the door with his shoulder.

Across the room, Derek lowered her gently to the bed. Shadows disguised all but his broadest movements. A sudden hiss warned her moments before a soft flare of light bathed the room with a tempered golden glow.

She blinked and looked up, abruptly and overwhelmingly shy. She was sprawled across the bed like a wanton, while he stared back, tall and strong and bold. She swallowed and moistened her suddenly dry lips with her tongue. His eyes sparked with a flash of brilliant blue light, following her every movement.

"The light," she whispered.

"I want to see you," he declared in a low, husky voice. "I want you to see me. I don't want anything between us, not even darkness." One knee on the mattress, he lowered himself beside her. "I've thought of it for too long."

His words sent a wave of longing through her. "I...yes." She reached for him.

He took her mouth in a kiss that differed from the urgency of before. Slow and leisurely, it was no less devastating.

Amber kissed him back, everything within her opening up to him, and he stole her breath, her heart and her soul. She didn't care, would offer it all again if he desired. She would give him anything if he held her, cherished her, loved her in return.

A heartfelt, abiding warmth spread through her, and she tightened her arms around him. Uncertainties about loving Derek had disappeared. Loving him was like breathing: automatic and necessary for her survival.

Amber held him close, matched him kiss for kiss, until he pulled away with a soft growl. He pushed himself up onto one elbow. "I want to see you." He repeated his earlier words and reached for the buttons of her calico dress.

She caught a ragged breath but didn't move, even when he fumbled. The buttons were small, running from the collar of her dress to her waist. "Damn things." He frowned and glanced up through the veil of his lashes. "Hell of a night for you to come looking for me in your *dress*."

She flushed and tried to offer a knowing smile, but it felt all too unsteady. "You've seen me in my nightgown too often as it is."

"Now I'll see you as I've always wanted to. Wearing nothing but me."

His words robbed her of her breath, and a finely drawn image flooded her mind. Derek, naked as he was surely soon to be, covering her equally naked body like a second skin. She shivered and her nipples peaked in shameful anticipation.

Derek pushed himself to his knees and began to ease the

dress from her shoulders with slow certainty. She watched his every movement until the blue fire of his gaze caught hers. Full-blooded desire sparkled there, and the knowledge that he could want her that much sent a new wave of longing through her.

Her heart pounded, and an emptiness she'd never known before settled low in her stomach. She needed…something. She needed *Derek.*

Reacting—not thinking—she raised her hips to accommodate him. A moment later she lay before him in nothing more than a dainty white chemise, petticoat and pantalets.

"Are you nervous?"

She whipped her gaze up to his. He traced one finger from the heavy beat of her pulse at the base of her throat, to her collarbone, over the rising slope of her breast, and then he flattened his palm over her heart. "Your heart is pounding."

"I'm…I don't think it's all nerves."

He smiled, a wolfish promise she couldn't misinterpret. *Passion, desire.* She recognized it on his face—and in herself, for the first time. Certainly, she'd known such emotions were said to exist, but she could never have guessed what they would feel like until she'd known Derek.

He tugged at the buttons of his shirt and shed the garment. She hadn't seen him shirtless since his wound had begun to heal, and she reached for him now.

"You mended well." She rested her fingers near the pink, slightly puckered flesh, soothing the wound with a gentle caress.

"Thanks to you."

"I hate it that you were shot. I hate that I may have been able to prevent it. I hurt—"

"Shh." He pressed two fingers against her lips. "Don't. It's over." He traced the fullness of her bottom lip. "Concentrate on this."

He took her hand and placed it flat in the middle of his

chest, fingers splayed wide over the smooth ridge of muscle. His skin felt so very warm, and her fingers flexed in involuntary appreciation.

Ever so slowly, as though he had all the time in the world, Derek reached for her chemise and pushed the straps over her shoulders, binding her arms to her sides. She dropped her hand from his chest reluctantly, disappointed to no longer touch him. Then she forgot everything except the sight of his hungry gaze as he pulled at the thin lawn fabric and bared her breasts.

Dear Lord. No other man had seen her thus, and a sudden shy desperation urged her to cover herself. He spoke before she could move.

"You are so very beautiful. Just as I imagined."

The hushed awe in his voice did much to ease the need to hide. He swept one hand over the fullness of her breast, his palm dragging across the summit, where her nipple had puckered in anticipation, and she forgot things as trifling as modesty.

"You make me feel beautiful."

He smiled, an extraordinary expression…a promise of satisfaction to come. The magnificence of his face distracted her, and before she quite knew how, he had whisked her petticoats and pantalets from her. In a heartbeat, she lay naked before him.

He knelt before her and stared, his eyes darkened to an indigo unlike anything she had ever seen, and his frank admiration warmed her, even reassured her. In that instant, Amber knew she had been made for this night, this moment. She had been made for Derek and he for her. Nothing else before or after could ever matter in this same way.

"I want to see you, too," she whispered, and started to sit, to reach for him.

"Lie back." He gave her a gentle push, and she fell back without protest. He rewarded her with a quick, fierce kiss, then stood. He freed the buttons of his pants and shed them and his drawers without ceremony. In moments, he was as gloriously naked as she.

His firmly muscled chest tapered to narrow hips and powerful thighs. At their juncture jutted the most elemental part of him, thick and huge. Even with an idea of what to expect, she had not anticipated he would look quite like…this. Dry medical descriptions and that part of him pressing against her, disguised by barriers of cloth, had not prepared her for the reality of him.

"*You* are beautiful," she breathed. "Splendid. But are you sure this will…work?"

"Men aren't beautiful." He sank to the bed and laughed, a low, husky sound that sent shivers racing down her spine. "You needn't worry about it working. I know what to do."

She might have said something more, but he took her mouth in another long, breath-stealing kiss. Amber sighed, welcoming him home, and gave herself up to be thoroughly seduced.

"Let me show you what I know." He pulled away and smoothed the loose tendrils of hair back from her face. He sent his fingertips on a journey over the curve of her jaw, the length of her neck, the plane of her chest. His hand moved lower, over the plumpness of her breast, the curve of her waist, the full arch of her hip. She caught a ragged half breath.

"Your skin is so soft." Derek whispered the words against her throat, and she felt them as much as heard them. He nipped her skin lightly with his teeth, then bathed the feigned wound with his lips and tongue. He shifted and repeated the tiny bite at her collarbone, then at the rise of her breast.

Amber arched against him, and Derek growled softly. "Do you like that, angel?" he asked. He tested the weight of her breast with his palm. "What about this?"

His fingers danced over her skin until they circled her nipple. She found herself straining for his touch there, but still he resisted. And then, so lightly she wondered if she imagined it, she felt the first brush of his fingertips.

"Oh!" She couldn't hold back the word, and then she lost her breath completely as his lips replaced his fingers. He lavished equal attention on both breasts, suckling one and then the other until they felt tender and swollen with need.

She shoved her trembling fingers into his hair, holding him close and urging him toward…something. She couldn't say what, and yet she knew it was there. Perhaps it involved the inexplicable dampness that suddenly appeared between her legs. She could only trust the instincts that urged her onward.

Derek shifted over her, and Amber moved with him. She ran her hands across his back, testing the muscled warmth of his skin and clasping him to her. She trailed her fingers down the ridge of his spine, as far as the curve of his buttocks, hesitating there, indecisive until he swept the decision from her.

"Touch me," he groaned, and caught her lips in a deep kiss that all but consumed her. He twisted onto his side, next to her, and pulled her hand to him.

He was hot and hard, yet smooth and soft. She tested the size and feel of him, her fingers curled around him, and found she approved. Very much. With a soft sigh, she stroked her palm up and down, gauging his length and appreciating how snugly he fit into her hand. She tightened her grip ever so slightly, and his erection flexed in her hand.

"Stop. God, stop," he groaned in a tortured voice, jerking her hand back, and he moved over her once more.

She blinked and tried to focus on more than pure sensation. Derek's face had become drawn, his eyes closed, and he clenched his jaw with obvious effort.

"Are you all right?" Was that hoarse, throaty voice hers? "Did I hurt you?"

He opened his eyes, and she thought she might drown

in their sparkling blue depths. Then he smiled with wry acceptance and gave her a quick, thorough kiss. "No, honey, you didn't hurt me. You did everything right. Too right."

"How can it be *too right?*"

"You're right, it can't." He nuzzled her throat. "Nothing tonight could be too right. It's perfect."

He caught her mouth in another soul-stealing kiss, and she gave herself willingly. Dimly she noticed his hand teasing her breast, her hip, her leg, and then back up. He toyed with the curls at the juncture of her thighs and she squirmed, embarrassed for him to find the unmistakable wetness there.

"It's all right, angel. Don't worry." He nibbled at her bottom lip, somehow avoiding her as she tried to catch his mouth with hers. "I want to be sure you're ready for me."

*Ready?* She had been ready for days, weeks, months— years. Perhaps all her life, only she hadn't known it until tonight.

His fingers swept between her legs, probing delicately until he found a tiny bud of pure sensation. "Derek!" His name came from nowhere and everywhere, a breathy cry that sounded foreign to her. She could hardly breathe as his fingers stroked her damp, swollen flesh.

"I know." He punctuated the words with a kiss that captured her attention. And then, before she quite realized it, he slipped his finger inside her. Amazingly, her hips flexed against his hand with a will of their own.

"I know, honey," he said again, withdrawing his hand. He shifted, settling between her thighs, and she parted them for him without a second thought.

"Wider, darlin'," he muttered against her mouth. "Wrap your legs around me."

She did as he asked, and recognized a different probing, but she couldn't deny the demands of his kiss. His tongue darted past her lips, imitating the motions of his manhood against her femininity, and she had neither the heart nor the will to deny him either. She *wanted* to be one with him, in every way.

"You're so tight. I'm sorry, angel, I may not be able to last very long this time."

"Derek?" He pushed against her, filling her, stretching her. She stirred, trying to accommodate his body, and then a sharp lance of pain pinned her to the bed. "Derek?" she repeated, gasping this time.

"Amber." He stared at her, heavy-lidded, his lips swollen from their kisses and his face drawn with obvious shock. She moved again, trying to find some comfort, and he moved with her.

"Don't!" He closed his eyes and clenched his teeth. "Jesus, don't move."

"Why?" Despite his demand, she did it again, searching for a more comfortable position.

"Christ!" He began to move then, pushing himself faster and deeper than she had ever thought possible. Somehow she found herself moving with him, and gradually the pain eased to mild discomfort. Still he thrust against her, over and over, until a curious sensation began to build within her. For just a moment, she thought she could catch a glimpse of the wildness that drove him.

"Amber. Oh, Jesus, honey." The words sounded torn from him. He threw back his head and thrust against her— hard—once more. A heartbeat later he collapsed against her with the bonelessness of a man who had nothing left to give.

Derek struggled to awareness after a few moments. No woman had ever responded to him as Amber had. She satisfied him in ways he hadn't known were possible.

She shifted beneath him, and her body clenched around his. Amazingly, he felt himself awaken and begin to stir again. And why not? She was so hot and wet and tight around him—

*So tight…* Reality intruded, abolishing the lusty, wanton thoughts. He pushed himself up on one hand and stared down at her. Her cheeks were pink, flushed from their love-making. Her eyes sparkled like crystalline green emeralds, and her lips were rosy and swollen from his kisses.

"Derek," she whispered, smiling as she brushed a lock of hair back from his face.

He pulled away before she could touch him again, carefully easing their bodies apart. She made a small, breathy sound, as though his movements caused her particular discomfort. And, he supposed with some detachment, they probably did.

He climbed from the bed and headed for the washstand in one corner. Dampening a cloth, he glanced down. There it was, the proof he had known he would find. The proof that exhilarated him. The proof he dreaded.

Blood. Amber's blood.

"Derek?"

He wiped himself clean, settled his features in the familiar, distant mask he knew he'd perfected, and turned to face her. She looked so very inviting, reclining on the bed with such innate sensuousness, propped up on one elbow. Her come-hither smile drew him inexorably nearer. Her magnificent auburn hair draped over her like a curtain, hiding most of her breasts from his view, though an impudent nipple peeked through.

*Holy Christ, what have I done?*

"Why—" His voice gave out abruptly, and he cleared his throat before starting again. "You were a virgin."

The smile slowly died. "Yes."

"You said you would never lie to me."

She pushed herself up until she was sitting, her legs tucked beneath her. Her gaze remained steady as she fum-

bled with the bedcovers, grasping a loose piece of cloth—
his shirt—and pulling it on. "I didn't lie."

"You were never Richard's lover."

"I never said I was."

"You never said you weren't, either." She shrank back
when Derek started forward, so he stopped. "You never
denied a thing—you refused to answer. It's as good as a
lie."

"You asked once, when you first got here. I didn't answer then—I couldn't." She shook her head, sending her
hair drifting about her shoulders. "But later, when I got to
know you, I *wanted* to tell you. I even tried, earlier tonight,
in the study. You wouldn't listen. You said it didn't matter."

The words echoed in his memory, and he even thought
he'd meant them—then. Now he regretted them with all his
being.

*What's wrong with you?* demanded a fierce voice that
somehow managed to sound markedly reasonable, as well.
*You care for Amber as you have never cared for another
woman. You should be glad she was never lovers with Richard. She's yours. Only yours.*

The words that came from his mouth, however, said different things, angry things. "How could you let everyone
no, encourage them!—to believe you were Richard's mistress?"

She rose to her knees. "The others don't matter. If it's
any consolation, I never meant for you to find out this way.
I meant to tell you tonight, to explain things before this—"
her hand fluttered around her "—went any further. But
Nathan arrived and Gideon was shot, and it didn't seem so
important anymore."

"Not important?" Derek stalked toward the bed, pretending he didn't see her flinch as he grabbed his pants. He
jerked them on with a fierceness that threatened to rip the
fabric. He almost wished he could tear them to shreds.

Maybe that would help ease the bitterness that threatened to choke him.

Amber scooted to the far side of the bed, watching through wary eyes. She pressed her lips together and waited until he'd fastened his trousers. Then she asked softly, "Can I explain?"

"What is there to explain? Everyone considers you a— a soiled dove, and until this moment, it was a lie. Until we made it true. You've had weeks to tell me, but never in all that time were you willing to be honest with me."

"A soiled dove," she said, her voice so brittle Derek wondered that she could speak at all. "Yes. Well, I was stupid, you see. I was sure I couldn't trust you at first. If people I had known for *years,* and who had known me, didn't believe me, why would you? I was afraid to take the chance.

"But then, when I got to know you better and things started to change between us, I wanted somebody to believe in me—just once—no matter what. I wanted someone to trust me, to know that I wouldn't do the things people said."

"How could I trust you?" he demanded. "You didn't trust *me.* It has to work both ways, or it won't work at all."

"And there you have it." She seemed to wilt before his eyes. "Two wounded souls who don't know a thing about trust. We expected each other to be all the things that we can't be ourselves."

He stepped back, feeling oddly as though she had just punched him, and shoved an agitated hand through his hair. "You could have trusted me. I thought you knew that."

"How? *How* would I know?"

"I proved it to you."

She shook her head sadly. "And I proved myself to you, more than once. But neither one of us saw it, did we?"

"I—" He wanted to counter the truth in her words, but

he couldn't. Dammit, this was all wrong! "I have to think."
He turned toward the door.

"Derek, wait!" He swung back as Amber stood up on
the opposite side of the bed. "Before you go, there's one
more thing. One more secret, and then you'll know everything."

An odd emptiness settled low in his gut. "One more
secret."

She stared straight at him. "You know you're the only
man I've ever been with. So you deserve to know everything."

"What?"

"The real reason I was never Richard's mistress."

His stomach clenched.

"It was because he didn't want me."

*"What?"*

"Richard never asked anything of me. He brought me
here, gave me shelter and work. He gave me everything I
needed. And he wanted nothing in return. God, that hurt.
To know he could do so much for me, so willingly, and I
had absolutely nothing to give him in return. So I offered
what I had. Myself."

Derek swallowed, but his voice, when he spoke, was still
hoarse. "You *wanted* to sleep with him?"

"I *offered* to be whatever he wanted in a woman. If that
meant his mistress, I would have done it. Gladly. But he
didn't want me, not that way. He thought of me like the
daughter he'd never had, he said. He offered me his home
and his protection as long as I wanted it, and I didn't owe
him a thing. So I kept his house and did his laundry and
planted that huge garden out there—" she flicked her hand
toward the window "—but it wasn't enough. He died before I found any other way to repay him."

Derek shook his head, hating what Amber's admission
meant. His already complex world had tilted completely
askew this night, and it didn't seem as if it would ever be

right again. All he knew for certain was that he couldn't remain in this room another moment. He couldn't look at the sad beauty of Amber's face or smell the suddenly overpowering scent of sweet vanilla mixed with the musk of sex. He couldn't listen to any other words, had none to offer.

God, he couldn't breathe!

He spun on his heel and charged from the room. And with him he carried the taste of Amber's kisses, the feel of her body pressed perfectly against his—and the sight of her stoic face as he left her.

## Chapter Twenty

Derek descended the stairs, his mood bleak. Long about daybreak he'd finally accepted that his frustrations were his own damn fault. The realization hadn't improved his mood.

He'd hardly slept since storming from Amber's room, his thoughts whirling like a windstorm. He'd gone from prowling the yard to pacing the length of Amber's garden. Finally he'd retreated to his bedroom, flinging himself onto the bed, but it was no use. Physically, he was exhausted; mentally—emotionally—he remained unnervingly alert. With the first hint of dawn, he'd risen to watch the sunrise on the far horizon, conceding at last to some hard truths about himself.

Reaching the first floor, he found his boots arranged precisely at the bottom of the stairs. He stopped and stared at them, knowing that Amber had placed them there. He'd left them behind last night, realizing it only when he would have stepped into the yard barefoot. Unwilling to return to Amber's room for them, he'd pulled on an old pair of Richard's boots he'd found in the armoire.

He'd left his drawers and shirt behind, as well. But then, Amber had been wearing the shirt at the time.

Derek swallowed and tried not to recall what a fetching sight she made dressed in his blue cotton shirt. Her bare legs, long and shapely, had tempted him from beneath the hem. She'd fastened two of the buttons, providing scant concealment for the sway of her breasts. Her hair had cascaded over her shoulders and down her back, a wild river of auburn waves.

Derek blinked, willing his body to forgo its physical response, with only marginal success. He changed boots with a grunt, depositing Richard's old ones in the study and heading for the back door. He studiously ignored the temptation of Amber's closed door.

*You've had all night to think,* he reminded himself as he stepped into the quiet early morning. *You know your mistakes—and what's next.*

Yes, he'd made his share of blunders—some new, some old and some terrible. Making love with Amber had been a wonderful gift, and her distress upon his selfish reaction showed him with amazing clarity where he had gone wrong. How could he have been so willing to believe the very worst of her?

But he knew, as perhaps he'd always known. If only he'd had the strength and integrity to look deep within his soul when he had the chance. But he'd been so damned consumed with protecting his own secrets, he'd used any excuse to keep others at bay. As for Amber, as long as he found a means of keeping her at an emotional distance, he'd fancied himself safe. If he didn't allow her too close, she couldn't hurt him.

Instead, he had hurt her. Deeply. Amends would not come easily, but he must try. He owed much to so many, and he knew where he must start.

He found Beau in the cookhouse and asked him to assemble the men—and Amber. He would explain himself— as much as he was willing—once. The men deserved that. But he refused to beg anyone's forgiveness.

Except maybe Amber's.

Derek strode toward the front of the house, relishing the

familiar noises of the men and their morning routine as the ranch came awake. The sounds had become such a part of his life, he had come to enjoy them...much as he had come to care for this place. It felt almost like *home*. Home in a way he'd never known. Home in a way he had never expected to find.

Perhaps the feelings came from knowing that his father had built the ranch with his own hands, defended it with his last breath and left it for his son. Even a son he had never known. Or perhaps it was the satisfaction that Derek himself found as he brought the place into operation again, getting to know the men he hired and overseeing the work they did. Or perhaps it was shedding his own blood that had made him feel he could call the Double F his.

He blinked, lips twitching with a warmth that wasn't quite enough to qualify as a smile. Surely the ready acceptance and respect from Micah, Gideon, Beau, even the Andrews brothers—and one certain woman—had seemed unduly welcoming. The almost-smile died. They had accepted him until last night.

It didn't matter. Derek shook his head. The Double F belonged to him, to his very soul, and he would do whatever it took to hold on to it. Starting today.

"As most of you are aware, the man who arrived last night is my brother, Nathan." Derek began his speech after the men and Amber had assembled.

He swallowed, knowing what must come next and that it could not be delayed. "It's true that I served with Union forces during the war, the Army of the Tennessee—but the specifics don't matter. I meant to leave the war behind me when I came here, perhaps as some of you did. Unfortunately, that was not to be.

"I realize this controversy has put questions in your minds. You want to know the kind of man you're working for. I'm not here to debate politics, but I'm not ashamed of my beliefs. I oppose slavery. I fought to preserve the Union because I believe our strengths as a nation lie in putting our differences aside and working together as a whole.''

He took a deep breath, weighing his next words carefully. He hadn't meant to bare his soul to these men, but once the words started, they seemed unstoppable. He had never explained the reasons for his choices—no one had ever asked—and yet he believed passionately enough in his ideals to defy his family for them. Perhaps he'd merely needed time and distance—this new start at the Double F— to find the will to share them.

A soft grumbling had begun to ripple through the crowd, and Derek held up his hand for silence. ''I don't expect you to share or understand my views. It's been three years since the end of the war, and I'd hoped we could put this behind us by now. That hasn't been the case. However, I want to make this perfectly clear—North or South, black or white, young or old—any willing, capable worker has a home at the Double F.''

He ran a deliberate, unblinking stare over the crowd, eliminating any doubt as to the seriousness of his announcement. His most trusted hands—Gideon, Beau, Micah and Six—all returned his gaze directly. Amber offered a brief nod—of approval?

''I invite you all to remain at the ranch,'' he proposed, ''but there will be no hard feelings if you choose to move on. I don't expect you to decide now—and perhaps it would be better if you waited to hear the rest of what I have to say.''

Did the growing murmur indicate interest in remaining or leaving? Derek couldn't tell, and told himself it didn't matter. He would build the ranch back up by himself if he had to, just as his father had. The only exception would be Amber.

He had realized during the long, lonely night that he

would do whatever it took to convince her to stay. His eyes darted through the crowd to find her. She looked back, her gaze clear and distant and noncommittal.

"Quiet!" He raised his voice to be heard above the crowd. "It's only fair you know everything as you make your decisions." The men settled back to near silence, and Derek nodded. "The Double F has been targeted by rustlers for some time now. Richard Fontaine was killed because of it. I was wounded, and Gideon was shot last night.

"Until now I've taken a careful, investigative approach, but no more. Today begins my *crusade* to find whoever is responsible for these attacks. I fired Whitley last night. I'll do whatever is necessary to stop the rustling and see that no one else is harmed. If you aren't willing to do your part, then the Double F is no place for you."

A great weight seemed to fall from his shoulders with the last words. Even with the uncertainties he still faced, a new confidence told him he had begun to move in the right direction. Would Richard—and the Andrews brothers—be proud of him?

Derek nodded toward Gideon. "That is all for now. Gideon has the day's assignments."

Derek turned and found Nathan standing silently in the open doorway. His brother leaned negligently against the door frame, arms crossed over his chest and one ankle propped against the other.

"Nathan."

"Quite a speech." His brother straightened.

Derek shrugged but didn't look away. "The truth."

"Or your version of it."

He nodded. "I can only tell it the way I know it."

Nathan nodded in return, though Derek couldn't imagine what it meant. Was it an automatic response, or was he beginning to understand? Perhaps even recognize that the two of them might have genuine, differing versions of *the truth?*

Derek remained where he stood, suddenly unable to approach his brother. There was so much he wanted to say, but the words bombarded his mind with a deafening rattle that immobilized him. He swallowed and uttered the first thing that entered his brain. "Have you decided what you're going to do?"

"Not yet."

"You're welcome to stay here."

"I need time to think." An unmistakable note of bitterness laced his tone.

"You don't have to live here at the house. You and Mariah could build a place. There's plenty of land."

"I'm not looking for charity."

"I'm not offering charity," Derek snapped emphatically. "If you stay, you'll work like everyone else. Damned hard."

He hesitated, certain Nathan was unwilling to hear anything more, but just as certain it must be said. "It's not Palmetto, Nathan, but the Double F is home to the Fontaines now."

Amber made her way down the hall, hurrying past the dining room. Fortunately someone—Carolyn, she guessed—had closed the door partway. Though it aided her in passing unnoticed, Amber couldn't help wondering just who it was that Derek's mother thought would interrupt them. Certainly no one at the ranch.

All of the Fontaines were at dinner, their first as a family in more years than Amber knew. Aside from understanding the momentousness of that occasion, *she* had no desire to attract the least bit of attention from any of them.

Particularly not Derek. Or at least not at the moment.

She slipped into his study, lighting the lamp on his desk and arranging the drapes for the evening, then moved on to the parlor. Once the lamps there glowed with a warm, golden light, she closed those draperies, as well.

At the doorway, she turned back and cast a fond eye over the room. It remained much as it had while Richard was alive. Derek seldom used the room and seemed to care little about things such as furnishings. Curiously, Carolyn and Mariah had made few attempts at redecorating the house. It seemed unlikely that Derek would cooperate, even if they tried.

*Cooperate.* She reconsidered the word. Until last night, she hadn't realized how much cooperation was a form of survival—and she had been so certain she had learned all there was to know about such things. She'd had all night to think about it, and the moment Beau warned her of Derek's surprise meeting, she understood that changes were afoot. She had already learned the disadvantages of willful opposition; survival—*her* survival—depended upon her ability to adapt.

As it happened, Derek had said nothing this morning that particularly surprised her. That he had called the meeting at all gave her some uncertainty, even now. After all this time, he had given up his secrets.

She had seen little of him or the other Fontaines since. Similarly, they spared little attention for her, though she had intercepted a speculative look from Nathan now and then. After his less-than-gracious greeting of the previous night, she had counted herself lucky that he had only looked and mostly disregarded her.

For her part, Mariah had been pale and withdrawn most of the day. By early afternoon she had pleaded a headache that required a nap, which had suited Carolyn just fine; it left her alone with Nathan. The woman had hardly let him out of her sight, fawning over him as though he represented the Second Coming of Christ—and, Amber supposed fairly, it *was* an astonishing feat that he had reappeared alive and well. But why couldn't the woman have shown a fraction of that attention to Derek when she'd discovered his unexpected presence at the ranch?

Now they sat together as a family. Amber toyed with the folds of a drapery panel, pretending to straighten it as she listened to the clink of silverware against china. She was only delaying the inevitable; Beau was expecting her in the cookhouse. He could manage alone in the kitchen all right, but it was her job to serve in the dining room, clear the dirty dishes and bring in dessert.

And face Derek at last.

She swallowed and took a dragging step toward the door. He had been so very angry when he left her last night, and she supposed he deserved to be. Or at least hurt. The moments they'd spent making love were among the most beautiful of her life, and she'd allowed them to be tainted by secrets and lies.

Perhaps Derek had contributed to the pain by so easily believing the lies that others told, but Amber could not deny her own part in the disaster. She had lied, too, despite all her claims of innocence. Worse, she had lied to herself. She had declared all manner of outrage and self-pity, refusing to answer his questions and insisting she wanted someone to *believe in her*...and it had been a sham.

Sometime during the long hours of the night, she'd discovered the fear that had driven her. A man, wonderful and decent and caring, had come into her life and made her feel again. But if he knew everything, wouldn't he turn his back on her? Knowing he didn't want her based on lies and misinformation afforded her the protection of knowing she had done nothing wrong—it was his fault. But if he knew the truth and then didn't want her, she would have no one to blame but herself.

She simply hadn't understood what it meant to her heart and soul to love a man the way she loved Derek. Completely. Unquestionably. Eternally.

Thunder shattered her thoughts with stunning abruptness, followed by a dull crash and tinkling glass. Amber spun toward the noise and gaped at the parlor window. The drapes billowed back, and a huge rock fell to the floor.

"Come out, Fontaine. We're waiting for you!"

She stared at the rock, unable to force her body to move. After a moment she raced into the hallway, intercepting Derek as he strode from the dining room. She collided with the solid wall of his chest, and he reached to steady her, his large, capable hands warm on her arms. She threw herself against him, her arms around his waist, and she clutched him to her desperately.

"Derek," she whispered, or thought she did, but the harsh grating didn't sound remotely like her voice.

"Move it, Fontaine. Get your blue belly ass out here before we decide to come in there after you."

Nathan, Mariah and finally Carolyn crowded into the hallway behind Derek. "What is the meaning of this?" his mother demanded querulously, as though irritated by this dinner interruption. Or was she outraged that her son and his housekeeper stood embracing in the hallway? Amber wondered a bit wildly.

She tightened her grip around him, and ignored the rest of them. "Derek, I don't know what this is about, but you can't go out there."

"Amber." He pushed her back a step and looked down at her, a twinge of surprise in his eyes. Her heart broke to think that her reaction dismayed him.

"Who is it?" he asked. "Do you know?"

She shook her head. "No. But you can't go out there."

His gaze flickered to the front door. "I don't think they'll give me much choice."

"I demand to know what is going on here."

"Mother, shut up." It was Nathan who spoke. "Mariah, take care of her."

Amber spared little attention for the women, noting only that Mariah put an arm around her mother-in-law's shoulders and pulled her back into the dining room. "Come on,

Carolyn. We'll go back to the table while the others take care of this.''

''But what is *this*? I don't understand—'' The dining room door clicked shut behind them.

Nathan strode past Derek and Amber into the parlor. He lifted a corner of the curtain, peering out with practiced stealth. He looked back at Derek. ''There's a crowd out there, maybe twenty.''

''You coming, Fontaine? You know which one we want. The one that hires darkies and doesn't give a damn about the South. The goddamn Yankee carpetbagger!''

The need to peek out the window and see what Nathan described tore at Amber, but she fought it back with the rival need to stay close to Derek. Her heart pounded so hard she thought it might explode. She could hardly breathe and her hands shook, but if she kept Derek with her, it would be all right. She could protect him.

''They've got torches, and they're wearing masks,'' Nathan added after a moment. ''Burlap bags and pillowcases with eyeholes cut out, from the looks of it. The Ku Klux Klan, they call themselves. I've heard about them.''

Derek nodded solemnly. ''I didn't know they were organized here.''

''What are you talking about?'' Amber demanded.

''We don't have time now. I need to get out there before they start more trouble.''

Derek tried to step around her, but Amber grabbed his arm with all her strength. ''What do you mean? I told you, you can't go out there!'' She fixed a frantic, vicious glare on Nathan. ''Tell him! I don't know what this means, but it isn't good. Tell him, Nathan!''

Nathan opened his mouth, but Derek spoke first. ''Amber.'' He pressed his fingers against her cheek, turning her to him. His hands fell to her shoulders, a heavy, welcome weight. ''I have to do this, angel. A man has to face some things in his life, and this is one of them. Those men outside aren't going to go away if I just hide in the house…and I've never been one to hide from my convictions. If I ever want to look myself in the mirror again, I have to go out there.''

''You may not be here to look yourself in the mirror again, if you go out there,'' Nathan observed bluntly.

Amber choked back a sob. ''Derek, please.'' She crushed herself against him, and his arms came around her. ''Don't go. We'll find another answer—you and me, if Nathan won't help. We'll do it alone. Please. I…love you. I can't lose you now.''

''Shh, angel.'' He bent his head and whispered in her ear. ''It'll be all right. I promise. Shh.''

''Fontaine! Dammit, you've got five seconds or we're coming in there after you. How about if we light this whole goddamn place on fire!''

''All right, I'm coming,'' he shouted. His arms tightened around her, but for only a moment. Then he released her and raised her chin to look at him.

''Don't worry,'' he said with a tender smile, but the edges seemed wilted with resignation. ''I'll do my best to come back to you. I promise.'' His eyes flickered, begging her to understand. ''You make me believe we've got some things to discuss.''

''Derek—''

He kissed her then, a deep, abiding kiss that rocked her. Her mouth opened automatically under his, and his tongue plunged forward, capturing her heart and soul. She gave them gladly, offering all that and more, and taking whatever of him she could. She tasted him, held him, savored the scent of him. She impressed her memory with the essence of him.

Too soon he pulled away. He started for the front door, leaving her to feel nothing but cold emptiness.

''I love you,'' she whispered again, wanting him to know it, to hear it one more time.

"I…" He stopped before the closed door and looked at his brother. "Nathan, if you never do another thing for me, you keep her safe. No matter what happens or what you hear, you keep her inside and protect her—with your life if necessary. *Please.*"

Tears filled Amber's eyes, spilling over her lashes and down her cheeks. She glanced away, swallowing, desperate to hide her reaction, but Derek knew, anyway.

"If anything happens, the ranch is yours, Nathan, as a Fontaine. Amber is my witness. Just make sure she always has a place here. A nice, safe place."

"*Derek.*" She could no longer pretend to hold back her cries.

"Swear it!" he demanded of his brother, suddenly, fiercely, and the doorknob rattled in his hand.

She looked up, but she could hardly see him through her tears.

"I swear," Nathan grated, and then Derek was gone.

# Chapter Twenty-One

Amber ran for the door as it closed behind Derek.

"For God's sake, get away from there." Nathan grabbed her arm and jerked her into the parlor. He resumed his position near the window, keeping a punishing grip on her arm as he shot her a highly formidable glare. "They could shoot you through that door as easy as if you were outside at midday," he hissed.

She tried to twist away, but his fingers tightened. She glared back at him.

"What do you think you're doing?" Her voice came out every bit the snarl she intended. "You can't let Derek go out there alone. He's committing suicide—and you're letting him!"

"You heard what he said. Now shut up so I can hear what's going on out there."

"What do—"

"If you want him to have any chance at all, just *shut up.*"

Any chance? Did that mean Nathan had a plan, that he would do something to help Derek? She opened her mouth to ask, but he fixed her with a severe scowl that changed her mind.

"...here. What do you want?"

Derek's voice. She realized that he'd been speaking and she'd missed most of it. The gaping hole in her stomach seemed to steadily well up with anguish. She pressed her lips together in an attempt to keep her fears from escaping.

"You. We want you, you goddamn Yankee bastard."

"Why me? The war is over. It has been for three years."

"Good boy," Nathan muttered. "Keep them talking."

Talking? What good was this pointless chatter? It seemed a better idea for Derek to get away from those men and back into the house—as soon as possible. But how?

The spokesman of the group laughed suddenly, a sharp, bitter sound that grated through the night. "Easy for you to say. You didn't lose shit."

"My family lost its share," Derek countered. "There's hardly a family that wasn't touched by the war. But it's over. So go on home to your wives and children and forget about this."

"Forget? You Yankee bastard, you think we could forget?"

A sudden thumping noise replaced the words, interspersed with curses and a low grunt of pain. Amber's stomach clenched, and she squirmed against Nathan's grasp. He didn't release her, and in spite of herself, she found herself clutching his arm in a death grip that earned her a brief glance.

"How do you like the Rebel way of doing things, Yankee?"

"The war is over." Derek's voice sounded odd, breathless, and Amber's gaze flew to Nathan's face. "I keep telling you…that. You're no more Rebels…than I am Yankee. Anymore."

"Goddammit," Nathan muttered under his breath. "Don't bait them, you stubborn son of a bitch."

"What is it? What's happening?" Amber demanded.

Nathan glanced at her with a brittle look, as though gauging her strength. "They roped him and pulled him down the stairs."

Her breath left her on a wheeze. "What will they do next?"

Nathan blinked, an oddly slow action, and shrugged in much the same way. "Drag him."

"Drag him—"

"You just don't learn, do you, Yankee?"

Amber sucked in a sharp breath, cutting off her words when one of the cowards, as she had begun to think of the masked riders, spoke again. The sound of scuffling and another pained grunt followed. She jerked on Nathan's sleeve, earning a low curse. Somehow, it didn't seem directed toward her.

"They got him to his knees, but he's back on his feet."

*Oh, dear Lord in heaven above.* It was going to happen again. They would kill him. As her father had been killed. As Richard had been killed.

For a moment it seemed that she couldn't breathe and her knees threatened to buckle. Amber closed her eyes against the weakness, the physical reactions, and willed herself to stand straight, to retain whatever strength she had left to her  whatever strength Derek might need.

She could do it. She had coped with her father's murder, then Richard's. She had withstood the memories and the consequences.

But if she lost Derek, how would she survive it?

"You think you're so high-and-mighty out here at the Double F, setting yourself up in your own little kingdom." The spokesman's angry voice demanded her attention. "How about we show you what it's like to be court jester instead of the king?"

A great round of guffaws followed the suggestion, the horses stirred, footsteps scuffled on the driveway. Amber noticed the sounds distantly as she concentrated on *that voice.* It sounded frighteningly familiar, even muffled behind his coward's mask.

She stared at the draperies as though they would magically part for her or somehow enable her to see the scene outside. They didn't, but she supposed it didn't matter if they wore masks.

If only the spokesman would speak again! She hadn't noticed at first, but something in the words and his tone snagged at a distant memory—vitally important, yet it wouldn't quite form.

"You've been stealing from the Double F."

"Dammit, Derek, don't goad them anymore," Nathan growled, but Amber shushed him as she concentrated on the exchange.

"Figured that out, have you?"

"Why this ranch?"

"Why not? Nobody here suffered from the war. Richard stayed here, nice and safe and *rich,* while the rest of us did our part for the Confederacy. Or most of us did." More scuffling sounds arrested the speech for a moment. "You didn't, did you, Yankee? You tried your damnedest to kill us instead."

A lengthy pause stretched Amber's nerves tight. She guessed that Nathan suffered similar anxieties; he released her arm and began rubbing the palm of his hand up and down his thigh.

When Derek finally spoke, his voice grated. "No more than you tried to kill me. That doesn't have anything to do with Richard. He was a good Confederate."

The coward laughed. "Not good enough. A *good* Confederate wouldn't have had a damn thing left when the war was over—the rest of us didn't have shit. A *good* Confederate would've fought alongside us at any age. A *good* Confederate wouldn't have called a traitorous Yankee-lover like Blair Laughton friend. A *good*—"

Amber gasped and missed the other words. Why would

these men mention her father—and now, after he'd been dead for two years? And then…there it was. The tiny nagging memory burst forth.

Jeff! The man—the *coward*—behind the group, this Ku Klux Klan, was Jeff Buchanan.

Jeff Buchanan?

"No!"

Amber hadn't meant to speak, but the word echoed through the room. Nathan shot her a startled look and she scowled back at him, stepping quickly out of reach.

"No," she repeated as she spun on her heel and ran for the front door. "He's done enough. Everything I loved is gone. Not Derek, too."

"Stop this nonsense right now!"

A dreadful certainty seized Derek's attention before the first word ended. Amber's voice. He would always recognize it.

She sounded like a governess in a roomful of naughty children. The thought would have made him smile if it hadn't been for the awful fear that followed hard on its heels. A fear he'd never known, not in the heat of battle or even in the cursed waiting beforehand.

Goddammit! He meant to keep her safe, above all others. He'd told Nathan to keep her inside.

A quick, shallow breath, all he could manage, refreshed his wavering strength. It wouldn't last, not with the way they had him trussed up. His arms and legs ached, and his shoulder felt like it had never healed at all. The rope around his chest bound him tightly enough to restrict his breathing, and kept his arms pinned to his sides. He felt blood on his cheek, the result of one of his falls. His elbows and knees were scraped from being dragged—a taste of what was to come?

"Amber, get back inside the house!" He put the best he had into his shout.

"Well, well, well. What do we have here?" The question sounded base and lewd, accompanied by a knowing laugh from the masked man who led the group. "You two lovers now? With Richard gone, you set your cap for the nephew?"

Derek stepped toward Amber, thinking only to protect her. The man who held the rope that bound him gave it a sharp jerk, and Derek stumbled backward.

Amber's soft cry carried across the night. Regaining his footing, he raised his eyes to the veranda. He could see her clearly, thanks to the blaze of more than a dozen torches carried by the men who surrounded him. She stood glaring at them all, one hand positioned on each hip.

"You disgust me, Jeff Buchanan."

"What the hell..." Dismay sharpened the muffled voice.

Derek glanced from Amber to the Klan leader. Jeff Buchanan? Her one-time beau? And the man who had been rustling Double F cattle?

She had unmasked him.

Derek laughed, perhaps a bit wildly—but he was entitled. These masked riders had stolen from him and now had come to kill him, and the beautiful, ardent woman whom he had both misunderstood and mistreated, had cleverly identified their leader from no more than his voice.

"Shut up." The rope man jerked on his tether, forcing Derek to scramble for balance.

"How could you?" Amber demanded. "You murdered my father!"

"Shut up, damn you!" shouted Jeff.

Amber didn't listen. "You took advantage of my father's hospitality night after night. Then suddenly you were busy—planning his murder! And me? Did you *plan* for me to be attacked by those animals? To witness my own father's murder?"

Buchanan whipped off his mask furiously. Every one of Derek's muscles tensed.

"I told you to shut the hell up!" the other man snarled. "So you identified me. You invented the rest of it to protect yourself, you lying little bitch." His sneer looked grotesque in the torchlight. "I didn't do anything, and you know it. You just don't want to lose your new lover. I'll come back later for a visit, if that's what you want."

Her eyes grew round and she took a half step back.

"Shut your stinking, filthy mouth." The snarling words erupted of their own accord as Derek strained against his bonds. The rope man allowed him little progress, yanking him back and laughing when Derek grunted, struggling to retain his footing.

Buchanan joined in the laughter, dismissing Amber with clear contempt as he turned toward Derek. "Haven't you figured out that she was in on it? She did anything I asked. It was a convenient arrangement, especially when she moved to the ranch."

He paused, flicking an insolent gaze toward Amber. "But I couldn't marry her after that. She was no good anymore—but still worth a fine time now and then."

"You're a filthy liar." Her voice was as cold as death.

Buchanan looked at Derek, his face falsely innocent. "She's an unforgiving bitch, but she knows how to keep a man happy."

"Don't waste your breath, Buchanan." Derek looked at Amber. "Your lies are old news. I know Amber better than that."

"The people in Twigg don't think so."

"That supposed to mean something to me?" Derek sucked in a quick breath, speaking as he slowly grasped the rope at his chest with both hands. "The place is full of idiots, but a few of them know better than to believe your lies."

He uttered the last syllable, and then jerked at the coarse rope with every ounce of strength left to him. The momentum sent him stumbling backward. Almost as if in slow motion, the rope man came tumbling off his horse and landed in a heap in the middle of the driveway.

Derek dropped to the ground and rolled toward the shadows, dragging the flailing rope man with him for some distance. At the same time, he fought to loosen the rope and regain the use of his arms, to escape before the man could tighten his tether.

He pulled the noose over his head and flung it away as gunfire erupted all around him. Scrambling toward the heaviest of the shadows, he cursed himself for being caught like this. Twenty men shooting at him, and he was unarmed!

"Derek! This way." The disembodied command ripped through the darkness at his left. A bullet whizzed past his ear, sending him into a crouch as he headed for the voice.

"Here." Gideon had a shotgun tucked under his arm, and he tossed Derek his Colt revolver. "We've got them surrounded."

Derek threw himself to the ground, checking to make sure the gun was loaded. He cast a quick, decisive eye over the confusion behind him. Thank God Amber seemed to have disappeared from the veranda, he thought, turning his attention back to the frenzied activity.

The bright torchlight made the men on horseback excellent targets. Well-aimed shots came from the darkness, and Klan members writhed on the ground, shot from horses that had bolted in the unexpected gunfire. The rope man lay where he had fallen, clutching his arm and making little effort to join in the ruckus.

Derek searched for Buchanan. He remained mounted, firing wildly. They were shots of fear, shots of desperation, shots from a man who knew, surrounded by the enemy as he was, that his choices were to surrender or die. Reckless hopelessness had looked the same during the war.

Suddenly Buchanan wheeled his horse toward the house. Amber, Derek realized, had remained on the veranda, crouched low behind a pillar so she was mostly hidden. Buchanan had spied her, too, and now he pointed his pistol in her direction.

Derek didn't think. He raised the Colt, aimed and fired with swift, careful precision. Buchanan jerked upright, his arm flung wide, and he fell gracelessly to the ground and lay still.

Without a moment to spare for Amber or her sensibilities, Derek turned his attention back to the battle at hand. The ranch hands seemed to be moving in closer. Six, Micah, Simon and Beau appeared, spaced evenly at the edge of the darkness. Farther out, in the other direction, were Carlos, Juan and several hands Derek knew only by name. All crouched, moving with impressive stealth through the shadows, firing at will.

The Klan fought back with surprising ineffectiveness. Their choice bullying tactics evidently left them ill-prepared for a gunfight. Or perhaps the Double F vaqueros were more adept.

Another shot zinged past Derek's head, and he ducked, firing back as he sprinted for the cover of darkness. His shot caught a man on a dirty brown gelding and toppled him to the ground.

Derek narrowed his eyes as he looked around, considering his next target. The unnatural light had begun to fade as injured Klansmen dropped their torches when they fell. The gunfire seemed to be dwindling and the ranch hands moved closer still.

Six held one hand over his arm, but that didn't stop him from seizing firearms from the intruders. Others took on the task of capturing and disarming men who continued to fight. With unhesitating efficiency, Simon dispatched a man who took exception to having a black man relieve him of his gun; he had the cleanest right hook Derek had ever seen.

Keeping low, Gideon moved up next to Derek. "Want me to send somebody for the sheriff?"

Derek shook his head. "We better be sure the sheriff isn't already here."

Gideon glanced back at the tangle of men and horses. "Right. I've heard the law and the Klan work together at times."

They moved in closer, Derek mentally sorting through the confusion as he spotted familiar faces among those captured: Frank Edwards and Whitley, for two.

"Why doesn't that surprise me," Derek muttered under his breath. Typically, Gideon said nothing.

Amber remained crouched anxiously on the veranda, her mistrust of the cease-fire obvious. Derek smiled gently, thinking it seemed such an oddly female reaction, when she had charged to his rescue with complete fearlessness. He started for the house, calling over his shoulder to Gideon, "I'm going to make sure Amber's all right."

Gideon waved him on.

"Look out!"

Amber's cry spun him around toward the captured men. Whitley, his face drawn with utter despair, pointed a gun at Derek. How the hell had he managed to keep hold of a pistol?

"Prepare to die, you sorry Yankee son of a bitch!"

And then, as though time slowed to a crawl, a gun roared, Whitley's arm jerked up, the pistol flew out of his hand and he pitched backward in an awkward somersault. The air went deathly quiet for a heartbeat, until he screeched in agonized pain.

Derek stared, his mind empty. For an agonized instant he had known that Whitley's bullet would find him; he had prepared himself for the fiery bite. Someone had saved his life.

He glanced all around him, and it was then he discovered Nathan standing at the corner of the house. Smoke drifted in a lazy plume from the barrel of his rifle, still leveled in Whitley's direction.

Nathan. Bitter, angry, resentful Nathan had saved him.

An odd mix of relief and euphoria swirled through Derek. Before he could find the right words to thank him, movement flashed at the corner of his eye. He turned in time to catch Amber as she catapulted herself against him.

"Derek!" She wrapped her arms around his neck and kissed his face, crying and laughing at the same time.

He grinned and adjusted his stance to balance them, legs spread and arms clutching her tightly to his chest. God, she felt good against him. When he glanced back to where Nathan had stood, his brother was gone.

"Shh." He bent back to Amber, consoling her with more tenderness than he'd known he possessed. "Everything's fine, angel. Are you hurt?"

She shook her head and snuggled against him. "I was so frightened. I couldn't have survived without you."

"I'm all right." He stroked her hair lightly, enjoying the silken feel of it with a new sensitivity.

"Well, now, what in the hell is goin' on around here?"

Reluctantly Derek looked up. Clem and Twigg Andrews rode up the driveway, the sound of their arrival cloaked by the other activities. They flanked a man Derek hadn't met, but the badge on his shirt provided an identity: Sheriff Gardner.

"Hello, Clem, Twigg." Derek greeted them mildly.

"Had yourself some excitement, eh, young Fontaine?" Clem gave his head a jerk toward the captured men.

"You could say that."

"Howdy, there, Amber-girl." Twigg waved at her. "This ain't all about the two a' you sparkin', now, is it?" He scowled at the rest of the assembly. "It looks like a lynchin'—or somethin' as bad. I ain't fond of shenanigans like that."

"Nor am I," stated the sheriff.

Amber made a soft noise and pulled herself from Derek's chest. "Hello, Twigg. Hello, Clem."

She didn't try to go far, nor would Derek have let her. Instead, he held her against his side and kept her close with a firm arm around her shoulders. She didn't seem to mind.

"Whitley, what kind of dumb-ass mischief've you gotten yerself into now?" demanded Clem, suddenly dismissing the rest of them. He stared at his nephew, who was still writhing on the ground and screaming obscenities. Clem used the same demented chicken-blink Derek had come to expect of the Andrews brothers when they were perturbed.

Twigg followed suit, hollering across the yard. "I knew you was up to no good when you said Fontaine fired you fer no reason. He ain't that kinda man—but what kinda jackass're you? It's a good thing yer cousin Bill is a nervous scaredy-cat, or we wouldn'ta knowed what foolishness you was up to."

The elderly men dismounted and headed in their nephew's direction, still quibbling. "You shoulda been keepin' a closer eye on him," Clem accused Twigg.

"What nonsense are you spoutin' now, old man?" demanded Twigg. "*I'm* the one who said Whitley was goin' all loco. *You* said Fontaine'd be good fer the boy, make a man outta him."

The argument continued as the men stalked in their bow-legged way toward their hapless nephew. Derek might have felt sorry for Whitley if he hadn't threatened Amber and the others, and the Double F itself. Any misplaced sympathy disappeared.

Still, the question nagged at him: why did Whitley hate him so? Last night's firing seemed only a symptom, the result of an angry discontent that had driven Whitley from the very beginning.

The Andrews brothers had nearly reached their nephew when Twigg suddenly stopped and turned back. "You sure yer okay there, Amber-girl? I didn't think to ask after yer health, what with all this commotion."

She smiled, a beautiful smile that lit up the night and

warmed Derek's heart. "I'm just fine, Twigg. A little shaken up, but no worse for wear. Thank you for asking."

Twigg nodded. "Fontaine took care of you, eh? Good thing, or I'da had to tan both his and Whitley's hides, 'stead a' just my dumb-ass nephew." He swung back in Whitley's direction.

Derek laughed, unable to help himself. Amber looked up at him, her surprise clear. He knew he didn't smile often, let alone laugh, but it felt so damn good. He'd never before felt so happy. Had never believed he could be.

"Don't suppose you'll be spendin' much time at them line shacks anymore, will ya now, Fontaine?" Clem called without looking back.

Derek didn't hesitate. "No, I don't suppose I will."

# Chapter Twenty-Two

Amber put a fresh kettle of water to heat over the fire, then turned to survey her medical supplies spread out on the table. She cast a sure eye over the myriad containers for a quick inventory of what she had used and what she might yet need. Thank God tonight's commotion had produced few serious wounds for the Double F hands. The men who had ridden with the Ku Klux Klan would be treated by Dr. Harris in Twigg; Derek had refused to allow her near them. His only concession had been to provide a wagon to transport the more seriously injured to town.

"Do you need any help?"

She looked up to find Beau standing in the doorway of the cookhouse. Shaking her head, she bent back to her work. "Not unless you want to be the one to convince Derek to come inside so I can see to his wounds."

"He hasn't been in yet?"

"He said he was busy. But he promised to come in later."

"I don't think he's seriously hurt. Scrapes and bruises, mostly."

Amber looked up, eyeing Beau carefully as she weighed his words. Was he trying to reassure her, or did he mean to make less of what Derek had been through? How did he—how did any of the men—feel after learning the truth about Derek and his time in the Union army?

"I'd still like to clean and treat the wounds," she said mildly. "It's been my experience that even small injuries will cause problems if you don't treat them properly."

Beau stepped closer. "Amber..." he began, but then he shook his head. "You're in love with him, aren't you?"

She glanced away, disconcerted by the unexpectedness of Beau's direct question. She forced herself to look at him; she had nothing to be ashamed of. "Yes."

He nodded. "He's in love with you, too."

A fluttering excitement stirred deep within her, and she pressed her hands to her stomach. "I'm not certain about that."

Beau shook his head and gave her that funny almost-smile that had once been all he could manage. "I've been watching you. Both of you. You've fought it, but it's there, all the same. That's...good."

"Good." She blinked and pinned him with a look intended to be both deliberate and skeptical. "Do you really believe that?"

"Absolutely." He glanced away, as though her directness made him uncomfortable. Or perhaps he'd spoken more emphatically than he meant to. Then he looked back at her. "Love seems harder to come by since the war. We need to find it again."

"Do you mean that? Even for a man who—"

"*Wherever* you can find it. There's been too much pain, too much hate, for too long."

She nodded slowly, and an uncertain smile tugged at her lips. "You forgive him then?"

Beau shrugged. "I'm not sure there's anything to forgive. Maybe he didn't do anything so wrong. He fought for his convictions the same as I did. Maybe our choices were different, but we followed our hearts. Can you ask any less of a man?"

"I—" Amber broke off when she caught sight of a dark shape in the doorway. Derek stepped in, looking as serious as she'd ever seen him, his eyes hooded and distant.

"Derek," she exclaimed. His name seemed to echo with embarrassing breathlessness. She gripped the folds of her skirt, fighting the need to run to him, to throw her arms around him, hold him close to her heart and cover his face with kisses. Her limbs and her heart urged her forward, but his expression held her back.

Instead she cleared her throat. "You came...finally."

He nodded. "I promised."

"Is everything cleared up out there?" Beau stepped forward.

"For tonight. The sheriff supports us in protecting the ranch, but I expect there will be more questions later. No doubt a formal inquiry when the judge arrives."

Beau nodded. "If you don't need me for anything else, I'll go on to bed."

Amber smiled weakly and nodded.

"Beau." Derek's voice stopped him as he reached the door. He turned.

"Thank you." Derek offered his hand. "I appreciate your part in defending the ranch—and saving my life."

Beau hesitated, tangling Amber's nerves in a jumble, but she relaxed as he accepted Derek's handshake. "You're welcome. I was glad to do it," he said, and then left the cookhouse.

Unbidden tears stung her eyelids. Blinking fiercely, she turned before Derek noticed. "Are you ready to let me see to your injuries?" she asked briskly, snatching up a basin and filling it with hot water.

"I'm ready." Derek strode around the table.

She nodded toward the chair. "Sit down."

She stepped as close as she dared, overcome by a sudden, inexplicable shyness. Sensations raced along her nerves, and she hadn't even touched him yet.

*You've touched him before,* she encouraged herself heartily. They had made love.

But that had been before she'd said the words. *I love you* somehow changed everything.

Why didn't he say something? Do something? Now that she'd shared her heart with him, why did he seem so unapproachable? An hour ago, in front of everyone, he had held her close with tender, caring concern. What had happened since then?

She clenched her hands tightly, willing them to stop trembling and her heart to stop pounding. She took a deep breath and dipped a clean cloth into the steaming water, then wrung it out. Carefully she dabbed at the scrapes on Derek's cheek and chin before cleaning the bruise at his temple. He sat stoically, staring straight ahead, and said nothing.

"Does this hurt?" she asked softly, when she could stand the silence no longer.

He shook his head. "It's nothing. I could have cleaned it up myself, but..."

"But you promised."

"Yes." He glanced up into her eyes. "I promised."

She swallowed, tearing her gaze from the striking blue intensity of his, and blindly reached for the nearest glass bottle and another clean cloth. Derek grabbed her wrist, stopping her in midmotion. "Not that damn tincture again."

She glanced at the bottle, then at him. "It's good for healing."

"And it stings like holy hell!"

Her heart lightened a fraction and she gave him an impish smile. "I know. And I'm sorry. But it's better if I use it."

He tossed his head with a disagreeable shake. "I think you just like to see me in pain."

Her smile died. "I don't. Not at all." She closed her

eyes and tried not to recall the sight of him when she had
stormed out onto the veranda. The blazing torchlight had
revealed blood on his face, a torn sleeve and even a jagged
hole in his pant leg. What other injuries had he suffered?

A feathery-light touch brought her eyes open. Derek
stroked his fingers lightly over her cheek, and he almost
smiled. "I know you don't, angel. It was a joke—a poor
one. I'm sorry."

She nodded and swallowed, bringing her fingers up to
trace the backs of his without thinking. His eyes, darkened
to a startling, brilliant blue, seemed to see clear through
her, and sent a shiver of excitement racing along her nerves.

She pulled her hand back nervously, fumbling to pour
the tincture onto the cloth. She dabbed at his scraped cheek
with light strokes, but he sucked his breath in between
clenched teeth.

"*I'm* the one who's sorry," she whispered. "I wouldn't
hurt you for the world."

"I know."

She worked quickly, until the wound on his cheek and
the raw spot on his chin were as clean as she could make
them. She stepped back, carefully placing the tincture bottle
on the table and dropping the soiled cloth with the others.

What next? Feeling awkward with nothing to occupy her
hands at the moment, she looked at Derek. His other injuries were not so obvious, and asking him to remove his
shirt so she could see to his arm seemed suddenly too risky.

"Are you sure everything is going to be all right?" she
asked instead.

He nodded and gave her that hint of a smile. "We were
protecting ourselves tonight. That group has a long history
of causing trouble—and outright murder. Once the sheriff
arrived, they were quick to tell everything they knew."

"What happens now?"

Derek shrugged. "I sent Gideon to San Antonio. The
army will help Sheriff Gardner deal with this. In the mean-

time, Nathan and Simon went to Twigg to act as temporary deputies.''

''Is this…'' She was almost afraid to ask the question. ''Do you think this is the end of it?''

''Yes, I do. Buchanan was their self-appointed bully and leader, and he's gone.'' Derek paused. ''I'm sorry I had to be the one to kill him,'' he said in a distantly hushed voice.

''I am, too.''

The words weren't enough, and she couldn't simply stand there and watch Derek struggle with regrets. She knelt beside his chair and peered up into his beautiful, worn face. ''I never wished Jeff dead, but after learning of his part in all this, I can't honestly say I'm sorry he is.'' She took Derek's hand in hers. ''I'm only sorry you had to do it. He isn't worth the heartache.''

His fingers tightened around hers. ''You loved him.''

She shook her head. ''I *thought* I loved a fantasy—a man who didn't exist. The real Jeff Buchanan had my father killed when he came close to unmasking a treacherous band of thieves. And Richard…'' She closed her eyes briefly. ''I don't know how involved he was in Richard's death. He could have—''

''He planned it,'' Derek interrupted, ''but no one seemed to think he carried out my father's murder by himself. He had the men who murdered your father killed as well, I'm told. And he—'' The words stopped abruptly.

''He what?'' Amber laid her free hand on Derek's arm, urging him to say more, pleading with her gaze. ''What else did he do?''

''He was one of the men who shot me. He and Whitley. Whitley admitted everything.''

She closed her eyes and gripped his hand. Hard. The news shouldn't have come as such a surprise, but it hurt to have the last of her illusions stripped away. Already she had seen enough pain, enough violence.

''I never thought them capable of such vile things.''

Derek gathered her hand between his. His skin, rough and callused, felt warm and alive, his grip safe. She reveled in it. "It's over now. They won't be doing those things anymore. With Buchanan gone, Sheriff Gardner intends to see this group of fanatics disbanded. If he doesn't—I will."

"Yes." She knew he expected nothing less of himself.

With earnest reluctance, Amber pulled her hands from Derek's and stood. She would have preferred to stay there forever—or better yet, crawl into his lap and wrap herself around him. But things remained too unsettled between them, and she was too much of a coward to take the chance.

"This Ku Klux Klan, it's a frightening thing," she said instead, fussing needlessly with her jars and bottles and boxes of medical supplies. "I've never heard of it before."

"It's more of the ugliness left over from the war. This is the first I've heard of them organizing in Texas. Gardner thinks the Klan gave Buchanan a sense of security, which turned things uglier. He eliminated the real rustlers—as you suggested, with Richard gone, there wasn't much need to steal cattle when they could just round up strays. Instead Buchanan found pleasure in causing trouble for those he didn't like or who didn't agree with him. My arrival didn't go unnoticed, particularly when I started asking questions."

"And that's when Whitley became a spy?" She shuddered, thinking of living with the young man so close.

"He and Frank Edwards. I thought Whitley was just young and stubborn, but it turns out he was young and angry. Angry that he'd missed the *big fight* and determined to make up for it. With the war over, Buchanan convinced Whitley that the South would rise again, they would be instrumental in it and everyone who didn't think as they did, with the same zealousness, wasn't a good Southerner. Edwards was just greedy, hoping to get hold of the Double F."

Amber shot Derek a confused look. "Frank Edwards

wanted to take over the ranch? Why did he go to such lengths to search for you, then?''

Derek shrugged. ''I don't think he expected me to be found. A lot of men have disappeared since the war's end. Look at Nathan. I reckon Edwards meant to make a half-hearted attempt. He knew Richard had family who might show up someday. He just underestimated the Pinkerton men he hired.''

''And they found you in Chicago.''

''It was a place to be.'' He shrugged. ''Better than Charleston.''

She could hardly disagree with his reasoning. ''What do you suppose will happen to Whitley and Mr. Edwards? Or any of them?''

''That's up to the judge, I suppose. Or the army.'' His eyes narrowed. ''I'm sure they don't want to leave it up to me.''

Imperceptible as it was, Derek had begun to relax as they talked. Now, with her thoughtless questions, she had put that fierce, angry look back on his face. Idiot! she reprimanded herself, pulling in a deep breath to clear her thinking.

''Enough of that talk.'' Amber straightened and bustled about the room like a woman with a purpose. She poured fresh water into the basin and took up a clean cloth, then turned back to Derek.

''Here. Let's get this off so I can see your arm.'' She reached for the top button of his shirt, making every effort to appear competent and indifferent. ''Your sleeve is torn, so I'm sure there's—''

''Amber.'' He wrapped his fingers around her wrist. Her knuckles pressed against the plane of his chest.

''Yes?''

''If you take my shirt off, it won't be to clean any wounds.''

''I...what do you mean?'' she asked, breathless.

"It will be because I'm going to make love to you—because you want to make love with me."

Excitement twisted her stomach into a series of intricate knots that refused her any peace and left little space for elemental needs like breathing. "You *want* to make love to me?"

He tugged on her arm, pulling her near until she was bent at the waist, so close she could feel the heat of his body. "How could you doubt it?" he demanded softly.

"You..." She swallowed. "I thought you may have reconsidered—regretted—things between us."

He blinked as though surprised by the suggestion, then his gaze roamed her face with unmistakable tenderness. "I was afraid," he admitted softly. "I thought *you* might have regrets. Not only about last night, but about what you said earlier."

*I love you.*

The words echoed between them. Could he say them back to her, simply repeat the words she had given him?

No. And how could she expect it of him? Had anyone else ever said the words to him? Jordan certainly had not—of that she had no doubt—and Carolyn had clearly demonstrated her ill-capacity for them, as far as Amber could tell. Mariah, perhaps?

Amber closed her eyes and refused to follow her thoughts in that direction. Derek may have been engaged to Mariah once, but he hadn't married her. She'd married his brother—was still married to his brother, as it turned out. Derek had promised that he would tell her about it someday, and she would take him at his word. She would trust him.

*I love you.*

Amber thought about the words and all they meant to her. She'd grown up hearing her mother and father exchange the sentiment often, with each other and their children. In the Laughton family, they were the last things said, even after goodbye or good-night, and they began each day. Even so, it had taken all her courage and the very real chance that she could lose Derek forever before she could say them. Derek had none of that.

"No." She opened her eyes and looked deeply into his, making no effort to conceal any part of herself from him. "I don't regret them. I don't regret a thing. But you—are you sure, Derek? You were so angry when you left me last night."

"I was wrong."

"I'm not so sure. I was wrong, too. I should have told you I—"

"Shh." He pressed two fingers against her lips. "We both made mistakes. Isn't it time to make things right?"

"Right? But Derek—"

"Shh," he said again, and rubbed his fingers over her lips, lightly, temptingly. "Later. We can confess to each other later. For now, tell me that you want me."

"I want you," she said softly, fervently, and sagged to her knees. "I want you now. I want you forever."

He stood, pulling her up with him, then shifted as though he meant to sweep her off her feet.

"No." She stepped back, sharing with him a smile of great tenderness. "We'll walk, side by side. No secrets, no lies, no misunderstandings. We're together because we choose to be, eyes wide-open."

"No secrets." He nodded and took her hand, leading her silently from the cookhouse.

The night was black and still, disguising all evidence of the earlier commotion. The house was dark and silent as well, his mother and Mariah having already retired to their respective rooms. Amber followed Derek's certain lead, her hand tucked snugly in his. No second thoughts, no regrets. She had never been more certain of anything.

He steered her past her bedroom and up the stairs, stopping only when they reached his door. "It seems right that I carry you over this threshold," he whispered.

"All right."

He swung her high, then settled her in his arms, cradling her against the breadth of his chest. She swallowed a surprised giggle and clutched his shoulders, hardly noticing when the door closed behind them.

Moonlight spilled in through the window, bathing the bed in a dappled light. Wanton anticipation stole her ability to think, to speak, to react as he lowered her feet to the floor. It was all she could do to stand when he released her.

A soft hiss, then the flare of a match, broke the spell of immobility. A moment later the room was aglow with dim, golden lamplight. Derek stood beside her, such gentle wonder in his eyes that Amber found herself blinking back tears. The faint shadows did little to hide his scrapes and bruises from her, but he had never looked more beautiful.

"Derek," she whispered softly, and held one hand out to him.

"In a minute, angel." He kept her gaze trapped by his and started with the uppermost button of his shirt. Slowly, one by one, he unfastened them all, then shrugged the shirt from his shoulders, ignoring it as it rustled to the floor. With the same lazy grace, he disposed of his belt and his boots. By the time his hands dropped to the waistband of his pants, nothing else in all the world could have seized her attention. Keeping his movements leisurely, he worked the top button open, then the next and the next, until finally he shoved the trousers down his legs and stepped free. His drawers followed, and the next moment he stood before her, gloriously naked.

"This is who I am." He spread his arms wide, as though demonstrating he hid nothing from her. "In truth, it is all I have to offer you. Myself. Other things are fleeting, not mine to claim. That lesson came to me at a dear price, and I need you to understand. All that I am—all that I will ever be—all that I have is yours. I will gladly share with you my wealth, my happiness.'' His voice tripped, as though the word was unfamiliar to him. ''But I can't guarantee you wealth or status or even that we will not face difficult times. I would give my life to protect you, but—''

''Are you telling me that you love me?'' An awe-filled joy trickled through her veins, picking up momentum until she thought she might jump from her very skin. She reached for Derek's hand.

He blinked. ''I—yes, I suppose I am. I haven't had much practice with the words.''

She released him. ''I'll teach you, then.''

Following his lead, she took her time in pulling each pin from her hair, dropping the handful to the bedside table when she was finished. Hesitantly, attempting a sensuousness she doubted she possessed, she gave her head a gentle shake. Loose auburn waves tumbled over her shoulders and down her back.

Derek's eyes, wide and uncommonly dark, were trained on her every movement. Her seductive grace came from some uniquely feminine place within her, a place she had not known existed. It astounded her, and yet nothing could have hurried her.

Her hands began a slight trembling that made her clumsy. She fumbled with the buttons of her dress, but Derek hardly seemed to notice or care. She unfastened them one by one, until finally the dress collapsed in a puddle at her feet. Her petticoat followed, then her chemise, and finally her pantalets. A moment later she stood as exposed as he.

She spread her arms as he had done. ''This, too, is all I am. I cannot give myself to you, because I'm already yours. I would spend the rest of my life caring for you, loving you, teaching you the words and all that they mean. My only regret is the precious time I wasted hiding the truth and keeping secrets that meant nothing. I should have been loving you.''

With one step, Derek crushed her to him and caught her lips with his. Tender kisses were not for this night, and his mouth opened over hers, urging, begging—demanding. She parted her lips, and his tongue delved deep. She welcomed him, brought her own tongue to the dance and urged him on. He tasted like…Derek, wild and heady and intoxicating.

She tangled her fingers in his hair to hold him close. When he would have retreated, she followed, searching out the recesses of his mouth, acquainting herself with his flavor, his texture, and making him hers.

''Amber.'' He tore his mouth from hers, his breath little better than a gasp. She had no more air, but what did it matter when he touched her, held her, kissed her as he did?

''Come.'' He pulled her to the bed, pressing her to the mattress with a delicious weight as he leaned over her. The firm muscles of his chest flattened her breasts, while his chest hair abraded her nipples to an excited fever. Instinctively she arched her back and pressed against him.

''Angel,'' Derek said tenderly. ''It'll be all right. Things will be different this time. You'll see.''

''Different?'' she managed to murmur, anchoring him to her with greedy hands at his shoulders, his back. ''I don't want things to be different. I want them as they were last night. Wonderful.''

He caught her bottom lip between his teeth and nipped, then kissed the spot with excruciating thoroughness. He did the same to her jaw, the curve of her neck. ''Wonderful? It *will* be. More than you can imagine.''

''Derek?'' What did that knowing smile mean?

''What, angel?''

''I…'' she began, but the words flitted away. Somehow her mind wasn't working as it should. Rather, it had tangled itself up in sensation, following his every move. Like now, as he traced his fingers lightly over her highly sensitized skin. He blazed a meandering path from the curve of her shoulder to the rise of her breasts, between them, down to her waist, her hip, and then back up again. She shifted restlessly against him, wanting—needing—more.

He seemed not to notice. Rather, he expanded his scrutiny, coming closer this time to the aching crest of one breast, to the mound of curls at the apex of her thighs, and yet just missing the places that needed—so badly—to feel his touch.

"Derek." His name came out as a querulous demand, a sob.

"Hmm?" He dipped his tongue to the indentation at her throat, where her pulse fluttered wildly.

"I want—"

"This?" he asked in a silky voice she hardly recognized. He shifted, slipping from her, and caught her nipple between his lips, suckling sweetly. He bathed her skin with a thorough tongue, scraping his teeth lightly over her sensitive flesh as he turned his attention to her other breast. He treated it to the same tender loving, then slowly began nibbling his way down her torso, to the curve of her hip, and lower.

"What—" Her breath deserted her as he kissed her there, her most private, feminine spot. The sensation was like nothing she had felt before and it hurled her to the far edge of desire.

"Derek." Could that deep, guttural cry have been her voice—his name? She reached for him, tangling her fingers in the length of his hair and meaning to push him away—yet she found herself caressing him, gripping his shoulders, begging him for…what?

"Please," she panted, writhing against him. "Derek, I—"

Her voice splintered as the sensations that had been building suddenly coalesced into an explosion of such magnitude it sent Amber hurtling toward the heavens. She cried out, clutching him against her, and then she knew no more.

Moments— or hours—later she found her way back to herself. Derek was stretched out next to her, smoothing damp, errant curls back from her face and smiling down at her with more love than the word could ever imply.

"What happened?" she asked, all she could manage.

"That? That was for you." He winked at her wickedly, with a satisfaction that warmed her from the inside. "That was to make up for my poor showing last night."

"Poor showing?" She shook her head and tried to imitate his wicked look. "You were splendid. As for the rest of this, I didn't know such things existed."

"Now that you do, will you be insatiable?"

"Insatiable?"

"Please?"

She laughed softly, and he joined her. Laughter, a beautiful sound they had never shared. She reached for him, brushed the tangled golden hair back from his face and gave him a long, leisurely kiss as his reward. Perhaps she could teach him more than mere words.

"If I'm insatiable, you know what that means."

"We're not through yet?" He widened his eyes with an overdone hopeful expression.

"We're definitely not through yet."

Her hands had never been more deft. She tested her fingers against the plane of his chest, the angle of his hips, the heart of his masculinity.

"Oh, no, angel. Not there." He pulled her hands from him and rolled her onto her back. "Not if you want to see what else I have in store for you tonight."

"There's more?"

He positioned himself between her thighs and teased her with a saucy poke at her most feminine entrance. "More. Much more. For tonight and always."

And then he proved it to her.

# *Epilogue*

"Are you ready?"

Derek turned from the veranda railing and found Beau in the doorway leading from the house. He nodded. "Yes."

"Nervous?"

He shook his head.

"No last minute jitters?"

Derek grinned, an expression he found easier to come by these days. Ever since Amber had begun teaching him about love. "None." He turned serious. "This is one of those days a man is destined for. I just didn't know it for a while."

Beau seemed to understand. "Congratulations. Someday...well, I hope to find it for myself."

Derek blinked, wondering what Beau had been like before the war. Amber said his heart had been broken once upon a time, and for the first time, Derek considered that she might be right. She had remarkable insights on everyone and everything, from the awkwardness in Nathan and Mariah's marriage to Gideon's unusual indifference, even for him. Derek was learning the wisdom of listening to her.

"I'll be there in a minute."

"Do you have the ring?"

Derek patted the pocket of his suit coat.

"I'll tell them to get ready." Beau turned for the door. "I think I'll check on the Andrews brothers before we get started. Clem had your mother cornered when I came out here. Do you think he might propose?"

Derek chuckled. "He told me he was never getting married. He just wants to do some sparking with her."

Beau's eyebrow shot up. "Sparking? With your mother?" He blinked several times. "Who would have ever guessed?"

Alone again, Derek turned back to his view of the ranch. The corral had all its boards in place, the bunkhouse appeared tidy, the barn door no longer sagged. He may have found a smithy to open up the blacksmith's shop again, and Amber would be filling the storehouse with canned goods from her garden soon. No more cattle had been lost or stolen since the night the Klan had visited, and Richard's meticulous notes were giving Derek ideas of how to bring the ranch back to its former glory.

The Double F. He had never meant it as more than simply a place to be. A place to figure out who he was and where he was going. It had done that, and more. It had given him a home—love. The land, the people, all had become part of him. He had never before belonged anywhere, not truly, and now his cup runneth over, as the Bible said.

In the month since Jeff Buchanan's Ku Klux Klan had caused its last bit of trouble, few other problems had risen. None of the vaqueros had left the ranch after discovering Derek's Yankee past. Sheriff Gardner had been true to his word and the KKK had been disbanded. Whitley, Edwards and several other leaders of the group had been arrested and taken to San Antonio, charged with stealing the Double F cattle—and with attempted murder. Eliza Bates declared her son-in-law's innocence to all who would listen, though the number was few; the activities of Buchanan's group stood for themselves.

Derek let out a small breath. All was not happy, however.

He and Nathan had not settled their differences, though they spoke with remote politeness on occasion. Things weren't right between Nathan and Mariah, but they remained at the ranch. For now.

"Derek?"

Amber stood just inside the doorway, so unearthly beautiful she stole his breath. He had not seen her all day, nor had she allowed him even a glimpse of her wedding dress. The Andrews brothers had presented her with the dress as a wedding present, made by Twigg's only modiste.

Amber seemed to float in yards of satin and lace. The low neckline dipped off her shoulders, and a wide ruffle adorned the bottom of the dress. Her hair was pulled back, crowned with a cluster of flowers—roses, perhaps—fashioned from the silk of her dress. A veil trailed down her back.

"Angel."

"Your mother is very cross with me. She says we shouldn't see each other before the ceremony. But I had to be sure."

He moved to her side. "Sure of what?"

"Of you. You aren't having second thoughts?"

"Those bridegroom jitters?" he asked with a smile.

"Yes."

"Beau was here earlier with the same question."

She flushed prettily, and Derek couldn't resist leaning forward to drop a quick kiss on her lips. "No second thoughts, no bridegroom jitters." He turned serious. "I didn't know what I was missing, angel. You're the other half of my soul, and nothing was right until I found you. I've been waiting for this moment all my life."

"Derek." Tears sparkled in her eyes. "How can you put into words exactly what I feel? I—"

"Amber-girl, you out there?" One of the Andrews brothers—Twigg, Derek thought—shouted from inside the house. "We ain't gonna have no sparkin' goin' on now, are we? You two only gotta wait a little longer, then it'll be all legal-like.''

Amber's eyes grew as wide as saucers. Derek grinned, then leaned around her to call into the house. ''No sparking, Twigg. We're saving it for later, when there won't be any interruptions. Now you'd better get to your seats or we'll start without you.''

''Humph.'' He thought it was Clem who made the disgruntled noise. ''If it were me, *I'd* be doin' some sparkin'.''

Derek turned back to Amber. ''Are you ready?''

''Ready.''

She stepped toward the house.

''Amber?'' He reached for her at the last minute, and she turned back to him. ''I love you, angel.''

Her face blossomed with a smile as radiant as the sun, a smile he'd come to depend on. It burned away the last of the shades of gray that clouded his heart and brought him into the light at last. ''And I love you,'' she whispered softly.

The sound of Six's fiddle signaled the wedding was upon them. Hand in hand, Derek led Amber forward to greet their future.

\* \* \* \* \*

Lookin' for some spicy Westerns seasoned
with just the right amount of sizzling
romance and rollicking adventure? Then help
yourselves to these Harlequin Historicals novels

## ON SALE MARCH 2002

### A MARRIAGE BY CHANCE
by **Carolyn Davidson**
*(Wyoming, 1894)*

### SHADES OF GRAY
by **Wendy Douglas**
*(Texas, 1868)*

## ON SALE APRIL 2002

### THE BRIDE FAIR
by **Cheryl Reavis**
*(North Carolina, 1868)*

### THE DRIFTER
by **Lisa Plumley**
*(Arizona, 1887)*

 Harlequin Historicals®

Take a jaunt to Merry Old England
with these timeless stories from
Harlequin Historicals

## On sale March 2002

**THE LOVE MATCH**
by Deborah Simmons
Deborah Hale
Nicola Cornick
Don't miss this captivating bridal collection
filled with three breathtaking Regency tales!

**MARRYING MISCHIEF**
by Lyn Stone
Will a quarantine spark romance between a
determined earl and his convenient bride?

## On sale April 2002

**MISS VEREY'S PROPOSAL**
by Nicola Cornick
A matchmaking duke causes a smitten London
debutante to realize she's betrothed to the
wrong brother!

**DRAGON'S KNIGHT**
by Catherine Archer
When a powerful knight rushes to the aid of a
beautiful noblewoman, will he finally conquer
his darkest demons?

 Harlequin Historicals®

HHMED23

Silhouette Books invites you to cherish
a captivating keepsake collection by

# DIANA PALMER

They're rugged and lean…and the best-looking, sweetest-talking men in the Lone Star State! CALHOUN, JUSTIN and TYLER—the three mesmerizing cowboys who started the legend. Now they're back by popular demand in one classic volume—ready to lasso your heart!

You won't want to miss this treasured collection from international bestselling author Diana Palmer!

**LONG, TALL Texans**

CALHOUN, JUSTIN & TYLER
(On sale March 2002)

*Available at your favorite retail outlet.*

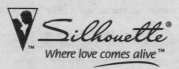

Silhouette®

*Where love comes alive*™

# This Mother's Day Give Your Mom 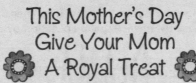 A Royal Treat

Win a fabulous one-week vacation in Puerto Rico for you and your mother at the luxurious Inter-Continental San Juan Resort & Casino. The prize includes round trip airfare for two, breakfast daily and a mother and daughter day of beauty at the beachfront hotel's spa.

## INTER·CONTINENTAL
### *San Juan*
RESORT & CASINO

## Here's all you have to do:

Tell us in 100 words or less how your mother helped with the romance in your life. It may be a story about your engagement, wedding or those boyfriends when you were a teenager or any other romantic advice from your mother. The entry will be judged based on its originality, emotionally compelling nature and sincerity. See official rules on following page.

### Send your entry to:
### Mother's Day Contest

| **In Canada** | **In U.S.A.** |
|---|---|
| P.O. Box 637 | P.O. Box 9076 |
| Fort Erie, Ontario | 3010 Walden Ave. |
| L2A 5X3 | Buffalo, NY |
| | 14269-9076 |

## Or enter online at www.eHarlequin.com

PRROY

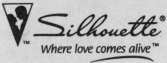